THE BASTARD HEIR

A WINTER HARBOR NOVEL, BOOK 1

WHITLEY COX & EMBER LEIGH

WHITLEY COX & EMBER LEIGH

CONTENTS

This book is dedicated to my whimsical and wonderful co-author! What a delightful journey we've taken!
~Ember

I dedicate this book to the pacing and hook drill sergeant, AKA my writing partner. It took us more than a while to get to this point, but we're finally here and I'm so glad I took this adventure with you.
~Whitley

CHAPTER ONE

HARLOW

"Are you fucking serious right now?"

I couldn't believe those words came out of my mouth.

No, scratch that.

I couldn't believe I spoke like that *to my boss.* The one in charge of my pending career advancement. The one I'd been quietly convincing to make me partner.

Dalton's lips thinned. "Harlow, I know your caseload is already bursting. But trust me when I say—*this will put you ahead.*"

I rolled my lips inward to prevent any unsavory outbursts that might ruin my standing on the spot. Spring sunlight filtered through the wooden slats covering his western-facing window overlooking the port. Here in Winter Harbor, damn near every day was picturesque. But the silently bobbing boats and the clear blue sky did nothing to quiet the storm inside me.

Dalton had a fair point. This case would give me the leverage I needed to prove to him and the other name partner, Troy, that I could hack it with my last name on the leaderboard. They were *Quick & Fairchild* right now, but if I joined the ranks of their Oregon-famous estate law firm, it would turn into *Quick, Fairchild & Jackson.* Elegant. And

1

something I'd been working for since day one of my legal career.

I just couldn't take on *this* case.

And I couldn't tell Dalton *why*.

"I hear you," I said slowly, almost robotically, as I stared out the window, trying to find solace in the lapping of the water against the docks. "I just wonder if I could prove my chops elsewhere, and we could assign the Winters case to Stephanie or ... or Ian."

Just saying the name of the client—*Winters*—sent a chill down my spine. I hadn't thought of the Winters family since my senior year of college. No, that was a lie. I thought of a certain Winters man practically every day since my senior year of college when he dumped me and left me in one of the biggest, most assholish fashion the world has ever seen.

But I'd never let him know that he'd ever graced my mind after that horrible day. And I would certainly never agree to take a case that put me in direct contact with him—or his brother—again nearly eight years after his inglorious exit from my life.

"I'm offering this to you because I want to see you succeed." Dalton barely concealed his sigh. "Because I think you're ready. Unless you want Ian to become partner instead of you."

And there it was—the audible snapping of the last straw. I couldn't dodge this. The Winters case had been managed for almost a year by a former partner who'd disappeared suddenly last week in a puff of scandal and gambling debt. I aimed to replace him, but apparently, it meant taking on the one case I would rather amputate a leg to avoid. The case I'd only found out about accidentally an hour ago when Dalton's secretary sent me a forwarded email from Callum Winters himself, confirming with the legal group when we'd be meeting him today.

"I was planning to take it myself—which is why you're just hearing about this at the eleventh hour—but I just took over the Ludgate estate, and that is going to take up all of my time." He heaved a big, weary sigh.

The Ludgate estate was a disaster. I did not envy my boss.

2

"I don't know, Dalton ..." For a lawyer, my argument was weak sauce. We both knew it.

"You can do this. I have complete faith in you, Harlow." Dalton placed a fatherly hand on my shoulder, his expression sympathetic, but I could also see that he was running out of patience with my resistance to this career-changing case.

I gnawed on the inside of my lip as I relegated myself to the facts. Dalton was giving me the case. The Winters brothers—all three of them, but two in particular who were noteworthy parts of my personal history—were about to be within three feet of me. And I'd be partner soon, so this would all be worth it. *Probably.*

Even if running into Callum Winters sent me to an early grave with no updated will in place.

I'm an estate attorney. I should know better.

"You're right," I said, propping my hands on my hips. "The case is mine. There's no problem at all. And I'll show you that you made the right choice."

Because if there was one thing worse than facing Callum Winters again, it was losing the promotion to name partner at the firm of my dreams.

Dalton only looked minorly convinced as I sent him a tight smile and marched back to my own office. My heels clicked on the expensive sandalwood flooring, age-old anger burbling back to life inside me.

How could it be that I was thirty years old and still not over the fact that Callum Winters was a dick to me eight years ago?

I'd graduated from college. Passed the bar in Oregon. Joined one of the most respected practices in the entire state. Branched off into estate law, which was my passion, even though it went against the grain of what my entire family of lawyers practiced. I owned a townhome just off the gorgeous main boulevard and spent my days proving my worth in the legal field. Add in the fact that I was now gloriously cancer-free and had been for two and half years, and life was what most normal people would call awesome.

So why was my entire body getting hot and prickly just thinking about seeing freaking Callum Winters again?

According to the email chain, Callum and Co had been corresponding with Dalton's secretary for the past week about what to do regarding their recently deceased father's will. They were coming to Winter Harbor—their father's hometown ... and *mine*—to wrap up his affairs. Which meant that they were very likely *down the street* from me, and I was supposed to act like everything was okay.

"Hey, Bets?" I paused at my secretary's desk—well, my shared secretary with Ian, but I knew she secretly preferred me. "I need the Winters family file, ASAP, with a cherry on top."

Betsy smiled as she clicked through screens on her computer. "You got it, Harlow. Anything else?"

"A martini, maybe," I collapsed into the chair facing her desk. She was a lifeline of the practice, and probably very underpaid. Once I became partner and made her into my main secretary, though, I planned to change that. "Possibly a massage after that."

She snickered as the printer kicked to life. "That's all doable."

"You're the best, Bets. I'll need you to send me your good juju for this meeting." I checked my phone for the time. Half-past eleven. The Winters brothers would be facing me in less than an hour. That was plenty of time to get up to speed on their case ... but not nearly enough time to fortify my heart for seeing my first—and only—love again.

Or his younger brother, the man who'd come between us.

"Good juju: sent," Bets replied as she collected the pages slipping out of the printer. "Though I thought you had plenty to spare."

I smoothed the front of my pressed black pants. Betsy had no idea about how much juju I needed if I was going to be facing down Callum *and* Carson Winters again. Hell, even I didn't know how much juju I needed. I was just sure that it wouldn't be enough.

"It's always smart to get a little extra." I took the print-outs from her.

"Especially if you're dealing with the Winters family." Betsy lobbed a sigh that held weariness. As though she had some experience with them.

"I haven't dealt with them, actually." Better to not admit my previous romantic attachment to someone who was suddenly my client. If there was one thing I would not give Callum Winters, it was the satisfaction of knowing he'd stood in the way of my promotion. "Have you?"

Betsy leveled me with her warm brown gaze, wisps of gray hair escaping her low ponytail. "The whole town has experience with the Winters. Not the kids, of course. Nobody knows about them since they've never come around." She waved her hand dismissively. "But the man whose estate you're handling now? Everyone above fifty-five in this town knows about Elliot and Camille."

She was right. My parents had murmured vaguely about the sad Winters story plenty of times during my youth, but I never paid much attention. It had always seemed like something antiquated and irrelevant. But I'd never thought that Callum *Winters* could be related to *Winter Harbor.*

The mention of Callum's mother made my stomach jolt. He'd always spoken about her with such fondness. It was strange to think that Callum's father and I shared a hometown, but that Callum had likely never even been here before.

Until now.

"Ancient history, right?"

Betsy didn't laugh or even smile. Instead, she reached for my wrist. "Let me just say, you need the juju. That family is bad news."

I almost laughed because I knew what level of bad news Callum truly was ... and his brother Carson, for that matter. But I didn't know why the rest of his family was bad news. Or why that meant I should care.

"Things will be fine," I told her, more to reassure myself than her. "This is a simple inheritance case and then, boom. All done. Easy as cake."

"As pie," Betsy corrected me.

"That's what I meant. It's easy like baking in general." Even though, for my kitchen-impaired self, baking was an intolerable chore.

"Mm-hmm." Betsy's little smirk told me exactly what she thought of that. "You were too young to know Elliot

Winters. He fled town before you were even born. But if those sons of his are even one-eighth as shady as he was ... well ..." Betsy glanced over my shoulder and down the hall, probably checking to see if Dalton or Troy, the other partner, was coming. "You need to check and double-check every single thing they tell you."

I swallowed a knot in my throat and forced a smile. Bets had no idea how right she was. And unfortunately, I'd already learned this lesson.

Because Callum wasn't just my first love.

His younger brother, Carson, was my ex.

I excused myself to get my things, drawing deep, fortifying breaths. I needed to get to the abandoned Hope Creek Manor where I'd be meeting the Winters brothers, and I needed to get there *early* so that I could get my bearings and prepare myself.

Even still, having a plan didn't keep my knees from feeling like mush as I packed my briefcase and headed out the door. Eight years had passed. Who knew where they were in their lives? Hopefully happily married and moved on. Where I should be, too. Where I would be, I supposed, if it weren't for Callum.

A sharp ache registered in my chest, and I took a deep breath of the crisp April air to distract myself. No need to get lost in the swirl of ancient heartbreak and *oh woe is me, my squandered soul mate*. No, I'd been down that road too many times—especially when drunk. I loved to torment myself with the ridiculous notion that Callum was the one for me. The one who'd ruined it all. The one who I might have a second chance with if only the stars aligned.

Well, now that the stars were aligning, they looked more like a comet heading for disaster. This churning in my gut—this couldn't be the marker of a soul mate. This could only signal a bad idea or food poisoning.

Harlow, get yourself together.

The salty sea breeze calmed me as I headed for my black two-door coupe at the front of the office on Main Street. Winter Harbor was a quaint and cozy town with plenty of locally-owned restaurants and a bustling port. It was not only my hometown but also my sanctuary. And as I navigated the back roads to the impressive plantation-style home, I vowed to not let this heartbreak blast from the past disrupt my peace and tranquility.

I had fought long and hard for this little slice of success. I wasn't going to let the ghost of my love affair with Callum Winters haunt me forever.

Right?

I squeezed the steering wheel the whole way, up until I sat in front of the impressive mansion. However decrepit it had become over the years, it was still a sight to behold. Overgrown bushes clogged the wooden steps to the wraparound porch, and huge oak trees crowded the expansive front yard. But the late 19th-century Queen Anne-style Victorian mansion was a gem, even with the cracking white paint and the echoes of the broken family that used to inhabit this space. The family that had started Winter Harbor.

The grandsons of which were scheduled to arrive any minute now.

Inside my car, parked in the big cul-de-sac driveway in front of the house, I drew a deep breath.

Because seeing him again after eight years wasn't bad enough. No, now I had to confront the distinct possibility that he and his brothers might become the newest residents of Winter Harbor. It was a good thing my parents were taking an extended vacation in Europe because, as lawyers themselves, they always loved to talk shop with me, especially when they were six thousand miles away from their own caseloads. And they would have plenty of questions about my newest case being tied to the only man responsible for breaking my heart. For now, I didn't have to tell them that my ex was back in our hometown requiring my legal services.

So maybe this whole situation was just reinforcing the truth that my parents knew all along: *it's best to stay in the family business.* I had to be the rebel who branched out into estate law, even though I had a cozy spot waiting for me at my mom and dad's intellectual property and contract firm. Their Winter Harbor practice had taken off so much that my brother had opened a Portland office. That could have been me. But no. I insisted on this career whose sole outcome was to lead me back to my ex.

But I just loved estate law. During my second year of law school, I was allowed to sit in on a case between three siblings, fighting over their inheritance. It got so ugly that it went to court. The entire ordeal grew so surreal that it seemed something more suited for a season of Melrose Place than real life. But that just played into my love of dramatic soap operas—thanks to summers spent being babysat by my grandmother when I was a kid. So after that trial, I was hooked and determined to go into estate law.

Gravel crunched on the driveway, jerking me out of my thoughts. Panic started a hot, insidious trail through my limbs. Truth was, I could tell myself I was ready for this moment as much as I wanted, but I'd never *truly* be ready to face down Callum again.

Through my rearview mirror, I watched as a broad-shouldered man exited a car. I didn't need to watch for long to know who it was. The way he raked his fingers through longish, dark brown hair stirred memories in me I thought I'd laid to rest. Ice-blue eyes. Square shoulders that had only grown wider, more filled out, in the eight years since I'd seen him last.

I was staring at Callum Winters.

The only man I'd dared to love.

The only man who had ever broken my heart.

And right beside him? Another tall, dark, and handsome man with equally piercing blue eyes. And that's when the truth hit me like a sucker punch.

My education didn't matter.

My legal career meant nothing.

My grit and grandeur in the courtroom?

Also meaningless.

Because nothing could have truly prepared me to take all the Winters brothers head-on.

Not when one of them hated me for dumping him ...

And the other one hated me for having been with his brother.

8

CHAPTER TWO

CALLUM

To say that the past month of my life had not been going well would be a gross, laughable understatement.

And as I stepped out of my rental car and looked up at that crumbling house before me, I knew right then and there my streak of bad luck was nowhere near close to being over.

I'd lost my job in such a humiliating way they could have started a Netflix series covering my epic failure. *Made a Fool in Manhattan? Wallstreet One-hit Wonder: How Callum Winters gained and lost it all in a New York minute.* I could see the Rotten Tomatoes comments now, and they made my gut turn over as if I'd just eaten a bushel of rotten tomatoes.

And because of that epic failure, that legendary firing, and tarnished reputation? My NYC condo was on the market, all my things in storage. *Jobless and homeless: check and check.*

And the coup de grace? I was back in Oregon for the first time since I'd fled after college graduation ... breathing the same air as my estranged brothers.

Revisiting strained family members: infinity check.

Two other vehicles pulled up behind me in the gravel cul-de-sac, yanking my attention from the quiet coupe closer to the house. I assumed my lawyer—sorry, *Dad's* lawyer—was in there, but I still couldn't quite wrap my head around the turn of events.

9

Dad was dead.

Not like his death was much different for me than his life.

He hadn't even bothered to tell us—or at least *me*—that he was sick. We had to find out after the fact from his doctors and lawyers that he'd been diagnosed with stage four pancreatic cancer three months ago and had just enough time to get his affairs in order.

Not enough time apparently to give his sons a quick call, or even an email to let us know that he was dying.

Typical Elliot Winters. Only thinking of himself.

He'd been estranged from his sons for years, with nothing but a thriving import business, a big fancy house, and a healthy bank account to show for his life.

I often wondered if Dad even knew my middle name or whether he remembered my birthday. He hadn't called on my birthday or sent a card in years, so I would hedge to guess that he had no fucking clue. Or maybe he'd just officially stopped caring about his spawn once he shipped us off to boarding school way back in our primary years.

I stepped out of my car, looking back at the new arrivals behind me. I hadn't seen my brothers in years, but there they were. A strange, familiar warm feeling washed through me, even though I'd told myself a long time ago to forget they existed. After what Carson did to me, I'd ruled out a relationship with him out of principle. And after enough years had gone by without truly getting to know my youngest brother Colton, it seemed like too many mountains to scale.

Just because we shared the same genes, last name, and blue eyes didn't mean birds of a feather flocked together. My brothers made that very clear.

Better to just forget about them.

As much as it hurt my heart to think that way.

It was probably for the best.

Leave the heartache in the past. Move on with my life and create the family of my dreams elsewhere, with someone else.

Even though at this point, I was pretty sure that person didn't exist. And if she did, well ... I'd fucked that chance up eight years ago.

"Wow. Look who it is." Carson's coarse voice cut through my thoughts.

I shoved my hands in my pockets, steeling myself to face him. We'd always struggled to truly get along—he'd been an asshole growing up—and I had a feeling now wouldn't be much different. Once an asshole, always an asshole? Should have been crocheted on a damn pillow somewhere.

"Brother." The word fell flat. Yes, we were biological brothers, but I knew this wasn't how it should be. Even though I had no idea how to change things. Whether I even should. Whether I even wanted to. Especially not after the shit he pulled, and what it cost me. "Been a while."

Carson scoffed, raking his fingers through his thick, dark hair. Like most assholes, he had great hair. Only slightly better than mine, not like I'd admit that to him.

Colton lurked behind him, looking stiff and much older than the last time I'd seen him. But then again, when I'd seen him, he'd been a sixteen-year-old delinquent. Who knew where he was at in life now? Or where Carson's life had taken him, for that matter?

The worst part was, I wanted to know but didn't know how to ask.

Pride was an intrusive beast and after everything that had gone down between Carson and me, I was too proud to be the first one to extend the olive branch.

A big part of me still wanted to beat him with that branch.

The three of us stared at one another in tense silence. This was worse than an awkward Thanksgiving. Worse than a ten-year family reunion with the *distant* side of the family. Not that we'd had either of those things. Dad always had some excuse not to invite us home for the holidays, and he was estranged from his side of the family. And we never met our mother's side, not even after her death.

This was pure fucking torture involving two guys who shared my bloodline and childhood.

I studied Colton for another moment, it was easier looking at him than it was Carson since I held no resentment toward my youngest brother. We were simply estranged. Like me, his jaw was lined with thick short scruff. Carson was clean-shaven. Colton's ears were also pierced and gauged with black wooden earrings the size of dimes. Not my thing, but I'll admit they suited him.

"Are you boys ready?" The feminine voice broke through our strained silence.

A voice I felt like I knew, though it had to be my imagination. I swallowed the painful knot in my throat at the unwelcome yank to my past—to the *ancient* past, back when I'd had love, lost it, and then set it all on fire for good measure.

"Harlow?" The incredulity in Carson's voice made all the hairs on my arm stand up.

I hadn't heard or spoken that name in eight years. It only arrived in my dreams. I turned slowly, anxiety prickling across my shoulders.

And then there she was. The proof that the past month of my life could, in fact, get much worse.

Harlow stood before us, backed by the impressive mansion. Her mahogany hair was up in a classic twist, with a few loose strands framing her face. But her eyes were what made my heart clench and my palms sweaty. It was those eyes, all those years ago, that had stopped traffic, stopped my heart, and made me chase her.

"Yes," she said, offering a brief smile. But it melted quickly, her gaze everywhere but on me. "Shall we get down to brass tacks?"

Birds twittered in the nearby woods as I struggled to understand why she was in front of me.

I wasn't dreaming, was I?

"Why are you here?" I blurted. My voice came out harsher than I'd intended, but the maelstrom of emotion inside me was something I couldn't understand right now, much less handle.

She didn't even flinch. "I'm handling the case for your late father."

"I've been corresponding with Leonard Rasmussen," I shot back. "Where is he?"

"Leonard no longer works for the offices of *Quick & Fairchild*. I am a senior partner, and several of his clients have been passed to me. One of those clients being Mr.

Winters. Sound good?" She sniffed, finally allowing those blue eyes to meet mine.

Heat shot through me. I clenched my jaw until an ache ran up to my temple. It was a bizarre kind of comfort, the pain. Almost felt like I deserved it for putting myself in a situation where I was forced to stare at the woman who'd broken my heart, the brother who'd caused it, and the other brother who was just a quiet statue of a relative.

I couldn't respond.

Carson cleared his throat. "Yeah. Great." After a beat, he said, "Callum? Colton? You guys in?"

Colton mumbled something in way of agreement. As for me, I couldn't rip my eyes off Harlow or convince my heart rate to slow down.

All I could see was the past. The slow mornings in her campus apartment when I'd surprise her with breakfast in bed. Watch the gratitude crease her face, the tears pool in her eyes when I'd surprise her with her favorite juice—mango—or pancakes in a new shape. I lived for the small touches. And the weight of their absence over the past eight years suddenly greeted me in the chest like a freight train.

The day we ended flashed through in my mind like a movie reel.

All her tears. Each one, shredding my heart into ever smaller fragments.

And yet, after what I'd found out—from Carson, of all people—I couldn't see any other choice but to end things.

Now, older—but possibly not wiser—I realized I had other choices back then. I'd simply been too proud, too stubborn, too hurt to see that forgiveness was a choice.

And oh, how different my life would be if I'd only made that choice, seen it through the thick fog of hurt.

Not a sliver of doubt careened through me that Harlow hadn't moved on. She was probably happily married with two-point-five kids, a two-story house with a white picket fence, and some fluffy dog with an atrocious name like *Precious* or *Darling*.

Maybe I'm a dick, but I'd never met another woman I wanted to do those things for. Sure, I'd dated and had girlfriends over the years, but I'd always compared them to Harlow, and unfortunately, not one held a candle to the woman who stood in front of me now.

"Let's get this over with," I muttered, my anger at myself for my current situation making my words clipped.

Harlow spun on her heels and headed for the house, dissolving my trip down memory lane.

We followed silently.

There couldn't have been a more awkward rag-tag crew in the Pacific Northwest.

I took up the rear, following behind Colton. His white T-shirt was tight across his back and see-through just enough that I could see the dark etchings of an enormous tattoo between his shoulder blades. Only a small sliver of the ink peaked out on his neck above the collar, but it wasn't enough to give me any indication what the tattoo might be.

"We'll start with the reading of the will," Harlow called over her shoulder as she navigated the top part of the gravel drive in her spiky black heels.

I couldn't stop myself—my gaze slid down the creamy curve of her calf, down to her dainty ankles. My neck went hot, remembering how many times those feet had been propped on my shoulders. How many times I'd kissed up the length of those legs.

Her heel wobbled on the brick path leading toward the wrap-around porch. She inhaled sharply, her ankle twisting suddenly. I rushed ahead, unable to stop myself from reaching her.

"Careful." My voice came out a rasp as she collapsed against me. I steadied her, the soft scent of her shampoo searing through me.

She glanced up, pink staining her cheeks. But she collected herself quickly, muttered a half-hearted *thanks*, and cleared her throat, striding toward the front door like nothing had happened.

"Once we read the will," she went on, the waver in her voice barely noticeable, "we'll take a tour of the house. Go over the complete list of assets. And I'll answer whatever questions you might have."

I had so many fucking questions.

Had Harlow finally gotten married, like we'd talked about doing all those years ago? When the future seemed so bright and so full of love and possibilities, nothing could stop us from achieving our dreams.

Clearly, she'd become a lawyer like she'd always wanted. Maybe she had a mini-Harlow running around somewhere, waiting for her to get home from a full day at work so they could have pancakes for dinner.

"This is quite a house," Carson said, his voice sounding distant.

I twisted to look at him. His gaze traveled along the rails of the porch, up the pillars toward the roof.

"Been a historical gem of Winter Harbor since it was built." Harlow rummaged in her things for the key. "And possibly your house for the next year, should you all choose to accept the terms of the will."

I blinked a few times as her words settled in. I could hear the birds again, but this time their tweets swelled like a storm. No longer joyful. Instead, it sounded like the birds were mocking me.

Colton snorted, the first reaction I'd seen from him in almost a decade. "What did you say?"

"Yeah, what?" Carson echoed.

"Why on Earth would any of us live here for a year?" I blurted. "I have an entire life in New York. Is that some kind of a joke?"

Except the only joke was my words themselves. I had no life in New York. Everything I'd known about that city was lost or on the market.

I was a free agent.

Drifting.

Listless.

Completely fucking lost.

And also, unable to come to terms with it all, hence the bald-faced lies.

I just couldn't let Harlow see me as the failure I clearly was.

Not when she was rocking her life.

I wouldn't be able to handle the look on her face if she knew the truth about me.

Pity. Most likely.

Or maybe relief. That she'd dodged the bullet that was Callum Winters.

Not to mention the look on Carson's face, which would probably be one of smug satisfaction.

I was jobless, homeless, and loveless.

The only thing separating me from a hobo on the train tracks was that I didn't have the polka dot rucksack on a stick to carry over my shoulder.

But one thing was for certain. Even though the demise of our relationship had brutalized my heart—my own doing, given how I'd handled things—seeing her today just proved beyond a shadow of a doubt that I wasn't over her. Eight years, and I still wanted her. Still craved her. I needed to check her ring finger—not that that meant much these days. But even still, I needed to see if she had a big diamond frosting her delicate hand.

I took a deep breath and climbed the stairs.

Time meant nothing when it came to Harlow Jackson.

The woman had burrowed herself so deep beneath my skin, she was tattooed on my heart. The only way I could move on and try to forget about her *again* would be to get the hell out of Winter Harbor ASAP and never look back.

CHAPTER THREE

HARLOW

It was hard to look away from Callum. He never made it easy, not with a jawline like his, or those piercing ice-blue eyes.

Amid all the confusion of this unintended reunion, one thing was for sure: I was still attracted to the devastatingly handsome force that was Callum Winters. If he'd been hot back in college, now the man was essentially combusting.

I supposed some part of me was secretly hoping that time would have treated him poorly. Like maybe he might have rolled into Oregon with a snaggletooth, a hairy mole between his brows, or a repulsive buttcrack-scratching habit.

But no.

Callum had to show up looking like the modern-day off-duty Don Draper.

Jury was still out of the buttcrack habit, though, and I had zero intention of hanging out with him long enough to find out.

"We'll go over everything inside," I reminded them. I knew they wouldn't take well to the news about the stipulations of the inheritance—talk about the mother of all bomb drops.

I cleared my throat, fumbling with the key to the front door. I dropped the damn thing on the faded welcome mat. I could feel their attention sizzling on me as I bent over to pick up the key.

"Need some help?" Carson offered.

"Not at all." I stood, avoiding eye contact with every single one of them until I could get my shit under control. When I tried the lock this time, it worked. The door swung open, a musty puff of air greeting us. Still, I could feel Callum's gaze scorching me while the truth screamed through my veins.

Callum and I—we had chemistry from day one. And apparently would have it until the last of days, as well. It was unnerving how the guy could still light me up after just a few heated glances and accidentally tripping into him. Unless this sort of attraction just meant I was verifiably insane and probably doomed to die single and still thinking about my first heartbreak.

As we stepped inside the expansive foyer, forgotten but still awe-inspiring, Carson let a low whistle. "Damn. Old grandpa Winters must have been royalty."

"That would make us princes, then." Colton's gaze moved up the columns in the foyer. "With Callum first in line to be king."

I forced a laugh. "Because your family founded the town, the Winters name is a bit like royalty around here."

"If we're rulers, then that makes Callum Caligula." Carson sent a jaunty smile toward Callum.

Callum's annoyance showed only in the twitch of his jaw. He said nothing, opting instead to send Carson an icy stare.

"It's so funny he forgot to laugh," Colton added softly, his gaze darting between his brothers.

I had to admit—it was a *little* funny. But I knew better than to encourage whatever was brewing beneath the surface here. I had enough ingredients in my own saucepan, I didn't need to add their mess on top of things.

"Well, let's get started," I suggested. I set my briefcase on a built-in ledge along the main hallway, bringing out the will and the copies for each brother. Once they were distributed, I fixed my eyes to the page and vowed not to look at any of them until I was done.

"I, Elliot John James Winters of 1467 Gregory Crescent, Portland Oregon, being of sound mind and body, hereby declare this to be my Last Will and Testament. I hereby revoke all previous wills. As I have no wife, my soul beneficiaries are my three sons: Callum Johnathan Winters, Carson Jeffrey Winters, and Colton James Winters ..."

The brothers were eerily quiet as I read; so quiet that at one point, I imagined they weren't even here with me at all. A helpful tactic, since some not-so-easy-to-swallow things lay ahead in this will.

"... I bequeath the entirety of estate to my three sons. In order to inherit the house, land, and all associated holdings, my sons must occupy the house in Winter Harbor together for the duration of one full year. During this time, my sons are granted full agency over the properties and all holdings, even during probate, as long as they comply with the directives of the will, and live at Hope Creek Manor for one full year."

I continued reading, hesitant to let any of them react or rail against their deceased father.

I didn't get far before Carson blurted out, "Whoa, wait a minute, so you were serious out there?"

I paused, considering my response.

But Callum spoke next. "There is *no way* any of us are living in this decrepit house for a year. It should be condemned. The city would kick us out if we tried to inhabit this place."

"I don't actually think the city would try any such thing," I said, unable to hide my smirk. The citizens might, based on what I'd heard about the Winters family recently. "They're extremely interested in this property, that's true. But they can't work around this will, unless the three of you cede your rights to the inheritance. So while your inheritance is on the line, the city will act in its own best interest. You can bet on that."

"Go on. Finish the will." Colton cocked his head, looking intently at me.

The only Winters brother I *didn't* have an intimate past with made him my favorite by default. I sent him a small smile before continuing , interrupted only by a few sighs from Callum. By the time I tucked my copy away, the brothers were each in their own stance of aggressive disbelief. Tightly crossed arms—Carson. Raking a hand through his hair while pacing the foyer—Callum. Squinted eyes and still cocked head—my favorite, Colton.

"How much money are we talking with these assets?" Colton demanded.

"In the ballpark of twenty million." My reply stopped Callum's pacing. "That's an estimate, for now, since a few of the holdings have yet to be appraised."

A tense silence stretched across the foyer.

"And if we don't accept the terms?" Callum asked. "What if we decide not to live here for a year?"

"The state of Oregon will become the new inheritors." I glanced at him only long enough to establish the bare minimum of eye contact. "Now, are we ready for the letters?"

"Oh goodie, there's more," Carson muttered.

I pulled the named envelopes out of my briefcase and dispersed them to the brothers. Carson tore into his envelope, followed by Colton. Callum stormed over to the far window that overlooked the overgrown back garden, where you could still faintly see a brick path and a long algae'd-over fountain. In its heyday, this house must have been something for *Better Homes & Gardens.* But now, it just looked like a candidate for the set of a sad period flick about estranged families.

I tried to mind my own business while the brothers read their father's final words. I really did. But the curiosity burned hot. And even if I would never again find myself on a friendly level with Callum Winters, it was hard not to watch the moody hunk as he scowled out the window and occasionally re-assessed the envelope in his hands.

Carson snorted at one point during the reading of his letter. Colton's face grew more and more serious as he read. Finally, Callum broke and tore into his letter. I examined my nails—my nude manicure still looked perfect, though I would have gone with a flashier color had I known Callum would be re-entering my world today. I might have chosen a more form-fitting skirt, or something that broadcasted how hot and unavailable I was, like an intentional crop top.

But why? This nonsensical need to attract Callum while at the same time wanting to run away and put miles between us once more—it was annoying as much as it was confusing. If I were a regular woman, I'd have been able to feel completely neutral about Callum by now. But desire and longing needled through me. Like there was something to revisit between us, which was absolutely absurd.

Colton scoffed suddenly, refolding his letter. "Okay. The man is nuts. I'm ready to go."

"No way in hell," Carson muttered, staring at his letter.

"Hopefully reassuring words from your late father," I said, which was just legalese for *tell me what's in the fucking letter.*

"Delusional, more like." Carson folded his letter as well.

A moment later, Callum scoffed and tucked his into his back pocket. "In summary, our father wants us to live together so we can mend fences."

"The fence is broken," Carson confirmed. "And nobody has the tools, so why bother?"

I couldn't hide my grimace. That was a death sentence of a father's dying wish if I'd ever heard one. "Well, the terms of the will are, of course, your decision. No pressure from me, or anyone else. I'll just need to know within two weeks what the decision is."

When I got no further feedback, only the intense stares of three estranged brothers, I nodded to myself. "Great. Let's take the tour."

I led the way through the foyer and into the vast living room. The house was built in the mid-1800s, which meant the ceilings were damn near twenty feet high and had amassed a fascinating collection of cobwebs through the years of neglect.

My heels clicked against the parquet floor as I led them deeper. "Dining room. Kitchen. Bonus room." I stopped along a back wall of windows in what had previously been used as a sunroom. "Five bedrooms upstairs. Three bathrooms total. Last lived in during the nineties. Plenty of renovation projects to undertake, provided the state of Oregon doesn't become the owner.

Colton peered up the wide staircase. "Twenty million in assets, huh? And this house isn't a negative in that tally?"

"Not unless the foundation is made of gold or something," Carson muttered, stomping the heel of his boot against the wood floor.

"Aside from all the other properties included in the inheritance, this house alone boasts an impressive wine cellar, along with twenty acres of land. As well as being a historical gem of the area. The Winter Harbor Historical Society would kill to have this house and turn it into a museum. And with the property values these days … yeah. You get the picture."

"You didn't include the wine cellar in your tour," Carson muttered.

I ignored his snarky tone. "You're welcome to keep looking around. Go check out the wine cellar."

Carson merely replied with a squint and a snort.

I shrugged off his cantankerousness, chalking it up to shock and awe. Even though he was also just a jerk and in the last eight years, I doubted that had changed at all. "That's the deal, boys," I finally said. "Live in the house for a year together, or cede it to the state. The choice is yours." *And please choose to get rid of the house.*

"My choice is a second opinion." Callum's voice had the same steely, emotionless tone he'd used the day he'd broken up with me.

Not like I still heard that voice in my nightmares on occasion or anything.

My brows lifted in slow-motion. Maybe this was the secret out I'd been waiting for.

At this point, if they requested a second opinion, I'd be able to spin it to my boss well enough. I could probably still eke out the promotion. And wouldn't that be the best-case scenario? Less time spent with the Winters brothers. Less time spent wilting in Callum's presence.

"There's no way our deceased father can command us to live inside a decaying house from the 1800s," Callum went on. "We live in America, not in Medieval England."

"Why would you bring medieval England into this?" Carson muttered.

Colton's brows went together. "How could a house from the 1800s be in—"

"Quiet," Callum's voice emerged as a growl. And that was where the first crack in his cold facade began to crumble.

They were still brothers, at the end of the day. I could almost see the three of them settling the Medieval England comment with a brotherly arm-wrestling battle.

Or maybe a duel.

But nobody took it further, even though back in the day, Callum and I would have.

"You're welcome to investigate a modern-day alternative," I said, unable to hide my smirk. "Feel free to review your packets at your leisure. The will has been read, and the documents have been dispersed. Unless you choose to contest the will, my job today is done until you make your decision, at which time I will provide you with a list of the holdings. Normally, you would receive that list before agreeing to the year-long term, but one of the will conditions is that you must agree to the year *before* you get a list of the holdings."

"Fucking Dad and his schemes," Carson grumbled with a head shake.

I agreed with him, but since Carson and I were *not* friends, I chose not to respond. I fixed my gaze on Colton since he was the only person in the house I *could* look at without feeling nauseous. "Do you have any questions?"

The brothers were silent, but I could *feel* the discontent radiating off Callum. Even with all this time apart, I could still intuit the soft parts of his heart. And now, I suspected that this unexpected reunion would strengthen that connection that we'd had since the beginning. The connection that still plagued me even while we were apart. After everything that had transpired in my life—and probably his—since we were last together.

"You three can contact me through the firm if you need anything. And if you choose to go with a different lawyer, well ... good luck. There isn't much wiggle room with this case."

I spun on my heels and headed for the front door, drinking in the interior of the house one last time.

Hope Creek Manor was the type of place I'd always wanted to live. Sure, I had a beautiful townhouse downtown, with a postage stamp backyard and plenty of herbs in my container garden, but this was the type of place that begged for a family. For a *legacy*.

Inhabiting a house like this, with a man I chose and the children we loved, that was the secret fantasy that lurked within me. The fantasy I'd chosen to cover up with relentless promotions and ladder climbing once the heartbreak from Callum had shattered me.

But once I'd been diagnosed with breast cancer, that secret fantasy had only grown more raucous. Not knowing if I'd ever have a chance to build the family of my dreams—that shit was scary for a twenty-something. And now, after kicking cancer's ass, I'd be damned if I didn't get exactly what I wanted out of life.

So if Mr. Right didn't come along and the children never happened, I'd at least have this sparkling career to be proud of.

Maybe I would only ever be a full-time lawyer. Dismal dating prospects had convinced me I'd never manage to attach the wife and mother tags to the resume of my life.

Which meant that finding out that Callum Winters was attached to this dream home made everything sting worse. Not only had he almost been that dream man, but he also had ties to my hometown. His family founded my Winter Harbor and were, for all intents and purposes, Winter Harbor royalty.

He had property.

He had a legacy.

Except the property was one that none of the brothers wanted to claim, and his legacy was one of notoriety. Callum Winters was nothing but a shell of a future that would never be mine. A dream that I just couldn't grasp.

And now that I'd faced down both Callum and his legacy in Winter Harbor?

I needed to start forgetting about him for real this time.

CHAPTER FOUR

CALLUM

Everything inside me was tight, including the strings of my heart as Harlow slid her svelte frame and tight ass behind the wheel of her car, started the engine, and finally—after sitting there with the thing running for a good solid minute—pulled away from the house. The crunch of the gravel beneath her tires echoed from the quiet yard and through the still-open front double doors of the house. Only once her vehicle was out of sight did I turn to face my brothers.

"I'll start making some calls about finding another estate lawyer," I announced.

"Bro, not necessary," Colton said with an eye roll. "I'm sure all *T*s are dotted and all *I*s are crossed. Harlow seems completely capable."

To my surprise, Carson nodded, agreeing with Colton.

I dismissed them with a handwave. "I'm gonna make some calls."

It wasn't that I thought Harlow was incapable of doing her job—on the contrary, she was probably fucking awesome at it—but I just couldn't handle seeing her again. The gut-wrenching pain, the ache in my chest so severe if I didn't know any better, I would think I was having a coronary.

I wanted a second opinion because I needed to protect my heart.

I was homeless, jobless, and loveless and if I had to see her again, either for work or personal, the facade I was trying to keep until my luck turned around, would crumble and she'd see me for the epic failure that I was.

Callum Winters, New York up and comer does the financial belly flop of the century. That was *not* how I wanted her to see me. Not when I knew with utmost certainty that Harlow's life was monstrously better than mine.

Hell, at this point, my brothers' lives were probably better than mine, too.

I took a deep breath. The letter from Dear old Dad was a hot lump of coal in the ass pocket of my dress pants. I grabbed it and unfolded it, my eyes once again scanning the words written in our father's perfect handwriting.

Callum

A man my age has many a regret.

I have too many to list in a letter like this. But I will say that one of my ultimate regrets is not tending to the relationship of my sons. Not making your bond with your brothers my number one priority. Helping you boys cultivate it into something with strong roots, sturdy branches, and shelter to weather life's worst storms.

I never had brothers. Or sisters. It was just me. Until I met your mother.

She became my everything, and when she passed, my heart shattered. My world crumbled. I did everything I could to provide for you boys after your mother died, to give you what I thought you needed: education, discipline, structure. But I know now that providing the luxuries you boys had was very different from what you needed.

You needed love.

You needed patience.

You needed guidance.

You needed me.

And I was not there. And for that, I am going to my grave a sorry man. When we lost your mother, I lost myself. I lost my soul. I struggled to look at you boys without feeling the pain of my loss at its fullest.

I cannot undo what is done. I cannot be a better father since I am nearing the end of my life. But what I can do, what I still have the power to do is bring my boys back together. To encourage you to rebuild the family that I destroyed.

Unite the Winters as they were meant to be. As your mother would have wanted you to be. This was my family's home. Where I was born. Where I was raised. It is now yours if you want it. The land, the house, and all the holdings that come with it—if and only if, you and your brothers can live in this house TOGETHER for one full year. Three hundred and sixty-five nights must be spent in a row in this house together. Otherwise, you forfeit the entire inheritance. I want my sons to be there for each other. To learn to love each other. To lean on each other. Learn to work together and get along as you once did when you were children. I want you to raise your families here together and create a new Winters dynasty. The kind of legacy that Winter Harbor deserved.

That our family deserved.

Call it eccentricity of a dying man, but these are my conditions. I look to you, Callum, as the eldest, the most level-headed and mature of my sons to convince your brothers that this is what is best for all of you. This town is meant to have Winters living in it. This roof is meant to have Winters sleeping beneath it. This land is meant to be trod on by Winters children, young and old. Be the guiding light Carson and Colton sorely need. The beacon I was too broken and distracted to be. You are the patriarch of this family now. You are the leader, and I trust you and believe that you can bring the Winters family into a new era of brilliance.

Good luck, my son.

Love,

Dad.

"What does yours say?" Colton's voice, too close for comfort, made me scrunch the letter in my fist and jerk my head in his direction. My brows knitted together as my baby brother peered over my shoulder.

"None of your business," I growled, turning away from him. I glanced back, curiosity winning the battle over my ire. "What's yours say?"

Colton's smarmy smile turned even more tempting to punch. "I'll show you mine if you show me yours."

Folding the letter again, I showed him my back and shoved the note into my front pocket this time. "Not a chance."

"We don't have to play pass the dead dad letter," Carson chimed in, wandering over from where he'd been rooted beside the enormous handcrafted wooden mantle to stand in front of the window with Colton and me. "But did your letters say that we had to spend three hundred and sixty-five consecutive days here?"

I grunted. "Yeah."

"Mhmm," Colton agreed. "Do you think that means that if one of us sleeps elsewhere for even one night, we lose the inheritance, or we just have to start over?"

"That's a question for the lady who just left as fast as those high heels of hers could carry her." Carson's tone held a level of asshole satisfaction I didn't like.

Colton scratched the back of his neck. "Well, I mean I'm game if you guys are. I'll have to move some shit around, of course. I'm a rather busy guy. But for twenty mil or whatever Harlow said this place and all the holdings are worth, I can postpone my trip to Ibiza until next year."

"Thanks for being so accommodating," I said sarcastically.

What was he going to do in Ibiza?

I knew very little about my youngest brother. We went to the same boarding school for a few years, but then when he started acting out, beyond that of a normal kid, he was expelled and Dad moved him to another school. And then another and another. And finally, military school. In reality, I didn't grow up with Colton, so I didn't know him.

Was a year in this house, in this town, enough to change that?

Did he want it? Did he want to know me?

"Well, I can't just abandon my construction job," Carson said. "I have a boss, projects, and clients that depend on me. Maybe in a month … but even then."

Where was Carson even living now? Since shit between him, Harlow, and I went down eight years ago, I hadn't seen the hide, hair, or slightly crooked nose of my brother. And

I didn't speak enough with our dad to get an update—not that I would have asked for one, anyway.

"I guess I could move some shit around ... for that kind of scratch." Carson was now murmuring to himself more than he was to us. "I'm going to go check out the upstairs."

"I'm gonna go find the wine cellar," Colton said, taking off toward what could have been the kitchen.

And I was going to start Googling alternatives for estate lawyers.

With the phone glued to my ear, I listened to the receptionist for the only other estate law firm in the tiny seaside town prattle on about how busy lawyers in her firm were.

"Mr. Yu is *very* busy. I'm not sure he can take on anything new right now. Particularly one where he's just fact-checking."

I rolled my eyes at the same time as I ran my index finger over the raised edge of the white wainscoted wall. Dust lifted off, coating the pad of my finger. I flicked it away. "What about Mr. Yu's associate, Ms ... O'D—"

"Ms. O'Dell is on personal leave. Which is why we're very busy. I can get you the number for Quick & Fairchild. They're the other estate office in Winter Harbor, and they have several attorneys who I'm sure could help you."

Grinding my teeth, I stuck my finger in my other ear as the *clomp clomp* of Carson's boots upstairs made it difficult to hear the woman. "I'll figure something out, thank you."

"You have a good day now." How could anybody be that chipper—ever? Nobody in New York was that happy.

Well, weed was legal in Oregon—maybe she had a couple of puffs on her lunch break.

Heavy footsteps upstairs again had me glaring at the ceiling. If we did end up doing this joke of a requirement to get our money, Carson could sleep in the basement. He sounded like a rhino wearing gumboots up there.

I worked my way through the enormous living room and dining room and down the dimly lit hallway with its wooden paneled walls and vaulted ceilings until I stood next to the banister. Dust covered every surface, and you could tell where painting or frames had once hung as the surrounding walls had faded, leaving various square and oval shapes of a darker green throughout the foyer. An enormous chandelier—uglier than fuck, I might add—hung above my head with more cobwebs hanging from it than drop crystals, and there were a lot of fucking drop crystals.

Harlow said the historical society wanted the house—but why? What was significant about this dusty old house with its rotting porch and overgrown yard?

"Found the wine cellar." Colton's voice boomed through the house as he pushed open the swinging kitchen door. He held three bottles in his arms and hand. "Grandpappy and Grandmammy had decent taste in vino."

He handed me a bottle. Like everything else in the house, it was covered in dust, but after I wiped the label, I saw that Colton was indeed correct. A Chateau de hiver from ... holy shit, 1975.

"Here's another one from the late sixties," Colton said, wiping off more dust. "Chateau de hiver ... why have I heard that name before?"

"It's because it's a very famous winery in the south of France," Carson said, appearing at the top of the stairs. "Hiver means winter in French. The winery is Winter Castle."

Colton's brows furrowed just as deep as mine.

"You don't think ..." our youngest brother asked, his thoughts undoubtedly going in the exact same direction as my own. Did we have ancestors in France who owned a winery?

I took the third bottle from him and wiped the label clean. "This one is different."

Carson clomp-clomped his way down the stairs like a speedy mule and snatched the final bottle from me. "*L'ete Eternel.*"

"Summer eternal. Or Eternal Summer, more precisely," he translated. Though he didn't have to. He and I both went to boarding school in Switzerland, where learning French had been mandatory. I'd also taken German and Spanish, while Carson thought that Italian would get him laid more, and Mandarin just made good business sense—which it did, and I was now learning Mandarin via app.

But of course, Carson was the know-it-all showboat, so he liked to throw that he was multilingual in everyone's faces.

"Okay, so Winter Castle and Eternal Summer, what the hell does all of this mean?" Colton's nose scrunched as he spun the bottle around in his hand to reach the faded label on the back. "You think this shit is still any good?"

"It means our grandparents and our father have more secrets than I think we could figure out in a year," I said, handing Colton the remaining bottle from my hand and heading out to the front porch. I needed some fresh air. The house was musty and stuffy, despite its high ceilings and empty rooms, and I was beginning to get claustrophobic. The past was closing in around me like the spiked walls in *Indiana Jones and the Temple of Doom*. The ghosts I'd never met and the secrets that they kept hidden—obviously for a reason—were creeping around, whispering words I didn't want to hear. I didn't need that headache. I wasn't into paranormal shit, didn't like mysteries, never had.

I liked facts.

I liked numbers.

I liked reality.

And even though my reality currently sucked, I was hellbent on changing that. A dead man couldn't force us to give up our entire lives for a year.

Could he?

I needed to figure out my life—which was complicated enough—I didn't need the enigmas and puzzles that came with this house and new long, lost family weighing down my already endless pile of problems to sift through and organize. Not to mention the possibility of seeing Harlow again and again and having that scab constantly picked.

I could handle a month here—tops. Just enough time to regroup, organize, and figure out the next chapter in my life, which the longer I thought about it, was not back in NYC.

There was nothing for me there.

Not anymore.

Gulping air, I jumped from the rotting porch onto the gravel. The grass on either side of the pathway down to the circular driveway was overgrown and thick with weeds. Bees buzzed from clover to clover and butterflies made purchase on the flowers in the jungle-esc flower beds that crawled over the corner of the foundation.

I followed the bees and blossoms into the shade and around the house—also away from my brothers.

God only knew the last time anyone had called this house home. The windows were still single pane, the exterior paint and trim were curling, the roof's wood shingles were rotted and peeling off. Random piles of newspapers, stacks of books, photo albums, and various garbage bags full of who knows what, dotted the rooms—pretty weird addition to the inheritance, if you asked me. The house needed work and a fuck-ton of it.

Would all the reno expenses have to come out of our own pockets or would the estate cover it? I wasn't exactly *flush* with cash at the moment.

I knew a lot about business, but nothing about wills, though I'm pretty sure there was something called probate we had to deal with. I needed to do some Googling.

It'd been a little over a month since the Raven Corp deal had gone south. I spent that month drinking, trying to find another job, and then finally giving in to the horrible realization that New York was done with me, and I needed to chase my dreams elsewhere. My condo was barely on the market a week before someone snapped it up, and they took possession at the end of the month. So, for all intents and purposes, I was homeless.

The sale of my home would pad my wallet for a little while, but it wouldn't get me far for long. I had plans—big plans—and I needed capital to do that. If everything went well, I'd be a resident of California sooner rather than later. I also wasn't keen on footing the bill for the entire thing while my brothers watched me open my wallet but didn't open theirs, only to take their cut of the inheritance and get the fuck out of town as fast as possible.

"Where do you think that goes?"

I nearly leaped clean out of my skin. From rhino in gumboots to tiptoeing field mouse, Carson made a point of hitting his shoulder into mine as he trudged through the grass past me toward a small door on the side of the house.

I grunted and called him a dick.

The rusty-hinged entrance had seen better days. Better years. The once-white paint flaked off and the vine and moss-covered concrete steps down to the not even five-foot high door were crumbling and appeared to have big purposeful chunks taken out of them.

"Looks like a hobbit door," Colton said, having followed us.

Carson descended a couple of steps and heaved on the door. It didn't so much as wiggle. "Is there a key for this?" he grunted, pulling on it again as if it might suddenly give way and gracefully swing open.

"Harlow only left three keys, and they're all for the front," Colton said.

"You didn't see any door down in the wine cellar?" Carson asked, studying the palms of his hands, which were now filthy with rust residue and years' worth of grime. He climbed the stairs and lifted his face to the sky. "Didn't see how to get to that balcony when I was upstairs."

All three of us stepped away from the house to find a widow's walk with dilapidated railings missing several rungs and posts. Windows closed in the cupola and the gutters above were teaming with leaves from the surrounding maples. A rocking chair, probably as old as the house itself and not one I would ever consider sitting in, seemed to rock of its own volition in the corner.

"Well, that's fucking creepy," Colton muttered. "Didn't see how to get to that door in the cellar. But the basement is huge. Only saw the cellar."

"I didn't see how to get to that widow's walk," Carson repeated. "Hidden door upstairs, maybe?"

"Only one way to find out," Colton said. Without waiting for either of us to respond, he took off back around the house toward the front door.

Carson smiled and glanced back at me, but that stupid grin fled his lips the moment he caught my lack of interest.

"You not coming?" he asked.

I shook my head. "Gonna check out the property a bit, then head out."

"And go where?" Carson probed. "Got a hot date? Little wifey back at the hotel waiting for you?"

My molars gnashed, and I made tight fists at my sides, which made an ache bloom in my knuckles. Knuckles that longed to make contact with my brother's face.

Eight years later or eighty, it didn't matter. I still harbored anger toward my middle brother and the hand he had in the demise of Harlow's and my relationship. He'd enjoyed watching our bond disintegrate.

Who did that to another person?

Who did that to their brother?

But I was better than this. I was better than him. I wouldn't stoop to his level.

I would spend my efforts on getting to know Colton. Carson had burned any bridge or opportunity for a real relationship with me.

Part of me wanted to get closer to him, but knowing who he was, what he was capable of, and the hurtful side of him made it impossible. I couldn't forgive. And I couldn't forget. Especially not now. Not after seeing Harlow again and realizing I was still madly in love with her. Carson had ruined that—on purpose.

He'd gone out of his way to implode my relationship with Harlow days before graduation, and hours before the biggest interview of my upcoming career. Carson had come to me with a bomb that had been designed to not just derail my life, but cripple it: *he and Harlow had a history, didn't I know? Interesting, she wouldn't tell me after a year that she was my middle brother's sloppy seconds? Say, does Harlow still like having her tits bitten?*

And thanks to his well-timed detonation, I'd lost the job. The girl. The happiness. No way in hell would I open myself up to heartache like that again with this asshole.

"Hmm, big brother? Haven't heard what you've been up to for the last few years. You a bigshot on Wall Street with a supermodel wife and brownstone in Brooklyn? How's the wifey going to take you having to live here for a year?" His chuckle made nails on a chalkboard sound like a beautiful aria. "Or have you pined after our lawyer all these years?"

His mention of Harlow and calling her *our lawyer* had me turning around. I gave him a look I hoped conveyed my irritation and that he best stop his goading. His sneer of response did nothing but elevate my temperature and make my fists itchy.

"Still an asshole, I see," I muttered, turning away from him again to head toward the house.

I would not stoop to his level.

I was the bigger person.

I was the *better* person.

"And you're still just a miserable bastard who thinks he's better than me. Who thinks he's better than everyone." He snorted. "Stop pretending like you're some fucking saint and the rest of us are all heathens. I went to the same boarding schools as you, remember? Same college too. Just because I don't drive a Lexus or have a tie for every day of the month, doesn't mean I don't know shit. I might have dirt under my nails now because my job is hands-on, but I'm proud of what I do. I like my life. Can you say the same, *big brother*? Do you like the man you turned into? Do you have everything you ever wanted? Every*one* you ever wanted?"

I turned around again slowly. The way he sang that last question made blood bubble magma-hot in my veins. I could hear it rushing through my head, my pulse pounding in my ears. He knew exactly what he was doing, exactly who he was talking about. I gritted my teeth for control, but the infinitesimal twitch of Carson's lip said he knew he'd hit his mark.

"You always had the biggest fucking ego out of all of us," he said. "God forbid the tables turn and you get *my* hand-me-downs—"

My fist drew up like an angry stone and made contact with my brother's cheekbone, sending a vibration through my hand and up my arm like an electrical shock—followed immediately by blinding pain not only in my hand, but also in my face as his fist caught me hard in the left eye. My head flew back at the same time Carson tackled me around the middle, sending both of us flying backward into the high grass and weeds, rolling around in the hot spring sun, fist flying, legs kicking.

How dare he call Harlow his fucking hand-me-downs. Like she was an old sweatshirt he wore, then passed on to me. Fuck him.

If this was how the next year was going to be, count me out.

We'd fought a lot as kids, but I'd always managed to get the upper hand on him. It'd been a while since we scrapped, and he'd put on the pounds—though apparently, it was all in muscle.

To be honest, I was probably more surprised than Carson was that I hit him. Sure, I was still pissed off at my brother for what he did to me and Harlow, but I'd like to think I'd moved on at least a bit over the last eight years.

Apparently, I hadn't.

Apparently, seeing Harlow and Carson in the same space brought back every raw, angry feeling I had hidden in the deep recesses of my mind.

And when he got on his high horse and started flapping his lips the way he was always prone to do, my fist reacted before my brain did.

"Stupid fucker," he grunted, squeezing his legs around my middle and flipping me back onto my back.

"You're the stupid fucker." I'd been taking Krav Maga for the past four years, so I knew how to fight, how to defend myself and hold my own, but apparently, Carson was taking some kind of dirty biker street-fighting because no matter how hard I tried to roll him off me using all my strength and every ounce of my training, the asshole kept me pinned.

I. Could. Not. Lose. To. My. Younger. Brother.

With me beneath him, Carson sat up, straddling my hips, his nose bloody, lip cut, and swollen. A chuckle bubbled up from his throat and he smiled, wiping the back of his wrist over his mouth and smearing the blood. His eyes narrowed into crinkled slits. The level of satisfaction I got from seeing my brother bleed was oddly disconcerting. "You always were so fucking easy to rile up. Can't come in second, can you? God forbid you get your little brother's hand-me-downs, huh?"

"Fuck you," I spat out.

"What the hell are you guys doing?" Colton came barreling out from the front of the house. The look of shock on his face was not one I was normally used to seeing. Ordinarily, there wasn't much that fazed my youngest brother. From what I remembered about him, when he wasn't stirring up trouble, Colton proceeded through life at a steady lope of *meh*.

Carson tilted his head at me. "You gonna come at me again?"

I jerked beneath him, not done pounding the shit out of him by a long shot, but knowing that he'd probably pound the shit out of me in the process. "Get the fuck off me."

He didn't budge. "You gonna come at me again?"

Through gritted teeth and heat in my extremities, I managed a reluctant *no*.

"Good." He climbed off me, but didn't offer me a hand.

Colton stood there just watching us. "Seriously, you guys. Is this still over a girl?"

Not *a* girl. *The* girl. There was a big fucking difference.

Rolling his eyes, Colton shoved his hands through his hair. "I'm starving. I'm gonna go grab some food, cancel my hotel, buy a sleeping bag or something, and then come back and spend the night."

"I'm not starting day one of three hundred and sixty-five tonight," I said, gingerly touching my eye. I was not looking forward to seeing what my face looked like in the mirror of my car.

Colton shrugged, the mask of indifference back on his face. "Do as you like. But I want to learn more about this place before I make up my mind whether I want to put in the effort to live here for a year or not."

"My note said we *all* had to stay for an entire year," Carson said, the purple bruise around his nose and mouth getting darker by the second. "So you can stay here for ten years in a row if you want, but unless we all agree, you get squat. And if you stay here too long, you'll be a *squatter*."

Colton turned to head back toward the driveway. "My note said the same thing. And I can tell this place has secrets. Like, are there legit skeletons hiding in some of these closets?" He headed off down the driveway toward a motorcycle, its shiny chrome tank glinting in the sun.

Like idiots, we stood there watching as our brother put on his helmet, retracted his kickstand, and revved his engine.

"He thinks he's a rebel," Carson said, taking off back toward the front of the house at the same time Colton's back tire sent gravel flying as he sped down the driveway to the main road.

Reluctantly, I followed Carson back toward the front door.

"You at a hotel too?" I asked, my lip feeling puffy and making speech surprisingly difficult.

He grunted, thundering up the wooden porch steps.

"You coming back here like what's-his-nuts?"

He grunted again, pulled one of the house keys out of his pocket and locked the front door. Making his way back down the steps, he didn't so much as glance at me as he headed to his truck.

"You going to even answer me?" I shouted back at him, the anger from our fight in the grass resurfacing and making the hair on the back of my neck lift.

"Harlow's our attorney for a reason." He called back, not bothering to stop or turn around. The light of his truck flashed as he unlocked it with the fob.

"What the fuck does that mean?" I hollered. Had he figured out that Harlow worked at the law firm ahead of time and orchestrated her being our attorney just to further fuck with me? After some of the shit I knew my brother had pulled in his younger years, it didn't seem too far-fetched.

And after his comments about Harlow being his hand-me-downs, it seemed more plausible than ever.

All Carson did was lift a brow at me and smirk. He opened his door and swung his big frame in behind the wheel.

I stood in front of the house and watched my brother drive away. Where? I had no clue. He could be heading to the nearest hardware store to buy a cot, so he and Colton could have a slumber party in the living room for all I knew. I would not be joining them.

I glanced back at the house. An eerie calm had settled over it since Colton and Carson left. A warm breeze from the nearby creek that quietly burbled not too far away ruffled the branches and leaves of the enormous maples that edged the yard, the only competing sounds were the chirp and tweet of songbirds in the apple and cherry trees by the overgrown fenced-in garden.

Potential possessed every inch of the yard, the fruit trees, fenced gardens, and abundant raised beds. All the life was still there, hidden beneath the overgrowth, it just had to be harnessed and tamed, rather than allowed to run free-range like some rogue goat who picked the lock on the barn door.

When I'd first arrived, the manor looked haunted. Unkept, ramshackle, and beyond repair. Too far gone for even one of those HGTV house flipper shows. But once inside, I realized how much character the house had. How much life it still had in it, how much life it had witnessed, been a part of.

The stories it could tell. The secrets it kept.

I wasn't a big fan of secrets—given the way my love life and family life had played out thus far, we could say secrets are a trigger for me—but the longer I stood there and stared up at the house that my father had grown up in, the more I realized I needed to know those secrets. I couldn't leave Winter Harbor in a year and still have those secrets *be* secrets.

I turned around to head to my rental car when a *chirp* followed by a *thwack* against glass had me spinning back around.

The grass was high, but even so, I could see movement just below the living room window I'd been staring out of earlier.

I wasn't sure what came over me, but I jogged over to the tall grass where a robin lay flapping one wing and struggling to get up.

Shit.

39

I was no vet, but even an idiot could tell it had broken a wing.

I was in a rental, so I had nothing but the clothes on my back with me. I couldn't very well leave the little thing to die, either. So, not really knowing what to do--but knowing I needed to do something--I unbuttoned my dress shirt, so I was in nothing more than a white undershirt, and I gingerly lifted the bird into my shirt where I ruffled it up until it was a nest of sorts.

"I gotcha," I said, taking in the bird's terrified gaze. "We'll getcha sorted."

I took another glance at the house and the imprint of where the robin had smashed into the window. We'd need to do something about those windows. There had to be something we could put on them to prevent birds from flying into them.

That thought struck me like an unwelcomed fork in the back of my hand. I was already thinking like I was going to live here for a year. Planning to fix the windows to save birds. What next, a hummingbird feeder? A birdbath?

With a deep inhale, I accepted my fate. I needed the money.

And as much as my past had left me soured when it came to secrets, as Colton said, I too could feel the mystery and all the burning questions we had about our family and mother hiding in this town and in the mansion.

We just had to go digging for them and be prepared for whatever—good or bad—may come to light. And that included real skeletons tumbling out of closets.

Now all I had to do was convince my brothers I was in this for the right reasons, convince them to stay for a year, avoid the hell out of Harlow for a simple three hundred and sixty-five days, not get murdered by a ghost, uncover all the family mysteries, collect my inheritance, and then my new life could start.

Easy fucking peasy.

But first, I needed to save this damn bird.

CHAPTER FIVE

HARLOW

Safe to say, three full days not glimpsing or even being in the same building as Callum Winters was not enough to push him out of my mind.

And despite Mr. Sunshine's warm reception to the details of his father's will the other day—which could only be described as *frosty* with a side of *totally rude*—I was not able to successfully keep my hand from wandering between my legs in the shower each night.

All thoughts inevitably drifted toward Callum. Because how could they not? Not only was he *still* the hottest man I'd ever laid eyes on—even all these years later—he'd gotten broodier and sharper in his handsomeness.

But despite this, I was officially praying for him to *leave*. The ball was in his—and his brothers'—court. They needed to either buck up to living in the house for the next year or move along. They had ten days to decide, and apparently, the Winters brothers planned to draw out their decision to the bitter end. I shouldn't have expected otherwise.

So this meant that I spent basically every waking moment of my life waiting for Callum. Waiting to hear from him. Waiting to see if he'd actually found some lawyer stupid enough to promise him a different result. Waiting to see if I'd accidentally cross paths with him somewhere.

And who knows—maybe all that thinking about him finally led him to my doorstep. Or rather, the grocery store. Because that Thursday, as I rounded my familiar path through Harbor & Home, the downtown family-owned grocery store, I found Callum in the toilet paper aisle.

It wasn't the most glamorous place to run into the ex-love-of-your-life. And granted, his back was turned to me, so I could have escaped without him seeing me.

What made it harder to walk away was the little old lady to his right. The local legend Maribel Malone herself. She pointed at a shelf, jabbing her index finger repeatedly as Callum tried for one TP brand after the other. I drifted closer without knowing why, or what my game plan might be. Maribel was known for being both town historian and disoriented old granny, so something begged me to stick around and see what happened here. Besides, my skin prickled with curiosity about what might happen between us if we were relatively alone in the personal hygiene aisle.

"No, the one with the pink bows," Maribel said.

"Oh, you mean this one." The rumble of Callum's voice was gentle. Almost soothing. Not at all the snark-edged knife that he'd wielded around me and his brothers.

I drew a fortifying breath. *That's the voice that's going to get you in trouble.*

The thought felt like a thunder crack from the heavens, but I knew better than to listen to crackpot missives from above. Even still, I needed to evacuate. Feigning my best *Oh I thought I needed something down here but actually I have to run far, far away* face of deep concentration, I tugged at my little cart and began backing up.

Just as Maribel pointed at me over Callum's shoulder and said, "I'll ask her!"

Callum twisted toward me and straightened. The alarm bells began shrieking inside my chest and everything inside me went hot and aware.

My mouth parted, and I wasn't sure what to do next. I felt like I'd been outed by the heavens I'd just rejected, and that there was some joke happening of which I was *definitely* not aware.

"What?" I croaked.

"Miss, can you come help me with a *personal item*?" Maribel asked. "This fine gentleman here helped me greatly so far, but I'd rather he not help with the next item on my list."

I opened my mouth to respond, but nothing came out. Callum's expectant gaze on me was so heavy and provocative I thought I might crumple to the ground under the weight of it.

"It'll only be a second," Maribel continued.

"Yes," I blurted, pushing my little cart toward them. I didn't know how to handle Callum, so I simply chose to ignore him. Except my cheeks didn't get the memo. Those bastard beacons of embarrassment were hot as a bonfire, and I couldn't do a damn thing. "What can I get for you?"

"I normally ask store employees to help me, but I haven't seen one for the past half hour." While she jabbered about the pitfalls of the recent generational shift of management within the owning family, Callum grabbed the handle of his shopping cart. Suddenly, Maribel stopped her yammering and looked at us.

"You two would make a good couple. You both happen to be single? Wouldn't that be a love story! Started in Harbor & Home. A couple of years from now, you could be in aisle six buying diapers for a baby."

My stomach shriveled into an acid nut and dropped to the floor. I couldn't think of anything to say, but I still managed to blurt, "Oh, don't be ridiculous. He's too old for me."

It was a throwback. One I definitely hadn't intended on. We'd always joked in college that Callum was too much my senior for us to be together, which was extra funny while we were both in our senior year. He was only two years older than me, but I'd entered college at a second-semester sophomore based on all my college credit courses I'd taken in high school. So while I was Carson's age—and had entered in his class—I made it into Callum's graduating class.

My mouth flapped uselessly as I struggled to make sense of why that comment had escaped me. Nothing made sense when Callum was around me. Nothing other than how much the man continued to light me up, whether I wanted him to or not.

Callum managed something similar to a pained grimace and walked away. I needed to get out of here—*now.* I got Maribel back on track—turned out she just needed some adult diapers—squeezed her hand, and dislodged myself from her sweet but talkative chokehold.

My cart nearly tipped over as I took the corner at the end of the aisle at full speed. I was racing to get away from Callum—or was I racing to get near him? I didn't know anymore, and that made me more upset, so I just needed to get out of the building altogether and pretend we hadn't had an awkward run-in by the toilet paper. Besides, that freak encounter answered a few of the questions I had for Callum: namely that he was still in town, which meant he was just as close to signing the deal as he was running away forever.

I speed shopped, largely unaware of what I was tossing into my cart. Just *knowing* that Callum could lurk around any corner made me jumpy and short-of-breath. I grabbed my essentials—forgetting entirely the toilet paper I'd originally come for—and hopped into a check-out line.

Right behind Callum Winters.

I stifled a groan, all of my muscles going tense. I could have backed up and sloooowly slid into the adjacent cashier's line without him noticing. And I intended to, fully, except he turned just as I'd begun a cat-like creep backward, and he pinned me with those frosty blues.

"You're following me now?"

All of the goodwill he'd garnered by being a good Samaritan in aisle five evaporated in a puff. "Trust me, I'm trying not to."

He hefted with a humorless laugh. "Thought maybe it was part of the estate lawyer package."

Something hot and electric seared through me. Time to test the waters. "Why would I do that? You're looking for a second opinion."

"You must have said something to all your little lawyer friends because nobody wants to take the case. How convenient."

My fingers curled around the handle of the shopping cart. *Little lawyer friends.* Callum always had a way of turning so few words into a full-blown war cry. "Well, I did warn you that would happen. Guess you just needed to find out for yourself, huh? Like a true man."

"Life doesn't give me a lot of reason to trust what other people say," he snapped.

His words landed like a spear because that's how he'd intended it. A spear lobbed straight from our sorry shared past.

And if there was one thing I was tired of, it was of people not believing me—or believing *in* me. And Callum had checked off both of these items from his list. First, by not believing me eight years ago when I told him that I hadn't lied to him about sleeping with Carson before meeting Callum. And now, his not-so-thinly-veiled attacks on my professional capabilities.

And really, his perfectly-aimed spear answered another one of my questions: *did he still care?* The answer was sort of. Eight years later, he still cared enough to needle me about it. And yes, I *had* slept with Carson a handful of times during a sad and lonely period of my freshman year. But the man was not my type. Not then, and not now.

"*Life* doesn't give you much reason to trust others?" I scoffed. "I think it has less to do with life and more to do with you, Sunshine." I couldn't stop myself. If he could lob the spear, then I could send one back. "Just because you don't want to give up your suspicious, bitter outlook on life doesn't mean that everyone else is lying."

If he'd been unaffected before, now I could see the hackles rising.

"Suspicious and bitter to you. Others might call it being a realist."

"Fine." I sniffed, the words tumbling past my lips before I could stop them. "Have it your way."

If there'd ever been a phrase to initiate a stand-off, that was the one. The phrase had always been charged between us. And maybe I'd used it to escalate a fight or two. But it had slipped out of me, unbidden, from the depths of our raucous history. And while I searched his face, I asked myself, *What did you ever see in this man?*

I just couldn't figure out if it was a rhetorical question or a challenge.

The air went tight between us, a cord desperate to snap, but the cashier cleared her throat.

"Sir, I can help you now."

Callum set his jaw and turned to her, his face stern as he unloaded his sparse cart quickly. Yes, I spied on him, and from the looks of his cart, his senior year self had decided to stay: ramen noodles, deli meats, a few packages of cheese.

Or maybe he just hadn't budged an inch since college—a young adult trapped in amber. If I was smart, I'd have moved on by now, but instead, I furtively watched him while he checked out. He produced a small wire cage from the bottom of the cart, but conspicuously left a shoebox in the front part of his cart, where a child would be seated.

"Is there anything in there I need to ring up?" the cashier asked.

"No," Callum said, just as something in the box chirped.

My brows shot into the air along with the cashier's.

"Did something just chirp?" I asked, unable to hold the question in.

Callum's jaw flexed as he turned to me. "Yes. But it doesn't concern you."

"Do you have live chicks for sale?" I asked the cashier. "He might be trying to steal one."

The cashier chuckled, but Callum ignored me as he shuffled along the side of the cart and opened the shoebox.

A live bird stared out at me, nestled in what looked like Callum's sleek business shirt from the other day.

"He's injured," he replied curtly, and then moved back to the cashier to pay.

"You some kind of animal-whisperer?" the cashier asked.

Yes, actually, Callum was. At least the old Callum had been, and it appeared the current Callum still was.

Callum lifted a shoulder. "If animals are hurt, I try to help. Done it a bit over the years, know what I'm doing now. Most vets won't take little wild animals, and if they do, it's expensive."

The cashier smiled. "What's your name, sir? Just in case anybody else comes across an injured critter and needs to know where to take it."

Callum's side-eye hit me hard. He cleared his throat and glanced back at the cashier. "Callum Winters."

The cashier's hazel eyes widened, and her smile dropped so hard I could almost hear it. "Winters."

Callum nodded. "Yeah." He tapped his credit card to the machine, took his receipt from the now stony-faced woman behind the till, and then he was gone. Deli meats, injured bird, and all.

I just wasn't sure if the heat prickling through me signaled relief or insanity. Because suddenly, I remembered what I had seen in Callum. It was the thing that had drawn me in like a fishing lure. His hard edges were laced with tenderness. A drive to nurture that was only slightly eclipsed by his drive to succeed.

He'd rescued countless animals throughout college. The man seemed to attract cats stuck in trees, too, which he'd always figure out a way to coax down to safe ground. We always joked that once we bought a house, he'd have it brimming with temporary animal residents by the end of the first week.

And with this house in Winter Harbor, it had taken three days.

Because Callum was the man who would save a bird in a town he'd decided to loathe. Which meant I already knew his answer regarding the will.

He'd be nurturing that house back to life with the family he couldn't stand.

Just as he was nurturing the bird. And I knew very well, he'd never been a fan of birds—at least not the kind that could shit on his car. But it seemed like he was able to put aside his ire for all things winged and beaky and was determined to nurse the robin back to health.

It made me wonder if he could put aside his distaste for birds, would he be able to put aside his rancor for me as well? At least enough to make the next year livable for the both of us?

Once I had been checked out and was safely back inside the confines of my neat townhouse, I got to work doing all the things that I knew would calm me down.

Watering plants, cooking dinner, and becoming the resident Down-There DJ.

They were easily in my top five activities, the type of things that would be included on my tombstone if they allowed things like that. But after all my peonies had been watered, a delicious roasted veggie dinner consumed, and *way* too many thoughts of Callum indulged in with my hand stuffed down my panties, I still didn't feel right.

There was something deeply unsettled inside me that needed attention, and I refused to give in. I needed someone to talk sense into me. Someone like my best friend Jayne.

She picked up on the third ring. College besties separated by a hundred miles, but never far from each other's minds. She'd known Callum in college too, which meant she was the *only* person who could set me right on this.

"Harlooow," she cooed. Pots and pans clanked in the background. She was probably getting dinner ready for her and her husband. If I knew her well, it was lasagna or lasagna-relevant.

"What's up, friend?"

"Just getting dinner ready. We're having raviolis."

I smirked to myself. "I wish I could have some."

"Move to Summer Hills already."

I sighed heavily. Summer Hills would only ever be an option because of my bestie, but in all honesty, Winter Harbor was my home. Now, and forevermore. I couldn't envision anything that would take me from here. Not the promise of Jayne's fantastic Italian menus. Not even if Prince Charming himself descended from heaven on a gold-encrusted steed and promised me a never-ending sex drive.

"If only that's where I wanted to live....." I said.

"I know, I know," Jayne conceded. In the background, a blender whirred. "Winter Harbor is where you'll die. I get it."

I snorted. "Most likely. Though due to recent events, I'm wondering if I should even stay."

She gasped. "What happened?"

I paused, suddenly unsure I wanted to dive into the sordid story. "It's ... well ... how can I put this? Callum is back in my life."

Jayne was eerily silent for a moment. Then sputtered, "What?"

"I can't get into the details ... you know, client-lawyer confidentiality and all that but—"

"Wait, he's your *client*?"

I sighed. "Yeah."

"Jesus. And he's being a dick? I can already tell he's being a dick."

"That's putting it mildly." Unfortunately, the mention of *dick* reminded me of his very own *nice* appendage.

I just needed to ignore that part of me with logic and reason.

"So, does he live in Winter Harbor now?" Jayne pressed.

"I don't know."

"And you can't say."

"And I can't say."

She laughed softly. "Well, if the town gets too small for you and him, you always have a room here. But I'd hate to see him chase you out of your hometown. It's *yours,* after all. And after what he did to you ..." She tutted. "He's the one who should be disappearing."

My throat tightened. She was right, but it didn't make things *easy.* "I know. But it's hard."

"I know, honey," she said, her voice softening. "Just tell me one thing. Is he still hot?"

I groaned. "Yes, of course he is. Hotter than ever, in fact. And he still rescues animals, which just ..."

"Doesn't help things."

Understatement of the century right there.

"No, it makes them worse. Much worse." I pressed a hand to my forehead, feeling suddenly dizzy.

"Whatever is going on, don't forget how much you've already overcome. You got over that asshole once, you graduated law school, you beat mother fucking breast cancer, you are just weeks away from becoming partner. Do not forget how fucking amazing you are.

I smiled. Her words settled something inside me, if only slightly. "Thank you."

We talked a bit more before finally hanging up. But it wasn't long before the discontent came swarming again. With the evening stretching ahead of me, promising turbulent loneliness, I knew that I couldn't just sit here, sober and mulling.

So what other option was there than getting fucking drunk?

CHAPTER SIX

HARLOW

I started with a nice glass of dry red wine, but by glass one-and-a-half, my weird emotions had only begun to multiply. At my ripe old age of twenty-nine, I knew better than to stay home alone to drown my sorrows.

No, I needed *people*. I needed commiseration, or at the very least, *distraction*. I didn't often head down to the most famous Winter Harbor watering hole, Beer & Moor, but when I did, it was always a good time. I just prayed that tonight it would help keep Callum out of my head—including thoughts about whether or not he'd named that injured bird yet, probably something annoyingly sweet like *Davie*.

Beer & Moor sat two blocks from my townhouse on a slight hill overlooking the sparkling Hope Bay, fed into, of course, by Hope Creek, which ran right next to Hope Creek Manor. Golden light from the setting sun bathed the town as I walked the two quaint and neatly manicured blocks to the bar, passing at least ten people that I knew, handing out friendly greetings like candy.

I sighed with relief once I saw the familiar sign of Beer & Moor, gladly entering the dimly lit yet kitschy-cute watering hole that nearly every tourist in the Pacific Northwest had visited at least once on their coastal route.

The scent of stale beer and fried food accosted me as soon as I stepped inside, already feeling better as I spotted the sparse yet motley crew of regulars lining the bar. Framed photos and signatures from celebrities A to D-list filled the wooden walls. I went straight for a stool with empty seats on either side, sliding off my trendy bolero jacket from my workday and hanging it on a tiny hook along the tall bar.

"Harlow! Long time no sip." The owner, a ruddy-cheeked and perpetually friendly old man named Burt Moor, was one of the main reasons behind Beer & Moor's notoriety. He never forgot a face and could talk to anyone for hours about almost any subject in the world. "What'll it be today? Another martini?"

I grinned as I slid onto the leather stool. "God, I haven't been in here in almost two months. You really never forget anything, do you? You must be an alien with that memory."

"That, or I always ate my vegetables as a kid. But it's definitely one of them. Hell, maybe both."

I snickered, assessing the line of backlit bottles behind him. "Yeah, a martini sounds like just the ticket. And make it extra filthy, my friend."

Burt sent me a warm smile before he got to work on my concoction. As I drank in the sights and sounds around me—the fast-paced, jazzy rock tune playing, the din of excited conversations, the clanking of the bottles as Burt readied my drink—I almost shot out of my seat when a rumbling bass said, "You still following me?"

I inhaled sharply, twisting to find Callum Winters, *yet a-fucking-gain.* Except this time, something looked different.

As he slid onto the barstool beside me, I realized what it was.

He'd been drinking. He'd loosened up. Which meant that the top three buttons of his button-up had been freed, the sleeves of his shirt rolled up his forearms, and that tantalizing patch of chest hair was out to play. He also had a smile on his face. It was small, but that did nothing to diminish its potency and what it did to my panties and their current level of dryness.

This man was trying to kill me. Rubbing one out in his memory had done nothing to allay the fire that he'd brought back to life between my legs.

"Don't even start," I hissed, trying to keep my movements casual even though there was a high chance we'd argue so badly Burt would ask us to leave. "I just came to enjoy a drink by myself. You're the one bothering *me* here."

"You sat in my seat." He gestured to an untended tumbler which, I'd admit, I'd assumed was abandoned.

"How am I supposed to know this was your seat? Where even were you?"

"In the bathroom. Giving a piss."

If he'd lobbed a mean spear at the grocery store earlier that day, then this was his spear to make amends. I stifled the laugh that wanted to spill out of me because I couldn't let him see that he was amusing in any way, shape, or form. No, I needed to stay mad. But dammit, we'd always joked about *giving* a piss, when so many people always *took* them. It was a stupid inside joke. One that I really wished still didn't delight me.

When I didn't respond, he nudged me with his elbow. "You remember, don't you?"

"Of course I remember."

"Then why didn't you laugh?"

"Because it's not funny anymore."

It was a lie, and apparently, he saw right through it. "Or let me guess, you don't want to engage with me now that I'm your *client*."

"It's definitely not recommended," I said, forcing a bright grin as Burt returned with my martini.

Burt jerked his chin toward Callum. "You know this guy?"

"Oh yeah," I said, receiving the perilously full martini glass. "Known him for a long time."

"Too long," Callum muttered. Once Burt looked satisfied and drifted back to a big group at the other side of the bar, I twisted to look at Callum.

"What is your fucking game here?"

"Game?" His bored rumble was both annoying and sexy. The man had always been able to turn me on with his voice alone. And I was here to confirm that his magic skill had only improved through the years. "I have no game."

"Why are you talking to me? You could have just picked up your—" I stumbled over my words as I tried to identify the liquid in his glass "—your stupid beer—"

"Whiskey," he interjected.

"Fine, you could have picked up your *whiskey* and just moved along, but no, you have to sit here and irritate me. Don't you have a bird to look after?"

"I could say the same about you. I was sitting here first, after all. And Jonas is *asleep*, I'll have you know."

Ugh, *Jonas*. Cuter than I'd expected, but I didn't let it derail me.

"Can't we just keep things professional?" I snapped, but in a restrained way, so that Burt and the other regulars wouldn't notice we were ten seconds away from taking this outside.

"But your cheeks just get so pink and sexy when you're mad."

That only caused my cheeks to get even hotter.

He used to enjoy teasing me or whispering dirty things in my ear just to make me blush. We'd rarely fought in our year together, so he did other things that would get my cheeks hot and pink. Truth be told, I liked it, too.

I took a long, concentrated sip of my drink. Stewing over my comeback.

"If you think I'm going to lose my shit," I said carefully, making sure to watch the other end of the bar, "then you never knew me at all."

"I'd say I knew you pretty well," he said, taking a pull at his whiskey. "More than pretty well."

"Not well enough to trust me, apparently."

I couldn't believe I went there. One sip into my martini and all bets were off. Every inch of my body was alert and expectant, waiting for him to serve me with something harsh and biting. But instead, I got an eerie silence. He drained his glass and set it on the bar. I tried not to look curious and focused on my own drink instead of his sexy forearm right next to me as he leaned in.

"I still know you well enough to say that when I walk out of this bar, you'll follow me." His rough voice scraped through me. "Just like you have been all day."

I laughed, but not because it was funny. Because he was *so* wrong, yet so confident about it. "You're nuts. I haven't been following you. They've been flukes. You're in a small town if you haven't noticed."

"Is that right?" He waved for Burt, who nodded in his direction.

I took a long sip of my martini—I'd downed half without even realizing.

"Yes," I said. "I'm sure you wouldn't understand, being that you look like you just showed up from a *board room meeting*, but here in Winter Harbor, it's not hard to run into literally everyone from town during a casual night out."

"Or in your case, run into your ex-boyfriend three times in five hours?"

The use of the word ex-boyfriend sizzled through me like it was a naughty word. Or maybe it was the way he was looking at me. Like he could consume me. Eat me alive.

And back when we were together, he damn near did consume me. Callum had been an intense lover ... but maybe I had been too. That was something I always relished about our past. We had always seemed destined for greatness. Like we could have actually taken over the world. I'd fantasized about our future so many times it had seemed like cold, hard inevitability: *Callum and Harlow will end up together, successful and rich, ruling their own personal kingdom. One that is full of rescue critters and stray cats.*

But instead ... he'd walked away from me.

"Listen," I began, suddenly exhausted. The bar hadn't been the rejuvenating distraction I'd envisioned. "Let's just clear the air. Say whatever we need to say. I don't want this to be a thing between us, now that we're going to be working together and living in the same town."

"I have nothing I need to say."

"No? Then you're just this snarky for no reason?"

His gorgeous lips curled into a sneer. "That's cute. You think I'm snarky."

"Bullish. Rude. Annoying. I have a whole list of other synonyms I could use."

"I prefer bullish." He signed the credit card slip that Burt slid toward him with a practiced polish. He looked like he'd stepped out of a business casual Gucci ad, but I still saw the shimmer of college Callum. The one who wore backward baseball caps. The one who'd woken me up every Sunday with breakfast in bed without fail. The one who'd told me that if he couldn't love me forever, then he'd never love again.

"Fine. If you have nothing to add, then I'll put it out there. Assuming that I'm your lawyer and you plan to stay in Winter Harbor for the next year, we need to keep things professional. We can act like we never knew each other. I don't want things to get weird if you're going to be living here."

A sarcastic laugh escaped him. "Pretend like we never knew each other? Not possible. I know *every* inch of you." That last bit was said more under his breath, but I heard it, and it had me sucking in my own breath on a sharp gasp.

Fuck.

He wore a neutral mask as he deftly slipped his credit card back into his wallet.

Coming here to distract myself wasn't just a failure, it was a horrible idea. I downed the rest of my drink and called out to Burt.

I stood up and waved at Burt, who was helping another customer. "I'll hit you later, Burt!" I couldn't stand another second at Callum's side, and I needed to get out of there *now*. Burt nodded—he knew I was good for my word—and I snatched up my bolero jacket and clutch before turning on my heels and vacating the bar as fast as my gin-filled legs could carry me.

The sky had faded into darkness while I was inside, the tiny sliver of the moon catching my attention as I stormed outside. I needed a brisk, bayside walk to cool off. A hand clamped my wrist a moment later as I started off down the sidewalk.

"Wait," Callum growled.

I snatched my wrist out of his grip, turning to face him. "What do you want from me, Callum? I offered for us to put the past behind us, but apparently, all you want to do is shove it in my face at every turn."

His nostrils flared as his gaze washed over me. Something tender creased his face, and for a moment, my anger dissolved. Illuminated in the golden light of the dangling sconces that lined the sidewalk, he looked both impossibly weary and the same Callum I'd fallen in love with.

"This is all really fucking confusing."

"Yeah, no shit."

His sadness shone through so clearly it broke my heart. In previous times, this is where I'd gather him to my chest and try to absorb some of his pain. Because even though he was so strong and bull-headed, he could never outrun his wounds. Not then. Certainly not now. "I didn't realize how much I missed you until I saw you again."

That made two of us.

My heart slammed against my ribs at his words, tempting me to fall face-first into his deeper meaning. But I was done going on the roller coaster that was Callum Winters.

I swallowed and straightened my spine. "Can we keep things professional now or what?"

"I have one thing I need to get off my chest," he finally said.

"What is it?"

"Carson said you're my lawyer for a reason." His throat bobbed, and he looked over my shoulder like maybe he was regretting saying anything. "But what reason is that? Did he ask for you specifically? Is he still hellbent on hurting us?"

The rawness on his face was heartbreaking. Emboldening. I took a step closer, remembering why I had always seized the opportunity to console him in times like these. The crack in his hard, bullish facade wasn't just an opportunity to help him. It was a chance to glimpse into the infuriatingly complex core of him. Where mesmerizing light and warmth spilled out.

And in a blink, we were back to where we'd always been.

I shook my head. "This case was dumped on me, and I took it because it puts me one step closer to a promotion.

I *assure* you, he had zero say in me taking this case. I did everything I could to hand it over to someone else," I said, unable to keep the teasing tone out of my voice. "I saw the name Winters on the file and nearly quit on the spot. Almost bought a one-way ticket to India to go and live in an ashram."

And then, there it was. The curl of his lips at the corners. Suddenly he was twenty-two again, hair flipping out from underneath his ball cap, and before I knew it he'd snagged me by the waist, gathering me up against him like something he didn't want to lose or let go of.

He was all steel and heat beneath those designer clothes, the same way I remembered but oh, so much more. His cedar scent washed over me, turning my knees into Jell-O, and I took a fistful of his pressed cream shirt.

"Still funny, I see," he murmured, his breath coming out hot against my forehead as his lips drifted along my hairline.

"Still a fucking tease, I see," I shot back. Everything inside me was pounding and wild. If he didn't kiss me, I'd combust, but I couldn't go further than that, because I was still so hurt and angry at him.

I couldn't bed the enemy, but I could certainly kiss him.

Just to find out if he still tasted as delicious as before. Because *yes—this was research.* Simply a taste, to lay that chapter to rest. And *then* I could move on.

Foolproof idea.

"You still want me, don't you," he murmured, like the egotistical prick he was. His lips actually grazed my hairline this time, and I melted against him, my pussy clenching with desperation.

I didn't just want him. I needed him. It was an ache I couldn't condone or even acknowledge. "Want you to stop stepping on my foot maybe."

He huffed a laugh. "I've never done such a thing."

"How quickly *he* forgets the broken toe of November senior year."

"How about *she* remembers how much she loves my tongue in her pussy and you follow me?" His lips grazed my cheek in their interminable trek toward my mouth. "Take my hand and see where it takes you."

I whimpered, pushing up onto my tiptoes. I'd get this kiss come hell or high water. But nothing else.

"I already know where it'll take me," I whispered, tilting my head so that our lips nearly brushed.

A soft grunt escaped him as his arms squeezed tighter around me. "And I don't want to go there."

Uncertainty swirled in his eyes. Even though he came across all calm, cool and collected, deep down, he was just as confused as I was. He was worried that if we slipped, it wouldn't just be a foot, it'd be down the whole damn hill. So was I.

When we ended, for a time I thought like my life had ended, too. Like a piece of my soul had been ripped from my chest.

I couldn't do that again.

Not now.

Not ever.

But just a taste?

I had willpower. I could eat just one cookie from the box and not devour the whole thing on my kitchen floor in shame.

Which meant, I could *just* kiss Callum Winters and not take it any further. My heart and soul could remain intact, while I also got my burning curiosity out of my system.

"So much has changed," I whispered. "So much has happened in eight years. We're not the same people."

A growl rumbled deep in his chest, like a Harley Davidson come to life. "Not everything's changed."

I don't know who moved first—maybe time and space simply contracted between us to make it happen—but our lips finally smashed together. Hungry, needy, fucking desperate. One kiss bled into a million. The warm velvet of his lips against mine was a balm I hadn't realized I'd been needing for the past eight years, but oh God, nobody could kiss me like Callum Winters.

And I'd tried to find someone—anyone—who could turn me on better than this man in front of me. But I'd failed miserably.

It was only him.

"Jesus, Callum," I croaked once we finally broke our never-ending kiss. I buried my forehead into the warm steel of his chest. Had I orgasmed already? It was possible. His lips were *that* magical still.

"Follow me," he insisted again.

I laughed weakly, lost somewhere between a fantasy and a tilt-a-whirl. "Where? To the dusty attic of your grandparent's house?"

"I have a hotel room," he whispered into my ear. "Or we can go to your place."

Something about 'my place' sent reason curling through my body. Replacing the lust with logic.

I needed to stay smart here. Remain strong.

"No, Callum," I said, drinking in the last deep inhale of his scent. "We can't do that. I'm your lawyer now. And that's how it's going to stay."

I released the front of his shirt and tore myself away from him.

That's how it *needed* to stay.

For as long as I could help it.

CHAPTER SEVEN

CALLUM

Thank fuck the Winter Harbor Motel was only two doors down from Beer & Moor; it made stumbling home with my throbbing cock pressing painfully against the zipper of my pants not nearly as agonizing as it could have been.

I could have followed Harlow, just to see where she lived, but that had bad idea written all over it. And although I'd imbibed on probably one too many whiskeys, I still had some common sense left kicking around inside me somewhere.

Of course, a town like Winter Harbor only had two decent motels. A bunch of luxury hotels along the water, and a few lodges and resorts, but those all came with hefty price tags. And I wasn't a millionaire—yet.

But because it was Easter weekend, everything had been reserved. Except, for some bizarre reason, for three rooms right next to each other. This meant, just like during my early childhood years, my room was located smack dab between Carson and Colton's room.

With my dick still somewhat hard and my keys in hand, I opened my motel room door and trudged inside.

Goddammit, Harlow knew how to get under my skin. She was as infuriating as she was sexy. As stubborn as she was smart. And as seductive as she was, a really bad idea to even consider hooking up with, even just for my short, forced stint of an address change.

But after that kiss outside Beer & Moor, I knew beyond a shadow of a doubt that I was still in love with her. And the way she'd kissed me back, gripped my shirt and made those sexy little noises that could render me coming in my pants like a teenager, I knew even if she still hated me, she also still had other feelings for me as well.

You didn't kiss someone like that when you didn't feel something for them. And considering she didn't bite my lip clean off or knee me in the balls, I'm pretty sure her hatred for me wasn't as strong as I initially believed it to be. As I deserved it to be.

I checked on Jonas, who was still asleep in his cage, his wing in a makeshift sling I'd fastened out of Q-tips, gauze, and surgical tape. He'd eaten a bit of the mealworm mash I'd made him earlier, but for the most part, he seemed to be content with sleeping.

I didn't even bother to turn on a light. I simply dug around for the bottle in my suitcase, grabbed a box of tissues from my nightstand, sat on the edge of my bed and unzipped my trousers.

I'd been doing a lot of this since seeing Harlow again.

A lot of self-abuse with my eyes glued shut and images of her ass in the air as I held onto her hips and pounded her hard from behind. The whimpers she made tonight as we kissed were some of the best noises in the world. Those were the melody of my dreams. The sounds I thought of as I stroked my cock from root to tip, squeezing on the crown until it filled with blood and turned deep dark purple.

She was smart turning me down tonight. She knew, as I did, that even one night together—for old time's sake, for closure, or for whatever—would just be a slippery slope.

Because even now, after just a taste of her, I was so goddamn close to going crazy it scared me.

Opening my eyes, I watched my hand slide back and forth over my dick, wishing with everything I had that it was Harlow's hot little mouth, her slick pussy, or her tight ass. She'd let me have her in all three. Something she said she'd never given another man.

She was trying so hard to hate me. And rightfully so. I deserved her ire. But her kisses didn't taste of hate. They tasted sweet and wholesome. Like home. And as always, she smelled incredible. Like a forest after a summer rain and the way she felt in my arms, the piece of my jigsaw life that I'd been missing had finally but put in its rightful place. Perfection.

Closing my eyes again, I brought up another image of Harlow. An image of her tonight. Beneath her jacket, she'd worn a red tank top with a low cut, and dark jeans. She had the best fucking tits I'd ever seen, and they were on full display tonight. Perfect, perky, and when I said I knew every inch of her body, her nipples peaked, calling for my mouth.

My dick pulsed in my palm and my balls cinched up. I was close.

It'd been impossible not to stare at her chest when she took my seat at the bar earlier and leaned forward. The low-cut tank top hit her just right, hugged her curves and smacked me in my face like a slap with a wet washcloth, showing me everything I was missing. Everything I'd given up.

I picked up speed and vigor, wishing like hell it wasn't my hand, but Harlow's lips wrapped around my dick. Her smile spread wide on her face as I came down her throat, and she swallowed every drop.

"Yeah, baby, that's it. That's it."

Knock. Knock. Knock.

"Hey, fucker. Stop yanking it and meet us by the pool. We need to discuss the house." It was Colton.

Of fucking course.

"Stop wasting all the motel's tissues and get your ass downstairs."

I growled.

Like hell was I going to be able to finish now.

I released my dick and stuffed it back into my pants, then went to wash my hands. I'd forgotten to buy beer at the grocery store earlier, which was why I'd ended up at Beer & Moor to wet my whistle, take off the edge, and drown my sorrows.

Only none of those things had actually taken place, and instead, I'd run into my old flame and wound up with an erection I could not satisfy to save my life.

Not that I could afford it, but saying *fuck it* anyway, I opened the minibar and grabbed the nine-dollar bottle of Budweiser before I stepped out of my room, locked the door, and went to go meet my brothers by the pool.

It was a nice motel, with a well-maintained but empty pool in the center courtyard, surrounded by two floors of motel room doors. A small gazebo with picnic benches sat beside the currently drained pool, and a concrete deck with over a dozen lounge chairs encircled the entire thing. An outdoor hot tub not currently being used bubbled and glowed off in one corner and a walk-up bar with a *Closed* sign would normally gather its mid-day shade from a dried palm frond umbrella.

Carson and Colton were at a four-top table with a retracted umbrella next to the pool, each of them with a bottle of beer in hand.

"'Bout time you showed up," Colton said with a laugh. "You get your rocks off?"

I shot him a look that said "Don't mess with me," and took a seat between them, but away from them. Even though he'd planned to buy a cot and a sleeping bag and start spending his night getting acquainted with ghosts right away, Colton ultimately decided to wait until Carson and I moved into the house as well, before he gave up the squeaky mattress of the motel.

"So, the furniture is set to arrive at the house tomorrow around noon," Carson said. "Beds, couches, tables. I ordered dishes and shit too. Linens and the like."

This was not the selfish Carson I remembered. I was actually grateful—albeit reluctantly. My head was so scattered about being in the same town as Harlow again and this goddamn will that it hadn't even occurred to me that we would need beds and forks and shit.

Colton nodded. "Got a call from Harlow's administrative assistant earlier. We've got a meeting with Harlow for nine-thirty tomorrow. She has the list of the company holdings for us."

Dread coiled inside me like an invasive vine, wrapping around my vital organs and suffocating the life out of them each one at a time.

I was going to be living with my brothers in the same house for an entire year. One of them I couldn't stand, both of them more like strangers than family.

But their commitment to this ridiculous demand of our late father was the only thing that could grant me financial freedom, so I needed to figure out a way to make this work.

And who knows, maybe you'll finally get that big, happy family you've always dreamed of.

I mentally slapped my conscience for even mentioning that. After the brawl between Carson and me at the house, I knew more than ever that we would never be close.

I could make an effort with Colton, though.

I squeezed my back teeth together and pulsed my jaw muscles. "So then we're doing this?"

Even though the furniture was purchased and set to arrive, there was still time to back out. But once the ink was dry on the documents, we would be committed to a year in this town and that house.

Maybe I was asking for their confirmation because I wasn't entirely convinced this was the right thing to do myself.

I took a deep inhale as both my brothers nodded and tipped up their beers.

I sipped from my own beer and savored the expensive liquid on my tongue for a moment before letting it slide down my throat and untangle my insides.

"I don't see how we can't," Colton said. "We all want the money. I mean, I don't *need it*, but I'm also not about to pass it up."

What the hell did he mean by he didn't *need* it? Was Colton rolling in the dough, and none of us knew?

"'There's plenty I could do with that money," Carson said. "First and foremost being a brand new pick-up truck."

Colton snorted a laugh and glanced at me. "What about you, big brother?"

"The money'd be nice. Got a few irons in a fire that could use some stoking," I murmured, glancing at the empty pool. I didn't need to tell them that my future success was wrapped up in California with my buddy Gary and a tech deal that had the potential to change my life if all went well. That was my private business. I'd serve my time in Winter Harbor and then get things back on track in California.

Carson made a dismissive noise at the back of his throat. "Whatever. So then, starting tomorrow, we will all begin living at the house. Three hundred and sixty-five fucking days with all three of us under the same roof." He blew out a breath. "Good thing that place is so big."

No shit.

Colton nodded. "I'll meet the movers and direct traffic for the furniture."

"I'll come too. We can grab the biggest rooms. Set the asshole up it the butler's closest," I said with a laugh.

Colton snickered when Carson flipped me off. "I will graciously give you the master bedroom, brother dear," he said to me. "The master suite for the master, of course." He made sure to toss on a southern belle accent and bat his lashes at me.

I snorted.

Colton and I shared a grin. But when I found Carson's smirking face, my smile dropped. "We done here?"

Colton finished his beer and nodded.

Carson lifted a brow before hitting me again with a smile too full of amusement to be genuine. "See you tomorrow at Harlow's."

The next morning, with a headache I hadn't been anticipating when my skull hit the pillow last night, I turned off the ignition to my rental car in front of Quick & Fairchild.

I threw my sunglasses over my eyes and locked my car door.

Harlow's coupe was already in the parking lot, as were my brothers' truck and motorcycle.

Great. I was the last one to arrive.

Would you rather be the first to arrive and then sit there in awkward silence with your brother or ex-girlfriend as you waited for the rest to arrive?

Touché.

I opened the glass door and approached the receptionist's desk.

"Are you here to see Harlow, too?" the grandmotherly woman asked.

I nodded. "Yeah."

"She's just down the hallway on the left. They're all waiting for you."

Rubbing at my temples, I made my way down the hallway to the partially closed door with *Harlow M. Jackson, Esq.* etched in glass on a fancy nameplate. I knocked with a single knuckle, even though I already heard their voices inside.

"Come in," she called, her voice immediately making my dress pants tighter and setting my nerves on edge.

I pushed the door open to find Carson and Colton sitting across from Harlow, who sat behind her desk with wary eyes. Was she remembering last night, too?

The bob of her throat and the sudden flood of pink to her cheeks said she certainly was.

I cleared my throat. "Sorry I'm late."

"Not late at all," she said, throwing on a smile I knew was fake. "Right on time. I was just saying to Colton and Carson that your family has a significant number of holdings, and it would behoove you all to visit each one and see what you own, as well as what you're dealing with."

I took a seat behind Colton, but kept my eyes on Harlow.

She continued, "So, I'm going to assume that since you're all here, you've decided to stay in Winter Harbor and live at Hope Creek Manor for the one-year duration, as per the conditions of the will?"

We all nodded.

Her gaze fell on me. "Did you manage to get that second opinion that you were seeking, Mr. Winters?"

"*Mr. Winters?*" Colton muttered, turning to face me. "Is she talking to you?"

Oh yeah, she was talking to me. Her tone held that cocky, teasing edge to it that normally got me all hot and bothered. My cock twitched. And apparently now was no exception. When she attempted to school me, it was hot as fuck, and she knew it.

She even had the cheeky audacity to let her gaze inconspicuously drift down to the front of my pants. Like she was waiting for my erection to wave *hello*.

Give it a second, sweetheart. It's still waking up.

Pushing my sunglasses up into my hair, I replied with a big ol' fat lie, "I found out what I needed, but we've decided to uphold the demands of the will anyway."

Her nostrils flared at my refusal to acquiesce to her little challenge. And only because I knew her so well, did I detect that flash of a lip lift. Just one corner, but it was there, and I saw it.

"Very well." Clearing her throat, she slid three copies of the same document across her desk to us. "This just indicates that you have all read the will and agree to the guidelines. If any one of you spends even one night *not* in Hope Creek Manor for an unapproved reason, then you all forfeit the inheritance. Understand?"

We nodded and murmured reluctant *yeses*.

"However," she went on, "there is a clause in the will that states medical emergencies, meaning overnight hospitalizations are exempt from this and do not count as a violation. There is also a clause stating that you only get one second chance, but then you also have to start over."

"Jesus," Carson muttered, scrubbing his hand down his face. "So you're saying if on day three hundred and sixty-three, one of us doesn't make it home for lights out, we *all* have to start over and do *another* year?"

"That is correct. Unless you wish to forfeit the inheritance." She was all business, and it was equal parts turning me on as it was pissing me off.

My mind wandered as Carson re-hashed the 365 days clause. Memories flood me of our senior year when she'd gotten all dressed up in a pencil skirt, blouse, and heels one day, then put her hair up in a twist and donned some sexy cat-eye glasses. I'd never seen a sexier sight in all my life.

We'd done a bit of role-playing that day when she got back from her meeting. I'd insisted on it. She performed the part of the tight-ass CEO who needed to be bent over her desk and taught a lesson on how to loosen up.

Now my dick was fully awake.

"One second chance *each*?" Carson asked, his voice pulling me from my filthy reverie.

She shook her head. "One second chance between all of you."

Colton groaned. "Christ almighty. I knew our old man was a twisted bugger, but I never thought he was capable of this fuckery."

I couldn't have said it better myself.

She placed three pens on top of the documents, but her eyes remained glued to mine. Deep blue I'd once gotten so lost in I wasn't sure I'd ever find my way out again stared back at me. Many moons ago I'd been A-Okay to get lost in the abyss and never resurface. Now I wasn't sure if it'd feel more like drowning than salvation.

Tell that to my balls, though.

One by one, we each read and signed the documents.

Harlow collected them. "All right then, that settles that. Effective today, Friday, April twenty-third, your one year at Hope Creek Manor begins." She pulled a large manila envelope from a stack of papers off the corner of her desk and slid it in front of us. "The list of your family holdings. A copy for each of you."

Carson took the envelope, opened it, and handed one to Colton and me.

I skimmed the list, but the pull to look back up at Harlow was too great.

Colton was the first to stand. "Are we all done here?"

Harlow nodded. "We are."

"'K good. Checkout is at eleven, so I gotta go pack up my shit."

He pushed past Carson, nodded at me, said a thank you and goodbye to Harlow and was gone.

My eyes shifted between Harlow and Carson.

His eyes were glued to the paper in front of him. "Says here we have a warehouse. Is there anything in it?"

Harlow shrugged. "You'll have to go and find out."

"And a sawmill?"

She nodded. "Yes, that I know about. It's a very successful enterprise. The only one within twenty miles, so it draws in a lot of customers."

Carson's mouth dipped into a contemplative frown and his head bobbed. "And what about this …" He leaned forward and pointed at a line on the list. "Is that a strip club? An adult sex store?"

Harlow's lips twisted as she tried not to laugh. "Doggy Style is a pet salon. I think it's in one of the strip malls your family owns. You may own a share in the company as well."

"Jesus, hell of a name for a pet salon," Carson muttered. He stood up and mumbled a deep, gritty thanks to Harlow before he locked eyes on me, lifted his brow, then turned to leave.

And then there were two.

"Is there anything else you wanted to talk about, Mr. Winters?" she asked as she walked around the front of the desk, scorching me with a look I felt in every square inch of my body. There was no smile on her face, but I could see her walls beginning to lose their foundation. They weren't scalable yet, but after last night, erosion had begun to take place. Her cheeks were also pink, so I knew she was feeling things.

Her eyes drifted back down to the front of my pants. I shifted in my seat, watching the flare of her lids when she realized I was hard.

There was plenty I wanted to talk about with her. Would I ever be able to see her again and feel neutral? Would I always carry around this cocktail of regret and anger?

But I couldn't bring these things up. In another place and time, she was my confidante. Now, she was just my lawyer, and I was just her client.

And I fucking hated it.

"What was that?" she said.

"I didn't say anything."

"You said you hate it."

I squashed the panic that burbled in my gut and cleared my throat, crossing an ankle over my knee. It wasn't exactly sexy to admit to your ex that you'd had a revelation at her workplace about how much you missed being her being your person; how important she'd been; how much it actually hurt to try to survive without her.

"This will," I blurted. "I hate it. I wish he'd just handed over the assets and been done with it."

She shrugged. "Clearly, he wants the three of you to make something of your family."

My throat tightened as I dared to look at her. "You've seen us. You think it can be saved?"

"There's no better time to start a new project than today," she said with a small sigh, as though reciting something she kept locked away inside her own head.

"Unless you're a procrastinator," I quipped, "and then it would be tomorrow."

She cracked a smile, leaning against the edge of her desk and crossing her arms beneath her breasts, pushing them up. My eyes were like two magnets.

"Sure," she went on, "but the point is, it's never too late to try. You guys might have had a rocky start, but you can still make something of it. You're young, and can turn your relationships around if you really want to."

"A rocky start," I said with a laugh. "It's been almost thirty years for me and Carson. That's a rocky introduction, second act, and intermission."

"But you haven't reached the ending, now, have you?"

"Certainly never thought a business named *Doggy Style* would be involved in our family saga," I muttered.

Harlow snorted with a laugh, covering her mouth as though it might hide her amusement. But her grin leaked out from behind her hand, and like always, it pulled a smile from me as well.

"Some families inherit lordship titles and vast acreage. The Winters brothers get *Doggy Style* and a sawmill," I went on.

Her squashed giggle turned into outright laughter. All I could do was lap up the sparkle in her eye and the sexy, professional lines of her.

"Don't be ungrateful," she warned, her laughter faded. "It could have been named *Reverse Cowgirl*."

This time, I snorted with laughter. "Not sure I'd trust any pets of mine to go to that place."

"I don't think it'd be a pet salon. Sounds more like a place you'd go to get your spurs sharpened or your boots shined."

"Both of those sound like Wild West Kamasutra," I said, remembering when we'd tried a few *interesting* Kamasutra positions ourselves.

The rush of pink to her cheeks said she was remembering that fun and sexy weekend, too. Clearing her throat, she glanced away from me and twirled the tip of her fingernail over a break in the grain on her wooden desk. "Hey, how's Jonas?"

Her inquiry touched me. She'd always received my rescues warmly throughout college, never complaining about my random detours to the pharmacy for late-night supplies or the re-routing of plans to accommodate a release back into the wild.

"Getting a lot better. Still has a long road ahead of him to heal, but I think he'll make a full recovery."

She nodded thoughtfully, crossing her arms. It looked like she might want to say something more, but had thought better of it. "Well, is there anything else you wanted to talk about?" The professional edge had returned, and she stood at attention again, smoothing down the front of her skirt.

My gaze drifted to her creamy calves. *Say no and leave.*

Against my better judgment, because clearly there was still alcohol in my system and I wasn't running on all cylinders or using all eleven percent of my brain, I said, "Yeah. Are you still thinking about that kiss last night?"

Because I certainly was. Hadn't stopped thinking about it. I hadn't stopped thinking about Harlow.

Her smile was saccharin. "Have you forgotten the terms of our agreement?"

Spoken like a true lawyer.

"No. You're my lawyer; I'm your client. But it's an honest question."

Everybody had a tell when they were bluffing, and Harlow's was a cute little nose wrinkle. Like she was some kind of bunny with an itch.

And her nose was twitching big time.

I honestly had no idea what my end game was here, or why I was pursuing her at all. I just knew I needed to. She was a ball of fire, and I was a stupid moth oblivious to the inevitable ramifications to my wings.

"It's an irrelevant inquiry," she said, leaning against the side of her desk again. Though this time, like she required the furniture to help support her. "Is that all?"

No. It wasn't all. She'd been the only one to penetrate my heart the way she had. I'd had countless women since her; nobody came close. Not a single ex in my sordid past cared about my rescues, much less asked after them. And sweet Harlow still managed to care, even with the simmering discontent and tension between us.

"Callum," she said, her voice sounding more urgent this time, like I needed to wrap it up. "Is that all?"

I stood and shoved my hands in my pockets, telling myself I'd head for the door. "Are you seeing anyone?"

"Another irrelevant inquiry." Her lips said one thing, but the rest of her body said another. Her pupils dilated, her nostrils flared and the way her chest rose and fell, causing the buttons of her blouse to strain with each inhale, did nothing to deflate that iron bar in my pants.

"Besides, even if I weren't, you know what they say. When the past calls, let it go to voicemail."

I smirked. "So I'm just a spam call."

"You said it, not me."

She made her rejection plain. Even though I could see through her words to the naked desire beneath. Like smoke curling up from a bonfire, I sensed her resolve drifting away and disappearing up into the ether the longer we stayed in this office together.

And even though I should have been done with this woman eight years ago, here I was, still weighing my chances with her. Wondering what might be, what could have been, if only things hadn't gotten so fucked up.

A sly grin slid across my face and, mirroring her, I crossed my arms over my chest as well and glanced down at her. "Judging by the way you kissed me back last night, you're either single or whoever you're with, he's not keeping you happy."

Her nostrils flared again and heat flashed in her eyes.

"Single then."

Her lips twisted, and she tossed her shoulders back. "My romantic life is none of your business."

"You're right about that, but I'm also not able to ignore what else is going on here."

Her brows pinched. "Which is?"

I raked my fingers through my hair, doubt clouding me for a moment. "This," I finally said, pointing back and forth between us and standing up.

Her throat bobbed, but she didn't move. The rejection was plain on her face. "Callum, I ... you're not drunk, are you?"

"Stone cold sober." I pressed my lips together and closed my eyes. This wasn't going as planned. Hell, I hadn't even planned this. I didn't even know what *this* was. I just knew I wasn't ready to walk out of her office. I wasn't ready to walk away from her.

"And what do you think *this* is?" she asked cautiously.

"We have a connection." I reached out and tucked a wayward strand of hair behind her ear, allowing the backs of my fingers to graze her cheek and remain there. Her skin was like silk. A beautiful pink bloomed beneath my fingers.

Her throat moved on a hard swallow, and she closed her eyes.

I needed another sign from her before I moved in closer. Before I took what I truly believed was still mine. Because that mouth belonged to me. Even after eight long, agonizing years, it was still mine.

Her eyes opened, and she jerked her face away from my touch. "Callum, don't," she said quietly.

There were so few people I'd let into my heart. Fewer than the number of people that had been in this very room earlier. And her office brought clarity. It reminded me of the basic truth I'd learned to be true.

My heart was a fragile piece of china. And loved ones were bulls.

And Harlow wasn't a missing piece of the heart-shaped vase, awaiting kintsugi. Continually throwing myself at her like this just gave her the hammer.

I didn't have nearly enough ducks in a row to be attempting to win her back.

Not yet anyway.

Those ducks were still aimlessly wandering around, quacking up a storm. But I had plans to collect them and teach them to walk in a straight line. I'd been emailing back and forth daily with my friend Gary from New York, and things sounded promising on this tech startup in California.

Her sigh was weary. "Maybe it's time we really talked. Now that you're sober and after what happened last night."

"All good," I said quickly, wrapping a protective mantle around my cracked and haphazardly reconstructed heart. "Strictly professional, you and I. Nothing ... *here.*" I pointed back and forth between us again. "Forget I said anything. No need to talk."

I was an unemployed thirty-year-old in the middle of a life upheaval. I literally had nothing to offer a successful woman like Harlow who appeared to have life by the fucking balls. I needed to retreat and go lick my wounds. Go sort out my shit—and my ducks—and show her I'd grown up before I tried to win her back.

Amusement quirked at her lips. "Fine. We won't talk. Let's just forget about it."

If only it were that easy. This woman owned my heart. I couldn't ignore that.

"We'll ignore each other in public and have zero contact outside of what is required for the estate case," she went on.

"If that's what you wish," I said, clearing my throat. Even though I'd be thinking about her non-stop for the next year, knowing she was a stone's throw away, lurking somewhere in Winter Harbor.

It seemed like the only solution that had a chance at working. Especially in a town the size of a toenail.

"I think it's best for everyone." At least for now.

We stared at each other for a long time then, long stretches of conversation passing between us even though we didn't say a word. I could hear her doubts, her unspoken desires, the ways in which she was both lauding and ridiculing me inside her head. She agreed with this as much as she railed against it. Just like me.

But the flush of desire was still there, and I wasn't immune to it. Her breathing picked up. Fuck, one of her nipples had gone hard under her blouse.

And now I had to walk away?

I already knew it would be impossible to stay away from her. Now that we were no longer on opposite sides of the country, but instead in the same fucking town, I could not stay away from Harlow Jackson. So she had to be the strong one for both of us.

Otherwise, she'd have me crumbling like a shattered vase at her feet. Begging the bull to piece me back together.

A knock on her closed door had me feeling as if we were teenagers and had been caught necking in a steamed-up car by the highway patrol.

"Harlow, your ten-fifteen appointment is here."

We both averted our eyes.

"Thank you," she called through the door. "I'll be one minute."

She straightened her blouse even though I hadn't laid a hand on her. "You need to go."

I knew I did.

Nodding, I adjusted my pants by tucking the list of holdings under my arm and shoving both hands into my pockets. She opened the door for me. I took a step forward and out into the cool, refreshing hallway.

I glanced back at her only once as I made my way back down the corridor toward the front entrance. But when I did look back, she was standing there watching me.

"Welcome to Winter Harbor, Callum. Good luck this year."

She needed the luck more than I did. I just needed to go home, regroup, and figure out a game plan.

Because if that kiss last night had taught me anything, it was that Harlow wasn't over me, just like I wasn't over her, and if it was the last fucking thing I did, I was going to get her back, and this time, I was going to fucking keep her.

CHAPTER EIGHT

HARLOW

In theory, it should have been easy to divert my attention to any of the hundred tasks on my to-do list. It spanned both work and home. I could have reorganized my office filing cabinets, prepared for an upcoming estate case with my assistant, finished weeding my garden or deep cleaned the bathroom.

Any of those tasks would have been preferable to thinking about Callum and all the feelings that we'd both been feeling in the tiny shoebox that was my office. A freshly sharpened machete couldn't have cut through that intricately woven tension.

I worked seventy hours a week on a *slow* week, and still, it wasn't enough to distract me from thoughts of Callum. He'd been right that there was something between us—an unbreakable connection—and it was there, alive as ever.

It was a good thing that I was strong enough to resist my basest desires. Even though I had slipped up once and *almost* slipped up a second time, I would *not* slip up a third time. After all, I'd gotten the taste I needed. Sexual chemistry still intact? Check. Best kisser in all the world? Double check. No further research was needed.

As long as I could re-immerse myself in the wonders of my to-do list, surely my body would fall in line with this decision.

My regularly scheduled Winter Harbor routine was so work-focused now that I had been gunning for the promotion. Most days, I didn't leave the office until eight p.m. I needed to inject some new life into the margins of my insane schedule.

If the last three years of my life had taught me anything, it was that our time here on Earth was precious and not something to be taken for granted. You could be killing it in court during an epic battle between two greedy sisters vying for daddy's fortune one minute—as I had been three years ago—then the next minute you're handed a devastating diagnosis after your doctor sent you to get a biopsy. And I was normally so good at checking for lumps in the shower.

Now I was a pro—at least on the one home-grown breast I had left.

But I was an impatient person by nature. This was why I sucked in the kitchen. I had no patience for anything to cook. I hated even waiting for water to boil. So my freezer was stocked with a lot of pre-made meals that just involved me poking holes in the plastic that covered it and popping it into the microwave.

Not the healthiest, or most economical, but I had no family to cook for. No kids to learn cutesy cookie recipes for. No husband to share pasta nights with.

I wanted those things. Desperately. But life just didn't seem to have that in the cards for me. So career success it was.

Rather than get my coffee to-go from *The Grind*—another Winter Harbor treasure owned by a Winter Harbor treasure, I ordered my latte in a real mug and sat down at the table, prepared to write in a journal or just eavesdrop on town gossip. Anything but imagine *Callum tearing my panties off with his teeth*, which was a fantasy that wouldn't leave me.

"Hey, sugar!" Ripley—the owner extraordinaire of The Grind smiled warmly at me as soon as he stepped out from his back office in the café. No matter what time of day or how long his line, Ripley—a town Winter Harbor staple like Maribel Malone and Burt Moor—had a greeting waiting for his best customers.

I blew him a kiss as he headed for the coffee bar to join his employees. I'd brought my journal today, where I would specifically not write about how much I still cared for Callum, the grumpy bastard who cared so much it made him cold. Morning thoughts, or something like that.

I took a deep breath, trying to orient myself in the dull roar of conversation surrounding me. I caught snippets of conversation from a table nearby where two middle-aged women chatted over coffee. I didn't truly tune in until I heard one of them say in a hushed whisper, "The Winters boys."

Every cell in my body tuned in after catching that. I cleared my throat, feigning interest in my opened yet blank journal, while I eavesdropped on the women nearby.

"Yeah, Ripley said that if they show *any* sign of doing to him what their grandfather did all those years ago, then he'd be hiring the best lawyers out there."

"But I can't imagine those boys would mess with such an established business here," her friend replied.

I adjusted my seat to be nearer to their table. The din of other conversations made it hard to hear well, and I needed every last speck of this dirt.

"Why wouldn't they?" Mrs. Know-it-all laughed sarcastically. "Then I guess you didn't hear the news. Dunlop Holdings is leaning on the state to declare eminent domain on the marshlands, and then sell it to them. They claim it's for the betterment of the city. They want to put in a new road which would cut right through the marsh, and then a hotel, spa, and casino. Say it'll bring in more tourists to this 'dying little seaside town.'"

The gasp from her friend was partially obscured by some loud laughter from a nearby table. Dunlop Holdings was owned by Robert Dunlop out of Portland, but the man owned hotels and all kinds of businesses all over the state. I knew of him only because of my involvement in the legal circles of Oregon. He was a shady asshole, and I'd hedged to guess just as hated or possibly even more than the Winters family.

"Striking while the marsh is under probate with those new Winters heirs," Mrs. Know-it-all said. "Knows with the mess that estate is in, he can probably just slip under the radar and have the state claim the land and resell it to him. He's probably greased so many palms nobody can turn a damn doorknob to save their life."

Her friend clucked her tongue. "Such a mess, all of it."

Holy shit. I knew that Robert Dunlop had been looking for a place to break ground in Winter Harbor.

I needed to look into this more.

Did the brothers know they owned the marsh? Had the state approached them yet about declaring eminent domain? Even though everything was in probate, they did have legal authority to act as managing parties of the properties and holdings as long as they were adhering to the terms of the will. But if the brothers were at war with each other, and too tangled up with other things, this could easily slip right past them. Particularly if a deal had already been in the wind.

I turned my attention back to my journal, finding the absent-minded doodle I'd drawn. *CALLUM*. So much for morning thoughts.

"I'm just assuming you want a latte to-go as well." Ripley's booming voice startled me out of my thoughts when he approached a moment later, holding a to-go cup. He set the drink down, resting his big hands on the top of the empty chair facing me. His bald head shone under the bright lights of the coffee shop.

I twisted to look at the front counter, realizing his line had died down. "Aww, Ripley, you're so sweet."

"That's what I'm here for." He winked at me just as the two ladies I'd been spying on shuffled to their feet, readying to leave.

I looked back at his front counter, spotting his all-star barista taking orders now. There seemed to be enough time for me to pry. Just a little. "You mind if we chat for a minute?"

"I can chat for an hour if that's what you want." He pulled out the chair and settled into the seat with a groan. The chair creaked beneath him, but then again, most chairs did. Ripley always joked how his nickname back in the day used to be Rip-ya-a-new-one because if there was ever a man in the room who could tear someone in half, it was Ripley. Even though his bodybuilder days were behind him, he was still muscly enough to put most thirty-somethings to shame.

"Well, I have to go to work soon, so an hour won't be necessary," I said, patting his hand. "But I appreciate you always being willing to help."

"I need to keep the area's best lawyer on my good side," he cracked, slinging a dish towel over his shoulder. The glow from the track lighting overhead shone off his bald head. A lot of folks likened Ripley's appearance to that of Mr. Clean, though he wasn't a fan of the comparison.

"Well, I'm not sure how to say this, but ..." I searched for a polite way to say I'd been obsessively thinking about Callum Winters and what it meant for both my hometown and my life, but nothing came to me. "What do you know about the Winters family?"

The start of a frown formed on Ripley's lips. "Plenty. Why?"

"Do you know anything about the sons? Callum, Carson, and Colton?"

His thick neck didn't move at all when he shook his head. "Not those three, no. But their daddy and granddaddy? Oh boy."

I rolled my lips inward, assessing my best fact-finding approach. Really, I wanted him to give me every last gory detail. But I was their lawyer. Even though this information didn't pertain to their case, I needed to tread carefully.

"Did you grow up with their dad or something?" I asked.

"Elliot and I went to school together right from kindergarten to our senior year. He was always a cocky bastard, but a kiss-ass at the same time. God rest his soul. His mom and dad owned the majority of this damn town, as you know. Well, that transferred to Elliot ... and now his sons. Elliot never gave a damn about anybody else. I'm sure his sons learned the same thing."

I massaged my temple. That wasn't the Callum Winters I'd known and fallen in love with. Maybe that was who he was now, but a person who didn't give a damn about anybody else, didn't waste their time rescuing wounded animals and making them makeshift beds out of expensive dress shirts and shoeboxes, right?

"So he was a callous jerk, I take it," I offered. *Like father, like son?*

"Worse. But once he got the hell out of Dodge with that lover he ran away with, Winter Harbor felt the wrath of his ashamed parents. I mean, don't get me wrong, I was glad not to see his arrogant face anymore, but him leaving really set his daddy off and ol' Errol took it out on the town."

I lifted a brow. "What does that mean?"

Ripley shook his head and pursed his lips. "Bought every piece of land. Jacked the rent. Tore down historical buildings to cram in strip malls and condos. Outsourced wherever he could to save a buck. Put a lot of folks out of business or their homes with his greed."

"Oh God."

"Mhmm. When Errol and Peggy died, Elliot Winters became my damn landlord. Was for the last thirty years, sugar. And now his *estate* continues to collect my rent."

Surprise trickled through me. I'd reviewed the holdings closely, but the most likely explanation was that various properties were owned under a different business name. I made a mental note to pry later.

"I can't talk too much about this part of things," I told him with a wry look. "I got handed their estate case recently, so I'm just trying to figure out some of the history."

He sighed, shifting in his seat. "All I'm saying is, if these boys try to pull one over me like what Elliot and his parents did all those years ago to *my* dad, then we're gonna have trouble."

"What did he do to your dad?"

"Opened his own fleet of fishing tours and put my dad's charter company outta business. Then, when my dad changed careers and started a fish 'n' chip shop, old Errol

82

bought the building the restaurant was in, raised the rent, and then evicted my dad. He had a mean streak, that bastard. Real mean. Especially to anybody that stood up to him—which my daddy did. But I've got the best lawyer on my side, right? I don't have to worry about them pulling the same shit on me." He sent me a wink.

"You do, but I'm also legally obligated to the brothers first, so let's not make this a Twister game."

"Fair enough. Though, according to Burt, you and that oldest boy might have something more than just legal going on."

Ripley's nod to my make-out session with Callum in front of *Beer & Moor* hit like a surprise punch to the gut. Word traveled fast ... and *everywhere*. My gaze dropped to the table. There wasn't judgment in his tone ... but that didn't mean there wasn't room for it.

"Callum and I have a history," I said quietly. "From our college days. That's all." Even though that wasn't all. There was so much more than just *history*. There had been a future, too.

Ripley nodded, looking out over the coffee shop.

His silence prompted me to add, "I had no idea that he was Elliot Winters' son when we were together. He talked about his family only in vague terms. It was a sore subject for him. In fact, I discovered his link to Winter Harbor two weeks ago when he showed up in town, and I was handed this case without any notice or preparation. I'm trying to make heads or tails of ... everything."

"Well, do me a favor," Ripley said, reaching to squeeze my wrist. "Don't start a second history with that boy. Because he's got 'don't give a damn' running through his veins."

The bells on the front door jingled and a new stream of customers walked in. Ripley smiled at them and waved, then squeezed my wrist again. "I gotta get back to brewin'. Just promise me you won't do anything stupid with that boy. I don't want to see my favorite latte lover with a broken heart."

I smiled, but I could feel the strain on my cheeks. "I promise."

"You can't see me, but I'm behind ya; that's how much I've got your back." He winked at me again and headed toward the counter, making a big, jovial commotion as the new arrivals made their way to order.

Ripley's words stuck to me like an uncomfortable, humid breeze. I wanted to shake them, but I couldn't. He was being smart. Wise, even. And the rational side of me knew that I needed to do everything in my power to keep from starting a second history with Callum.

But logic didn't obey lust. And when Callum Winters was still as hot as ever, with a probably-growing menagerie of injured animals collecting inside his new property, ignoring him did not come easily.

And now, Ripley's future was tied to the brothers. His words cycled through me more than I wanted to admit: *I got your back, you've got mine.*

He was right. That's how we'd been raised in Winter Harbor. Everyone looked out for each other, as much as they could. You couldn't always see them, but they were there.

I needed to look out for Ripley. Which meant that I had the perfect marriage of excuses to get back in front of the irresistible and infuriating Callum Winters.

CHAPTER NINE

CALLUM

The day was hot when I heaved open the hefty wooden door of the Winter Harbor Library and the scent of old books and ink flowing up my nostrils while my eyes adjusted to the darkness.

There were a few windows along one side and the sun shining through them lit up the dust particles in the air, turning them into gold pixie dust.

The place was dead empty, and there was only one woman working behind the desk.

I plastered on a big smile. "Hello," I said, making sure my volume was library-appropriate.

She was probably around my age and grinned at me, tucking her strawberry blonde hair behind her ear and blinking big brown eyes behind her thick black-framed glasses. "How can I help you?"

"I'm looking for anything you have on the history of this town, particularly around the last thirty to forty years. I read all the newspaper articles I could. But they don't have what I want." I leaned against the counter and flashed her an even bigger smile, checking out her nametag. "Do you think you could help me, *Pria*?"

Pink flooded her cheeks. "I'll do my best. Are you looking for anything specific? The more we narrow it down, the more I can keep you from wasting your time."

Her fingers started tapping on the keyboard of her computer.

"I'm looking for anything you have on Elliot Winters, his marriage, why he left town, the woman he married, and Errol Winters, his father. Roughly thirty to thirty-two years ago. If you've got anything on that, I'd love to see it."

She grimaced. "The Winters family, huh? And you didn't get what you needed from the newspaper archives?"

"The Winters family owns the newspaper. So I'm assuming they only printed what they wanted to print. I couldn't find anything about Elliot Winters marrying a woman named Camille."

She typed some more.

Her teeth snagged her bottom lip and her brows wrinkled. "I'm just getting the newspaper articles, too."

Had my father or grandfather deliberately come into the library and had anything negative about them scrubbed from the history books? I didn't think that there were textbooks or history books written about my dad and mom, but I at least figured there might be an article, or even a wedding announcement somewhere.

While Carson worked on the exterior of the house, I'd been taking care of the interior, and part of that meant chunking out all the old stacks of newspapers in the living room. My fingers were still black from the ink, but my questions remained unanswered. I thought for sure something in that stack would help solve the mystery of who our mother was and why the town hated our dad and grandfather so much. But I'd come up with zilch.

"Hold on," she said, drawing me from my wandering thoughts. Pria's brows lifted, and she smiled. "I have a wedding announcement here, but it's not for Elliot and Camille, it's for Elliot Winters and Melody Summers."

"Melody Summers?"

She nodded.

"Who the hell is that?"

Pria shrugged. "I've only lived in Winter Harbor a couple of years. But maybe she was from Summer Hills, which is like forty-five minutes south?"

Winter Harbor and Summer Hills.

Elliot Winters and Melody Summers.

Was this for real?

There was that bottle of wine in the cellar called Summer Eternal.

"Is there a Summers family dynasty in Summer Hills?" I asked. "Can you Google that for me, Pria?"

"Sure thing." She glanced around the still empty library. "It's not like I'm busy or anything."

I chuckled. "It's the middle of the week. I'm sure things pickup on the weekends.

"Not by much," she murmured. "Ah, here we go. Yes. The Summers family founded Summer Hills around 1846 and, much like the Winters family here, they bought up land and pretty much controlled the town. Melody Summers was the only child of Roger and Gloria Summers, and she was engaged to Elliot Winters."

Engaged.

Okay, but obviously that didn't pan out, because my dad married my mom—Camille—and they had me and my brothers.

"Any wedding announcement for Elliot and Camille?" I asked.

She tapped away, then shook her head. "Not that I can see."

"Okay. Anything else?"

Her lips twisted. "Between 1984 and now things are pretty sparse. There are the obituaries for Elliot and Peggy Winters, but other than that, not much."

"Yeah, I found those when I was searching the newspaper archives."

I grabbed a sticky note off the counter and a pen, then I scribbled down my number. "Can you call me if you come across anything else pertaining to Elliot or Errol Winters between 1984 to now? And I mean anything. We never know what might hold some significance."

Nodding, she took the sticky note. "I can totally do that." Her smile was flirty. "Do I get to know your name?"

"Callum Winters."

The flirty smile dropped like a stone in a pond, and an invisible force field immediately went up around her. Even somebody who had only lived here a couple of years knew to turn the cold shoulder when a Winters was around.

Fuck.

"Thank you," I said, continuing to smile warmly, even though the frost coming off her was enough to freeze my fingers off.

She nodded curtly. "I doubt I'll find anything else."

"You never know. But I appreciate your time and your help, Pria. I really do. You have yourself a great day."

Curiosity softened the sharpness in her eyes.

I turned to go.

"The whole town hates your family," she said after I'd taken two steps toward the door.

I faced her again. "I know. And I don't know why. That's why I'm here. I'm looking for answers. Up until two weeks ago, I hadn't stepped foot in this town, and now, I find out my family founded it, and those who live here hate us. So I want to know why, and I want to make things right."

Her harsh expression softened even more. Her brows unpinched and the force field was losing its shielding power. "Oh."

I nodded. "If you know of anybody, a town historian or even a grandparent who was around about thirty-two years ago, see if they'd be willing to go for coffee with me. Or even just give me their name and number and I can do the rest. I'm not trying to make enemies here—we've already got enough."

The rest of Pria's force field dropped and her eyes turned sad. "I'll ask around. I'm still new here."

"Not so new that the moment I told you my last name, your shields went up and your put on your cold shoulder," I teased.

Pink dashed across her cheeks again. "The ladies of the Winter Harbor Welcome Wagon literally brought a welcome basket to my front door and some of the first words out of their mouths were, *Never trust a Winters. They're cheats, liars, and scum.*"

My mouth dropped open. "If you can get me the name of these ladies, I'd be very grateful."

Her head bobbed. "I'll see what I can do."

"Thanks, Pria." I turned to go, but then stopped and glanced back at her. "Does the library accept volunteers?"

"We do," she said eagerly. "The volunteer form is on our website."

"Thanks." Then I left, only I had even more questions circling around inside my head now than when I arrived.

Our dad had been engaged to someone else.

To someone from another wealthy, founding family.

But by the looks of things, they never got married.

What happened?

Did our mother happen? Was she the reason our dad and Melody never got married?

Who was our mother?

She'd died when Colton was one, so I was only five, and barely knew her real name, let alone her maiden name. To me, she was just *mommy*.

We never met any of her family members—or our grandfathers.

My memories of our time together as a family were sparse. But flashes of amazingness and togetherness would sometimes come to me. We had very few family photos with our mother to reflect back on, but the ones we did have were moments like this. All of us together, all of us smiling, all of us happy.

I'd walked to the library, seeing as it was only about twenty minutes from home, and it was a nice day.

I was nearly home, my hands in the pockets of my dress slacks, when a godawful snarl and a screech echoed from under a bush.

I stopped in my tracks, then jumped back when a black cat darted out from under the bush and sprinted across the street, causing a car to throw on its brakes and honk.

Instinct told me to not keep going, but to look under the bush. Something spooked or scratched that cat, sending it flying out from under the juniper.

On my hands and knees, I peered into the shrub. Barely moving and barely breathing was a little brown blob with a bushy tail.

Fuck.

It was an injured squirrel.

My pockets were empty, but just like with Jonas, I had a white tank top on under my dress shirt.

Why was I still wearing Armani when I wasn't going into the office? I don't fucking know.

Dress for the job you want. Not the job you have.

Ah, that's right. And because I wanted to be back on top in the financial world but currently had NO job, I was dressing like a top executive and not the hobo schlub that I currently was.

With a sigh, I unbuttoned my shirt, reached under the bush and carefully pulled the squirrel out, cradling him—or her—in my hands in the shirt.

Since I decided to name the bird Jonas, believing him to be a boy, I was going to give this one a girl's name.

As I walked back home, I took in all the business names in the strip mall lining the street.

Harbor Pet Supplies.

Perfect.

"We'll call you Petra," I said, taking in the injuries that stupid cat had inflicted. Petra had a rip in her ear, a bloodied paw, and part of her tail had lost its fluff.

I turned down our long gravel driveway, picking up the pace so I could get Petra home and into triage with some Q-tips and gauze. There wasn't much I could do about the ear, besides maybe put a bit of Polysporin on it to stop any infection.

Colton's motorcycle wasn't in the driveway, neither was Carson's truck. It was just me. Well, me Petra, Jonas, and the ghosts. But so far nobody had given me any grief, not even the ghost that I'm dead certain hung out in the cupola with me each morning as I took my coffee.

I opened the front door and headed into the sunroom, where Jonas was recovering, grabbing my supplies from the window ledge.

I had Petra bandaged up and with some water in no time.

I was just washing my hands when the crunch of gravel under tires outside drew my attention.

I checked out the window only to have my heart do a complete fucking flip-flop and my dick twitched awake. It was Harlow.

Shit.

I needed to play this cool.

Because if I wanted to make things right and show her that I wasn't the cold-hearted bastard that she thought I was—that so many people thought I was—I needed to show her that I was capable of change.

Another glance out the window showed that she was still making her way to the cul-de-sac of the driveway, so like an idiot obviously in love and wanting to make the woman of his dreams swoon, I raced upstairs and changed into some gray sweatpants.

Because every man knows, gray sweatpants are equivalent to women wearing a negligee.

When we first got together, Harlow said I wasn't allowed outside the house in gray sweats. That the only men who wandered around in public wearing gray sweatpants were single and trolling, but no woman in her right mind let her man out of the house in gray sweats.

Until Harlow and I started dating, I didn't even know this was a thing. I wore gray sweats all the time to and from the gym, all the while having zero clue that I was "sending women into bouts of silent mass hysteria," as Harlow so eloquently put it.

"If I ever catch you wearing those outside the house, particularly without any fucking boxers on, there will be hell to pay," she'd said, her hands on her hips as she stood over me one night, while I sat on the couch grinning at her, in nothing but gray sweats—no underwear.

"You gonna spank me?" I asked.

She climbed onto my lap, straddling me and rocking against my growing cock. "Among other things."

"You're just begging me to disobey, then. I'm curious what these other *things* are."

Then she told me to shut the fuck up and made me do just that by kissing me and eventually sitting on my face.

I was at the top of the stairs in my gray sweats when I decided to run back to my room and ditch the boxers, too.

Grinning like an idiot, I practically flew down the stairs as her svelte frame sashayed, hips swinging, up the walkway toward my steps.

There was etched glass in the middle of the front door, so I could see her, but she couldn't see me.

I slowed my breathing, told my dick to settle down, then stood on the other side of the door waiting for her to knock.

CHAPTER TEN

HARLOW

It felt like an addict's bargain: *I'll stop wanting Callum, as long as I can see him regularly.* My entire body was wound tight as I drove through town, heading toward Hope Creek Manor. Part of me worried Callum would see right through this tactic, but the other part of me didn't care. If nothing else, I needed to get a feel for what Callum and his brothers intended to do with their holdings, now that they fully understood what they were inheriting. I might not be able to interfere, but I was curious about what the consequences might be for my hometown ... and my friends.

The brothers owned far more than I'd even realized in my cursory glance through the paperwork when I took over the case. They owned enough to really change the face of Winter Harbor—the place that had become a treasured gem to so many thousands of people—for better or for worse.

By the time I eased my car into the gravel cul-de-sac in front of Hope Creek Manor, my stomach was in knots. Only one vehicle was parked there—Callum's rental—which spiked my anxiety higher. I stepped out of my coupe and straightened my back, reminding myself of my totally-invented-yet-rock-solid purpose for coming: a fabricated weekly check-in. *You are an idiot, Harlow.* My heels clicked softly against the wooden wrap-around porch as I approached the front door and knocked.

Silence settled around me, punctuated by birdsong and the distant *shhh* of the breeze moving through the trees surrounding the property. God, this place was heaven. I just hoped the Hellspawn that lived here realized that.

Slowly, the doorknob turned. When the door swung open, Callum stood on the other side, his handsome face perfectly neutral as he looked at me. He barely blinked, yet it was enough to send every nerve ending in my body on high alert.

But this time, he wasn't wearing his business casual attire from whatever board meeting he normally lived in. He'd traded navy slacks and a button-up for gray sweatpants and a white shirt.

Fuck him.

He knew what gray sweatpants did to any red-blooded woman. And he most certainly knew what they did to me.

I was unable to keep my eyes from drifting south to the front of his sweats, and I could tell right away he wasn't wearing any fucking underwear.

Fuck him. Fuck him. Fuck him.

Wait, was that my brain *telling* me to fuck him?

I was so confused even I couldn't make sense of my own thoughts.

My mouth was dry. I could not say the same for my panties.

To make matters worse, his hair was tousled like maybe I'd caught him mid-workout session. His eyes were bright and there was a bit of a flush to his cheeks. And dammit, the tank top put him on display, exposing those thick, strong forearms that could take me halfway to heaven on sight alone.

"Can I help you?" he asked in lieu of a greeting, his bored, neutral tone somehow lighting me up.

All of my preparation for this moment withered on my tongue. I blinked dumbly, trying to remember how to speak. How to say anything that wasn't *can we please fuck now* or *I can sort of see your dick in those sweatpants.*

"Just a courtesy check-in," I finally said, forcing a smile. "I need to make sure that you three are obeying the requirements of the will."

"Irrelevant inquiry," he deadpanned.

I snorted with a humorless laugh. I'd used the same words on him a week ago. "Unfortunately, this is terribly relevant."

"So you'll be dropping in every Friday at five-thirty to check on us?" He pushed the door open wider, jerking his head toward the interior of the house. "Take a tour if you need. Check the beds. They've all been slept in."

Has yours been slept in only by you?

I mentally slapped myself for having that thought. Who Callum slept with was none of my business, so long as he *fell* asleep and woke up in Hope Creek Manor. Alone, not alone. Didn't matter one iota to me.

Keep telling yourself that, Harlow.

I stepped inside the house, already noticing that the place felt *different.* Weeks ago, it had been an abandoned wonder that only hinted at former glory. And now I could tell that the brothers were actually *living* here. The mustiness was gone. Fresh air dominated. Someone had gotten *rugs*, for God's sake.

"This place looks so different already," I said, unable to keep the awe out of my voice.

Callum kept his hands shoved in his pockets as he walked down the hallway toward the kitchen. I followed him, taking this as a quiet invitation to see the house.

"You got a dining room table," I noted as we passed the formal dining room.

"Haven't used it yet," he said. "It's hard to get the three of us to agree to stay in the same room for any length of time."

I snorted. "I've noticed." My heels clicked on the wood floor as we came back into the main hallway, right in front of the grand staircase. I looked up at the second-floor landing. "What are you up to this evening? Where's Jonas?"

"Jonas is in the sunroom with Petra."

"Who's Petra?" I asked, wondering if in fact he *had* shared his bed with another woman, and she got to see, taste, and feel what was taunting me behind those sweatpants.

"Squirrel I found about half an hour ago. Was caught by a cat, but I managed to save her." He paused, squinting at me. "Is this part of the weekly check-in? Reporting on my activities and what I ate for dinner?"

I blinked a few times, giving my heart a chance to deflate a bit from his mention of saving a squirrel.

His, "Hmm, Harlow?" had me shaking my head and rejoining reality.

I smirked to hide my fluster. "No. It was good-natured friendliness, actually, which I see you're immune to." Clearing my throat, I stepped around him toward the sunroom off the living room. "Can I meet Petra and Jonas?"

He grunted and followed me.

Two shoeboxes sat on the wide window ledge side by side.

I peered into one to see a little robin with a DIY Q-Tip and gauze splint fastened to his wing. His eyes were closed, and he was breathing evenly.

"Jonas seems to be recovering nicely," I said, turning to face Callum.

His cheek twitched, the start of a smile curling at his lips. He didn't meet my gaze, but I could feel the warmth blossoming between us. *Fuck.* This was always how it had been. Callum hadn't been over-exaggerating that day in my office when he made mention of our connection. I still felt it. Still was ruled by it. And making it out of here without answering to it was a fool's hope.

But maybe that's precisely why I'd come.

I turned back and looked down into the other shoebox. My heart clenched at the sight. So little. Petra was no bigger than soda can and had a nasty tear in her ear. But it was shiny with what I assumed was an antibiotic cream. One of her paws was bandaged, and the middle portion of her bushy tail was no longer bushy.

But she was breathing.

"Poor little lamb," I said, facing him once again.

His face had softened only slightly, but after a moment, it hardened again. "Is this really necessary, Harlow? The pretend pleasantries and small talk?"

I shrugged a shoulder. "Does our new social stipulation require me to be a bitch whenever we *do* speak?"

"It was a social stipulation *you* put into place, remember?" he said with a single brow lift. "It seems like it would make things all-around easier. Less likely to fall headfirst down a dangerous slope."

I knew exactly what slope he was talking about. The one he'd tried to push me down that night outside *Beer & Moor.* And he had a point. "Ah. It's just easier if you hate me. Got it."

Some of the mischief in his gaze dissipated. We'd hit a speed bump in the banter, and he'd opted to stop the car instead of forging ahead.

"I never once said I hated you," he said in a low, almost threatening voice. "I could never hate you."

His clarification promised to send us down a dark, emotional path. One that I wasn't ready to venture again. I popped on a bright smile.

"So, what have you guys been doing to occupy your time? Besides saving woodland creatures, that is."

His jaw flexed. "Do you really care?"

"You three have uprooted your lives to come to this town you have no connection to. I'm aware of how hard that must be. I merely hoped you three were settling in okay and felt good with it all. Jesus, are you going to give me the third-degree every week like this?"

He smirked. "So it *is* a weekly thing. Great. I'll let my brothers know so we can be sure to tidy up and put our Sunday's best on, so we can convince you that we're a happy little family out here."

"Sunday's best wouldn't fool me on that one, sorry. Remember—I *do* know you."

"So, is this weekly charade also a requirement of the will? I don't remember reading about this in the paperwork. Unless you just wanted some excuse to see me?"

I tried not to let my strickenness migrate to my face. I'd been here less than ten minutes, and he'd already called me out. *Wonderful.*

"You are impossible," was all I could muster, however weak it sounded.

"At least I'm not transparent," he said with a mischievous smile. "Do you want to see the upstairs?" The question felt like an olive branch. But one lined with thorns, if I knew Callum.

I hesitated, looking back at the front door. "You have a bunch of orphaned duck eggs under an incubator lamp you want to show me?"

That earned me a devilishly handsome grin over his shoulder. "Maybe. Maybe not."

Dammit. I had a hard, if not impossible, time denying this man, particularly when he wore what could be considered lingerie for me. I took a deep breath. "Sure. I can't stay long, though."

His footsteps clomped up the stairs. "Why? Got a hot date?"

"Yes, actually," I lied.

"Well, you better tell him you keep fucking up and making out with the Winters boy," he intoned. Electricity snapped between us. Of course, he'd gone there. *Of course.* The man probably believed it was illegal to go a day without reminding me of this sexual connection.

"It was *once*," I corrected. "I made out with *the Winters boy* once, and I think my hot date will be fine," I said, my heart racing. "I'd never *fuck* the Winters boy, which is the most important detail."

Callum appeared unfazed, but of course, all I could see were his broad shoulders straining at the white fabric of his t-shirt. Every inch of my body begged to see the reaction on his face, to see the desire shining through his eyes.

"But oh, you used to fuck him," he said, his voice grittier. "And you loved it, too. Particularly liked sitting on his face, if I recall."

My neck went hot at his words. It had been stupid to come here, knowing this would be the outcome. But God, it felt so right, too. This was the forbidden fruit I was dying to taste.

"I don't see how that's relevant." I cleared my throat. "Nor do I understand why you continue to dredge up ancient history every time we see each other."

He reached the landing, hands stuffed in his pockets as he turned toward me. His face had hardened into a mask of indifference, at odds with the heat and grit in his voice. I could only imagine it was because he was fighting this losing battle alongside me. And we were both willing victims.

"What else is there to talk about besides ancient history?" The smirk that emerged on his lips was both sexy and infuriating.

"Clearly nothing else, since you can't move on."

"But have *you* moved on?" he asked.

The question rooted me to my spot. I had tried like hell to move on. But every second spent around him reminded me that I hadn't. Not in the ways that counted.

"I offered to talk about it with you, but you didn't want to," I spat. "Does this mean you want to have the conversation now?"

Callum strode down the wide hallway. He jerked his chin toward a smaller door tucked into the wall. "Let me show you something."

I deflated slightly. Now he was deflecting. "What?"

"The perfect place to air our grievances."

Well, that was slightly more promising, at least. "What is it? A padded room and a couple of baseball bats?"

He chuckled and opened the small door, revealing a narrow staircase. He started up the rickety stairs, occasionally pausing to test a step and pointing when I needed to avoid a loose nail. When I stumbled on a particularly high step, his hand shot out to grab my bicep, catching me even though I was in no danger of falling.

The cracks in his mean-guy facade sent butterflies swarming in my belly. His smile hit me then, that same twinkle appearing in his eye that gutted me every time he let it out to play. The sparkle that reminded me of the old Callum. The Callum that had made me fall head over heels for him back in college.

But the Callum I'd started to glimpse over the past week ... this man was just as attractive and beguiling. And maybe that's why I'd fabricated the weekly check-in. He had the college-boy energy mixed with something refined, hardened.

The top of the staircase opened up into a tiny cupola with a glass-paned 360 view of Winter Harbor. I gasped, looking through the dazzling clean windows at the expanse of forest to the south, the bay to the north, and the edges of downtown to the east.

"This is an amazing view. And an oddly clean little room."

"I spruced it up myself. I come here every morning to drink coffee and have breakfast with the ghosts." That last bit was said with a cheeky smile.

"Ah. Your sanctuary." Part of me felt special that he'd taken me straight here to share the magic. But I knew better than to read too far into it.

"I need it, living with these guys."

"I'm surprised you or Carson hasn't ended up in the ER yet."

"There's still time," he muttered, his jaw clenching as he gazed toward the bay. That impassive mask was back, harder than ever as he studied the horizon. "I'd like to think he's matured or grown since college, but ..."

"I would hope that too," I said, trying to follow his gaze. "Do you really think you three will make it a year in this place?"

"We have to, right?" He looked toward me then, and I could see all the gears turning inside him just below the surface. The conflict and the pain. The impossibly high walls that he'd always maintained around his heart. The deep well of emotion that he regularly shoveled sand into, hoping to keep it level, only to have it sucked into the void. "Besides, maybe this is a chance for ..."

"For what?"

He released a sigh that sounded more like a hiss, scrubbing at the side of his face. "Harlow, I—" He faltered, which was unlike him. My fists balled as I waited to see what he'd reveal to me. Which part of his soul he'd uncover or hide away.

"What, Callum?"

Another sigh. "I regret the decisions I made when I was twenty-two." His jaw flexed as he stared at me. More intensely than anyone has ever looked at me. Like he was a breath away from just exploding altogether. "I could have been content living the rest of my life not seeing you again. Well, I could have survived, let's put it that way. But the truth is I fucked up. I should have heard your side of things.

I let my brother come between us and ruin what we had. I'm sorry, and I've been sorry every day for the last eight years. I did this to us and seeing you again—"

I swallowed a knot of emotion. It was like a hundred-pound weight had been lifted off my shoulders. I rolled them and inhaled a deep, rattly breath. "What?"

"I didn't make the right choice our senior year of college, and I've made a lot of bad decisions since then. And the longer I'm around you, the more I want to keep making bad decisions."

I narrowed my eyes, fearing the worst. "Like what?"

"Like begging you to blow off that hot date you've got lined up." His gaze turned hungry now, which was even more dangerous. "Taking you somewhere for dinner. Spending the next ten years of my life asking for forgiveness. But I also know that I don't deserve you. At least not yet—probably not ever. You've got your shit together and I ..." He ran his hand though his hair and glanced outside. "I've just got shit in a bunch of different fucking piles and no system in which to organize them."

"Callum ..." I swallowed a spike in my throat, trying to stare past him and pull an unaffected air. But it was hard when he was like this. The wounded alpha male, struggling to bare his heart. "Your dad just died. It's okay to have shit in a bunch of different piles. It's okay to feel ... lost." I scoffed a laugh and broke eye contact. "And believe me, my life isn't nearly as put together as you might think."

The heat of his eyes on me pulled me back, and my breath snagged harshly in my throat. His smolder was enough to burn off all my clothes and leave me in nothing but my toe rings. He'd always had that uncanny ability to see past whatever facade or brave face I tried to put on.

I hadn't counted on this today when I'd convinced myself just to drop by and see what happened. I thought maybe I'd catch him mid-workout. Maybe snacking while using his laptop. Not erasing the scars he'd left on my heart.

He looked out into the yard. "I can't fucking handle myself around you." He glanced back at me. "So if these weekly check-in things are actually real, I need to know when you're coming by, so I can leave. That is unless ..."

I swallowed and my pussy clenched. "Unless?"

"I'm ten seconds away from pinning you to the wall and having my way with you, so consider this your warning. Here's your out." He jerked his head toward the cupola door. "Leave now. Put the space between us that you keep saying you need. Because if you stay, I'm gonna tear off your fucking clothes."

His voice was pure sex and rasp.

I took a step closer.

"Is that supposed to be a turn-on?" I asked, intending to sound condescending when even I could catch the aroused quiver in my voice.

His gaze dropped to my blouse, and he dragged his tongue across his bottom lip.

"Looks like it was a turn-on regardless," he said, a devilish smile curling at his lips.

I shook my head. "Whatever."

He was more than right about that, but I couldn't let him win so easily. Even though I probably wanted what he was offering more than he did, I refused to give him the satisfaction of knowing it.

"I'm leaving because what's done is done between us. No need to revisit. I appreciate your apology, but I honestly think too much time has passed. We're different people now. I'll message Colton and let him know when I plan on coming by again for a check-in." Which would most likely be never. If my willpower held out. I doubt it would because it was hanging on by a fraying thread right now.

My hand hit the doorknob, but when I tugged, it didn't open. I tried again—the door was stuck. I looked back at him, both panic and excitement winding through my veins. In addition to his next-level sexiness, the man was getting hard. Which meant that the door made my decision for me.

"Are we trapped up here?" he asked, looking completely unconcerned.

"Uh." I swallowed hard, trying the knob again. "Yes."

His smirk melted into a shit-eating grin. "Looks like I'm going to have to break one of these windows."

My heart pounded in my chest now. One more second of being this close to Callum, with that growing hard-on making itself evident in his perfect gray sweatpants, and I'd start by tearing off *his* clothes. "Listen. I think it's pretty clear." My mouth went dry as I raked my gaze up and down his body. The truth sparkled inside me, clear for the first time ever. "We just need to get this out of our system."

His grin widened. "You mean the fucking."

"Of course I mean the fucking."

"But you said what's done is done, Harlow." He wet his bottom lip, that hungry gaze turning absolutely fatal to any shred of composure I might have had left.

"Yeah. That's done. But this is … something new. Something else."

He bridged the space between us in two steps, cupping my face roughly in his hands. His lips found mine next, and whatever hesitation or questions that remained were washed away by the cedar scent of him. All that existed now was Callum. This kiss. The intense passion pumping through my veins that reinforced what I already knew: I needed this man inside me.

We kissed so hard that my lips went numb at one point. Because now, nobody could see us, or stop us. Hell, we couldn't even get out if we wanted to. Callum groaned through a kiss, fumbling with the buttons on my blouse until my shirt hung open. His big hands found the dip in my waist then, and finally he broke the kiss to pull back and look at me.

"Fuck, Harlow." His lips were swollen from the kisses. He grunted as he brought me up against him.

"Yes. Fuck Harlow," I breathed. "Fuck her now."

He chuckled and his wily grin made my pussy throb. "Still impatient, I see. But I don't have a condom."

I shook my head, pushing up onto my toes to find his mouth again. "I don't care. It's just this once. Besides, I have an IUD and I'm clean. Are you?"

He nodded, and we resumed kissing, hungry and angry and bursting with passion. I'd never felt anything like this, not before Callum, not since.

He pushed my blouse off and went to unhook my bra, but I stopped him, grabbed his face and brought his mouth back up to mine. Curiosity flashed but for a moment

103

behind his eyes. I'd loved having my nipples sucked and bitten to the point of intense pain, but ... things were different now, and I wasn't ready to reveal that side of myself to him yet. This was supposed to be one and done.

He broke our kiss and scraped his teeth down the side of my neck, pulling something both feminine and animal from the back of my throat. I clamped my mouth shut, and he palmed my breast over my bra in his big, warm hand. His stubble raked along my jawline—something he'd always done, knowing it took me from zero to horny in a second flat. I grabbed at his hips, bringing his body crashing against me. I hooked a leg around his ass, desperate for more.

"Jesus, Harlow. How can it be just once when you do shit like that?"

I gritted my teeth as I struggled to focus on removing his shirt. When I failed, he tutted with a knowing grin.

"Never imagined you'd be so dressed-down today," I teased.

"Never imagined you becoming undressed inside my dead grandparents' house," he murmured, sliding the shirt off and tossing it over the back of a lone chair nearby. He palmed the thick ridge in his pants, his gaze scorching up and down my body. "Fuck."

"What is it? Performance anxiety after all these years?"

His gaze darkened, and he brought me crashing against him, the ridge of his cock pressing into my low belly. "I know you haven't forgotten how good it was." His palms sizzled down over my hips, his fingers seeking the hemline of my pencil skirt. He yanked it up, causing me to gasp, until the fabric bunched at my waist. "Something tells me you're still going to like it just as much."

He hoisted me up, his big palms cupping my ass cheeks as he pinned me to the glass window overlooking the bay. He claimed my mouth with his, inviting urgent, sloppy kisses. I clutched the sides of his face, the throbbing of his cock pressed up against my pussy too delicious to bear. How many times had I imagined this scenario? The mind-bending heat of him sinking into me, his powerful arms around. I thrust against him, suddenly so desperate to have him fill me that I thought I might pass out if I didn't get it *now*. A low moan escaped me as I fumbled to remove my panties without breaking the kiss.

"Please, Callum," I mumbled around our kiss.

He grunted, his breath coming out in hot puffs at my chin as he arranged himself against me. His biceps bulged around me, and then I felt the steel heat of his cock sliding against my soaked pussy. I buried my face in his shoulder and moaned.

"Fuck, Harlow." He flexed his hips, his fat cockhead easing inside me. I hadn't seen it yet, but I knew it from memory. I could practically sketch it even still, which said a lot about how much I used to suck his dick back in college.

The air hissed out of me as he buried himself inside me, somehow both urgent yet reverent. Yes, we were angry and frustrated and bursting with passion that neither of us could understand, much less rid ourselves of. But this still felt tender somehow. Like it might matter to him as much as it did to me.

I thrust against him as he drilled into me, welcoming every last inch of him. Once he was buried to the hilt, I was already fucking close. My chest heaved as I looked at him.

"You look so fucking sexy right now," he said, something raw slashing across his features.

"Don't forget it," I teased, feeling saucier than ever now that he was buried balls-deep inside me. "You'll want to remember how good this was when you have to jerk off to my memory for the next year."

His jaw flexed and in one fluid move he spanked my ass, enough to sting a little. "You think you'll be able to stay away? Now that you're riding this cock again? Baby, please. You'll be back on my doorstep in a day, two tops, begging for it again. And I'm here. At your service."

It was hard to keep up the front. Because he was right. Something about this felt like coming home. We'd always had an insane connection, but this, right here—this was next level shit.

"Why don't you fuck me like I want it? Then we'll see if I can stay away."

A grin tugged at his lips, but he dove into a kiss, stealing my breath and my response. He'd steal my heart again if I wasn't careful, too, which was why I needed to keep the teasing edge with him. If I really started opening up—if it got too tender and *meaningful*—then I'd be a goner.

It had to be one and done. Right?

Callum hoisted me again, and I hooked my arms tighter around his neck. He pumped into me, starting an urgent but thorough rhythm that had my ass pressed up against the cool pane of glass. Our bodies slapped together in time, and my head dropped back, making a *thud* against the window.

"Fuuuuck, Callum," I moaned.

"Yes. Fuck Callum," he said, mimicking me from earlier. "Fuck Callum every day."

I huffed out a laugh. Even in the heat of the moment, the man always, always knew how to make me smile.

His lips dropped to the hollow of my neck and he sank his teeth in. It was both possessive and tender. Just as I always loved.

He scooped me up closer to him, smashing my breasts against his chest. Emotion clamped my throat; an unexpected consequence of giving into passion.

"I'm close, babe," he murmured into my collar bone.

I squeezed my eyes shut. The pet name shouldn't have affected me, but this man was ripping me in half without even realizing it. There was so much more emotion and pain and betrayal underneath the surface; so much more than I'd counted on.

"Me too," I whispered, arching against him.

He groaned, drilling into me over and over again until I felt the familiar hot prickle working up from the base of my spine. I dug my fingernails into the sides of his body as everything washed over me: his cedar scent, mingling with the sweat of his exertion; the relentless rhythm of him, pushing into me over and over again; the feel of him filling me, in the way that only he could. The way that only Callum ever had.

I cried out, the fireworks of pleasure erupting hot and bright behind my eyelids. And then finally a gruff shout filled the cupola as he came and heat filled me.

He pressed his lips to my forehead, his chest heaving. For a while, nobody spoke. Nobody moved. We just breathed together, his lips brushing across my forehead. The two of us caught in a quiet reverie.

Relishing the fact that life had at least granted me this one last chance to satisfy my curiosity.

Wondering if I could really ever keep this to *one and done.*

CHAPTER ELEVEN

CALLUM

I'd yet to wipe Harlow's ass print off the window in the cupola. And every time I went up there and saw it, I got hard as a fucking rock and had to talk myself out of calling her to come over for an encore.

She'd said one and done. Not that I believed it for a second, not the way she'd begged me to fuck her or the way she's moaned my name.

But the spell we'd cast in our glass-enclosed sanctuary was ultimately broken when the orgasm fog faded, and we saw Carson climbing out of his truck in the driveway.

Harlow banged on the cupola windows until he noticed us, and with a smirk and what had to be the slowest fucking walk on the planet, he came up and rescued the prince and princess from the tower. The dragon doing the rescuing? That had to be a fairy tale first.

Then Harlow, with her disheveled hair, haphazardly buttoned blouse, and smeared lipstick, had bolted out of Hope Creek Manor with enough speed and determination you'd think we'd just told her the place had a bedbug infestation.

And I hadn't heard from her since.

I didn't want to push—well, that's a lie—I wanted to push my way back into her life full throttle and pick up right where we left off eight years ago. I was still hopelessly in love with her, and I could tell she wasn't entirely over me, but I'd hurt her and there were wrongs to right and grand gestures and declarations to be made. I needed to do this right if I wanted Harlow to take our second-chance seriously. If I wanted her to become as invested in our future and all the adventures, travels, and new possibilities it entailed.

So, even though I would have much rather spent my Sunday worshipping Harlow's body and apologizing over and over again to her clitoris with my tongue, I gave her some space and chose to be productive instead. Perhaps the weekend wasn't the best day to explore in-person all the family holdings, but it was the first free day I had. So there I was driving around Winter Harbor checking out each and every strip mall, warehouse, and apartment complex.

To be honest, I felt like a bit of a creeper, and based on the weird looks I was getting from people as I drove by slowly, they all thought I was a creeper, too.

But I'd been busy all fucking week. Between poring over paperwork regarding our dad's import business, and all the other businesses we apparently now owned, I'd barely gotten up from my laptop.

Well, besides that four-hour window yesterday where I added to my "growing zoo." At least, that's what Harlow used to call it.

I'd come across an ad for some guy needing to get rid of his tank and fish. *Free to a good home.* He was moving across the country for work, and if somebody didn't take the critters off his hands, he was going to have to flush them all down the toilet.

Fuck that.

I'd called him immediately, and with Colton's help, drove over to his place, which was a shoebox of an apartment on the fourth floor with no elevator. And because he was a dick who would flush live fish rather than make any real attempt at re-homing them, he refused to help me and Colton cart anything down to my car.

The two of us only needed to make four trips up to his crappy little apartment—but we got every last fish into a plastic bag and every last plastic plant and tiny ceramic castle into a cardboard box, before dumping the water in the guy's bathtub and carting everything down to my Honda Civic, then home.

Then I spent two hours setting up the tank in the living room and telling Jonas and Petra to leave their new scaled siblings alone.

It was actually a really nice addition to the space, with the bright, tropical colors and the soothing gurgle of the filter. I already knew this room would be my second favorite in the house after the cupola.

But, I couldn't spend all day staring at my new finned family. I had work to do. So, with my clipboard in the passenger seat of my car, I pulled out of the parking lot of the bustling strip mall my brothers and I were now the proud owners of.

The building itself had seen better days and could probably use a new roof, a fresh coat of paint, and some scrubbed gutters, but the shops along the sidewalks were fully loaded with customers. I planned to come back another day—probably mid-week—when the parking lot wasn't so full and inquire with each proprietor whether this kind of consumer volume was year-round or simply because we were entering tourist season.

For all its "quaint" and almost kitschy qualities, Winter Harbor was gorgeous in the springtime. Flowerbeds and trees with vibrant green leaves lined the barrier boulevard between lanes and everywhere you looked, someone was enjoying the weather with a smile on their face. I think I even spotted a couple with a surfboards on their roof rack. Was there really somewhere to surf nearby? I'd have to investigate later.

The light turned green, and I hit the accelerator just as a flash of blue, black, and white to my right had me nearly swerving into the curb.

It was a runner. A female runner. With a white hat pulled down over her eyes, a dark ponytail swishing behind her, a blue spandex tank top and black spandex pants that left absolutely nothing to the imagination, she ran down the sidewalk at a steady lope.

Though I didn't need my imagination to know what was under those pants. I'd recognize that ass, those hips, and that stride anywhere.

We used to run together. Often finishing off with a race to the shower, followed by a fuck-a-thon fueled by adrenaline.

My dick jerked in my pants as I watched her jog down the sidewalk, her tanned skin glistening with sweat, her ass cheeks ripe, round, and fucking perfect with each graceful stride. She had earbuds in, and sunglasses on. Combined with her hat visor pulled way down, I wouldn't have known it was Harlow if I didn't know the rest of her body so damn well.

She jogged on the spot as she waited for a vehicle to cross in front of her, and I came to another red light. I was right beside her now, but she hadn't looked over yet.

Should I roll down my driver's side window and say something?

My dick said yes.

My brain said no. Though that organ now held little authority these days when it came to Harlow Jackson.

I was about to let my dick take over and roll down my window when she turned down another road off the main drag.

Shit.

If I followed her now, I'd look like a stalker.

Ah, fuck it.

I turned right down the same road she did, only she was gone.

It was a dead end with no other roads stemming off from it. Where the hell did she go?

Had I imagined her completely? Was I so hung up on Harlow, so desperate for another fix, that I was now seeing her in other women? Or seeing her when she wasn't even there? When no one was there? Was she off grocery shopping or gardening, but my horny, confused man-brain had me seeing her running down the road and then disappearing like a phantasm?

If I were wandering the desert for days with sand coating my tongue and my brain screaming for water, would I envision Harlow standing on the top of a dune, the wind in her hair, eyes glittering in the sun instead of the logical mirage of an oasis with freshwater and shade?

All signs seemed to point to yes, until I spotted the trail mouth.

It wasn't very obvious, had no signage, and was fairly overgrown. But there was a trail there.

Even if it was broad daylight, I didn't know Winter Harbor well enough to judge whether a woman was safe running in the woods by herself.

Not to mention the thought of bears or cougars. Did they have them here?

They must. Winter Harbor was located on the Pacific Ocean. There were fishing boats coming in and out of the mouth of the river all day long. Where there were fish, there were bears. And cougars seemed to roam everywhere and anywhere they damn well pleased—typical cats.

Now I feared for Harlow and not just because some crazy rapist son of a bitch could be lurking in the woods ready to peel off her face, but a bear or cougar might be waiting there to do the same.

I parked on the side of the road next to a small copse of leafy trees, making sure to take advantage of their shade, locked my car, and took off in the direction of the trail.

My pulse raced. Why on Earth would she do such a thing?

I thought she was smarter than that.

The trail was severely overgrown and bushes whacked my face as I followed the path. She'd torn down any spider webs, having gone before me, so at least I didn't need to worry about taking sticky netting to the face with a big eight-legged beast finding a new home in my hair.

The further into the woods I walked, the denser the bushes became, until there wasn't much of a trail at all and I was forced to blaze my own.

Where the hell had she gone?

Had she been snagged, gagged, and hauled off to some nomadic-drifter hobo's lair?

But as soon as I thought the trees and bushes were going to close in on me and swallow me whole, they opened up to reveal a creek bed.

A beautiful, picturesque, clear, babbling brook.

That's when I realized where I was.

I'd walked so far back toward home, that I was home. This was my property. Or my family's property. I hadn't walked the entire perimeter of all our newly procured acreage, but I knew enough of the map to know that the stream in front of me was Hope Creek and the mansion was no more than a quarter of a mile south.

But I still could find no trace of Harlow.

It made me stop and wonder once again if I'd made seeing her up entirely, but then the sound of splashing on the other side of a hill had me running.

It wasn't so much a hill per se, as it was a rocky bluff that sent the stream into a small waterfall. But I climbed it, slipping on the damp rock and bashing my elbow something fierce.

I pressed on, though. Through the pain.

Then I saw her.

Like a mermaid in a lagoon. Because it was damn near as close to a lagoon as I'd ever seen one.

A deep pool of water, once again transparent as glass, was fed from a small waterfall, and in turn fed the first waterfall I'd come across.

She swam around, oblivious to my presence. Steam rose up around her from the water.

Holy fuck, this was a hot spring.

A hidden hot spring on our property.

Her dark hair was slicked down against her head and back, but then when she sunk down into the deep, so only her face remained out, that hair floated around her head like a dark halo.

My cock throbbed in my pants and I adjusted it, though that did very little to ease my discomfort. Seeing Harlow frolicking in the pool like a water nymph made me rock fucking hard.

Her pants, tank top, and hat were all folded neatly on a stump, as well as her phone and earbuds.

That seemed careless. Swimming naked in the woods and leaving all her clothes, her phone, and her keys out so anyone could take them?

Or was that the way Winter Harbor was? A town where you didn't have to lock your front door or set the alarm on your car just to run out and grab the dry cleaning. You knew your neighbors, and you trusted them.

Maybe she didn't have to worry here like I had in New York. Pickpockets and scumbags were everywhere. And no way in hell would I feel comfortable letting Harlow go for a run in the woods on her own in New York. I knew women who did run in Central Park in broad daylight and were still assaulted. I couldn't stomach the thought of that happening to someone I loved.

The hot blood coursing through my veins like lava tributaries racing down a volcano, and the now painful ache of my dick and balls said otherwise. It didn't matter that we'd had sex two days ago, and I'd rubbed one out three times since then. The thought of being back inside Harlow made my chest tighten and my cock run the show.

"This is private property, you know?" I finally said, loving the way she jumped and spun around covering her chest, the look of a deer in the headlights only making her all the more gorgeous.

I pushed down my groan; the memories of our time on the cupola at the house on Friday make me want to fill that *O* with something I knew she used to love. And judging by the way she'd moaned and begged me Friday, she still loved it.

When she realized it was me, her expression turned coy, and she dropped her hands but sunk down deeper into the water. "It's okay. I know the owner, and I'm pretty sure he'd be okay with me being here."

I shrugged and stepped over a log to reach the edge of the pool. "I'm not so sure about that. The owner can be *quite* the jerk from what I've heard. Actually, all three of the owners can be dicks. The oldest owner, of course, *having* the biggest dick."

She swam closer to me. "Sorry, did you say the oldest owner *is* the biggest dick? Because I'd have to agree."

I smiled, letting my gaze roam her face—bright blue eyes, rosy cheeks, full lips—she really was the most gorgeous thing I'd ever laid eyes on. Clearing my throat, I glanced away and jerked my chin toward her clothes on the stump. "You're sure it's safe to leave your clothes and valuables out like that on that stump while you go all Little Mermaid in here naked?"

Laughing, she pushed away from me again and dipped down below the water, only to emerge closer to the waterfall. "I've been coming here for *years*. Because it's private property hardly anyone knows about it."

"I bet drifters and hobos know about it." I shoved my hands in my pockets and pulled the front of my shorts away from my body to hopefully mitigate the appearance of my raging boner.

"Don't get a lot of those types around here," she said. "We're located at the mouth of a river, and don't have much to offer the vagabond type. Winter Harbor is lucky that way. Quaint, quiet, and safe. Everyone is your neighbor, and every neighbor is your friend. I honestly can't remember the last time I locked my front door or my car."

"That's going to take some getting used to. And Jesus Christ, always lock your front door."

She giggled. The sound was fucking music. "There's something to be said for small towns. People have your back. They're not just waiting for an opportunity to stab you in it."

I did nothing but grunt. I wasn't convinced that Winter Harbor was the end all and be all yet. It had its perks, sure. But it was also a town with bloodlust for my family, and even though Harlow didn't have to watch her back here, I was learning that wasn't the case for someone with the last name Winters.

She swam back toward me and lifted a dark brow on her damp face. "I know you can't see this part of the creek from the house. Did you follow me here?"

I cleared my throat again and tried not to look through the water to where I know she had nothing on but her beautiful bronzed skin. "I saw you running and then you headed into the woods."

"So you followed me." Her smile had all my resolve to not strip down naked and join her in the stream dissolving by the bucket loads.

116

"I guess the woods here are a lot different from the woods in New York. Never in a million years would I let someone I love go running into the trees on their own, daylight or dead of night."

Her sharp inhale and the little O on her mouth again had me going back over what I'd just said.

Oh fuck.

I'd said *someone I loved.*

Son of a bitch.

Well, fuck it. I did love her. Hadn't fucking stopped. I set my jaw firmly and held her gaze.

The O closed and her surprise faded. "I can assure you, I'm one hundred percent safe here. You don't need to follow me into the woods again ..."

Unless you want to.

She let that last bit hang unsaid. But we both knew it was there.

Rubbing the back of my hand over my forehead and coming up damp, I let out a deep breath. "It's hot as balls out. Is it normally like this in early May?"

"Not usually. It's an unusually warm spring. But this hot spring is massaging my achy muscles perfectly." She pushed off the rocks and swam away from me. "You afraid to go swimming in the *crick*, city boy? Worried about leeches?"

My smile dropped like an anvil. "Are there leeches?"

Giggling, she dipped back under the water, only to surface as close to me as she'd ever been. "Too hot for leeches. But I hear the mermaids can be wicked bitches."

"Yeah? Irresistible sirens leading men to their doom?"

She snickered. "Something like that." Not bothering that it made her breasts leap out of the water and bounce, she sprang up and splashed me, essentially soaking my clothes and causing my shorts to plaster themselves against my erection.

"Oh, you're gonna pay for that," I said with a grin, toeing off my shoes, peeling off my drenched socks, and the rest of my clothes until I was in nothing but my boxers—which poked up like a ten-man tent.

She swallowed, her eyes zeroing in on my crotch. "Quite the impressive tent you've got there, Callum Winters."

I smiled, my eyes laser-focused on her breasts beneath the water. "You always knew how to help me pitch a good one." Finally, I pulled down my boxers and jumped in next to her.

She blinked spiked lashes at me as I came up for air right in front of her. The smile on her face from earlier was gone, replaced with a look of sincerity and hope. She crushed her bottom lip between her teeth before she reached out and cupped my cheek.

"You know, there is a legend about this creek," she said, glancing around us through the steam.

"Yeah, and what's that? The mermaid's voices are like sweet honey for your ears, but their sting is deadly like a murder hornet's?"

She snorted, and her grin made my chest tight. "No. They say ... and by *they* I mean the *town*, say that if you swim in Hope Creek with someone, your lives will be entangled forever. That *Hope* springs eternal." She rolled her eyes at the pun. "And to swim together is a bond for life."

I tangled my fingers in her hair. "I'm okay with that."

A small, sad smile creased her face for a moment. "It's why I've come here alone for so many years."

"And I'm glad you did. Because there isn't anyone else I'd want you to swim with, but me." I tilted her chin with my free hand. "You never have to swim alone again, Harlow."

Her expression turned serious but hopeful. "I've missed you, Callum." The huskiness of her voice made my dick throb and emotion snag painfully in my chest. She always had been able to render me a puddle just from a simple look. Just like a junkie, I would do anything to get more of Harlow.

"Yeah?" With my fingers in her hair, I tilted her head up to look at me. Air fled her lungs in a whoosh, the puff hitting my lips as she gazed up at me, startled, with those incredible blue eyes.

I walked her backward until her back was to the rock wall. Pushing my knee between her thighs, her legs widened slightly for me. My right hand, which was still threaded in her hair, slid around to the back of her head more and I bunched it into a ponytail with my fist, tugging the handful until her face tilted up and her neck was exposed.

"How long have you missed me?"

The pulse in her throat pounded as hard as the pulse in my dick. "Since the day you left," she whispered.

CHAPTER TWELVE

CALLUM

Fuck me.

I'd missed Harlow every fucking day since I left, too.

I ran my lips over her pulse, feeling it speed up even more as I pushed my knee against the V of her legs. She ground down against me, a whimper of need bubbling up from the back of her throat. Snagging a peaked nipple between my fingers, I twisted and tugged until she groaned, shut her eyes and swiveled her hips against the top of my thigh. Her throat moved under my mouth as I scraped my teeth across her delicate skin, swirling my tongue around the hollow, only to work my way back up to that sensitive spot just below her ear.

She gasped when I caught the lobe between my teeth, biting hard enough for her to feel it. The shiver that shot through her made me smile against her neck.

I would like to say that it was the absence that made me want Harlow as bad as I fucking did. But it wasn't. Yes, we'd been apart for eight years, but I knew that even if we'd been together all that time, I'd still want her the way I did now. Still crave the taste of her, her touch. Once an addict, always an addict?

I took her mouth, sucking her bottom lip, scraping my teeth over it, then exploring the inside. Her tongue tangled with mine, twisting and sucking, stroking it like she would if it were my cock. She'd always given the best fucking head. This woman could suck the chrome off a bumper.

But even though she could make me come with just a couple of good sucks and strokes, what turned me on more than anything in this fucking world was the noises she made, and the way she squirmed when I was face down between her legs.

That sweet gush of her honey across my tongue as she tugged on my hair, jammed her hips up so hard I struggled to breathe and called out my name as she came was a permanent memory in my spank bank.

Nothing, and I mean nothing, was hotter than Harlow Jackson coming when I ate her out.

She squawked when I released her hair, broke the kiss, and roughly gripped her by the hips. "Callum!"

I plunked her perfect ass up and out of the water on the slate rock edge, palmed her thighs wide and pushed my face into her heat.

"Oh!" was all she said as she reclined back against the rock and scooted her butt closer to me.

Like a dog staring at a steak—pink and juicy—my mouth flooded with saliva as I spread her lips and latched onto her clit.

Her hips shot off the rock and her fingers flew down her body and into my hair, holding me in place. She'd always been a bossy little thing when getting head. Not afraid to give instructions. But that just made it all the better. I was a quick learner, and soon the only things that came out of her mouth as I was ears deep in her pussy were things like "fuck yes" and "oh God" and "Jesus, Callum."

No more direction needed. I was a Harlow Jackson pussy-eating master.

And just like riding a bicycle, I never forgot in our years apart, just what made my woman gush, scream, and damn near snatch me bald.

Sucking hard on her clit, I swirled my finger around her entrance, dipping it in and out, teasing, and tormenting her. I knew what she wanted. She kept pressing down, trying to force my finger deeper into her channel.

But not yet.

I was enjoying her grunts and groans of frustration. The tightening of her fingers in my hair and the eventual demand of, "Fucking, stick your fingers in me already, Callum."

"So bossy," I chided, pushing one, and then another, inside her. She sighed and bucked up into my mouth as I circled her clit with my tongue.

"Not bossy. I just know what I want." Her clit swelled and her juices coated my fingers and hand.

"And that's me with my face between your thighs and my fingers—"

"That's you shutting up and making me come," she breathed, pushing my head harder so I struggled to get air in through my nose.

Chuckling against her cleft, I did as I was told, and dined on a delicacy I hadn't tasted in eight long, agonizing years. I ate Harlow out like both our lives depended on it. Sucked her clit until she gasped, pumped my fingers inside her, stroked her walls, pressed on her G-spot, and laved at her folds until she exploded around me.

Her body stilled, her back bowed, and her fingers fisted my hair until pain shot down my skull and into my spine.

But none of that mattered. This was what I loved most in the world.

This was what got my engine revving like nothing else.

I flicked open my eyes and watched as she rode the waves, reached the crescendo, and then slowly began to coast down the other side.

I continued to lazily slide my fingers in and out of her until the last wave of the orgasm waned. When she released my hair and her body relaxed, I pulled my fingers from her and licked them clean.

You couldn't waste a drop of the good stuff when you're an addict like I was.

With my dick now raring to go and getting mighty demanding about it, I pulled her from her post-orgasm coma and back into the water with me, settling her on my hips.

Her smile was soft, the same as her eyes when she finally opened them. Her arms rested on my shoulders and her fingers toyed with the hair at the nape of my neck. "I didn't pull your hair too hard, did I?" The huskiness of her voice had my balls pulling up and my dick getting even harder.

"Nothing I can't handle, babe," I said, settling her down over my cock, both of us sighing as I filled her,

Home.

That's what it felt like to be inside Harlow.

It felt like home.

And having never really had a true *home*, the sensation was pretty fucking overwhelming.

With her breasts mashed between us, bobbing in the water, I reached up and went to tug on her right nipple, but she stopped me.

I lifted my head and the look on her face that met me was something I'd never seen on her before. I couldn't place it. Worry mixed with conviction..

"I had a mastectomy two years ago," she said quietly.

My stomach dropped to the bottom of the pond. "What?"

"I was diagnosed with breast cancer in my right breast, and the best course of treatment was a mastectomy."

"Oh my God."

It didn't matter that we were in a hot spring. A terrifying chill raced down the length of my spine, and I sucked in a sharp breath.

Her lips pursed together. "Don't look at me like that, Callum. Don't ruin this moment with pity. I don't want your pity. I'm fine. I'm cancer-free. I have an implant." She took my hand and made it cup her breast. "Feels real, right?"

I squeezed it gently and nodded.

Harlow sighed. "I just wanted to tell you because, well ... you can tell the difference, but not *that* much, right?" Fear lingered in her eyes.

The difference didn't matter to me. But I gave her what she needed and nodded. "Can barely tell at all." It was tough to get the words out. My throat was tight, my chest hurt. I knew she had her family here in Winter Harbor, but I hated myself for not being the hand she held when she went to the doctor's appointments, or for her treatments.

"We did radiation, but chemo wasn't necessary."

I nodded and swallowed.

Her soft, delicate hands came up and cupped my face, forcing me to look at her. Though, I didn't want to look anywhere else anyway.

"I'm okay, Callum. Seriously. I'm fine. I froze a bunch of my eggs in case the radiation messed with my fertility. I have twenty in a freezer in Portland. And the doctors say that I should be able to breastfeed with my one natural breast. But if it's not enough, then it's formula for the win, right?" Even after eight years, I could tell when she was putting on a brave front. Her voice quavered, and she spoke really fast. But it was the terror mixed with conviction in her eyes that gutted me the most. She was worried I was going to see her differently.

But that was impossible. To me, Harlow would always be perfect, real breasts or not. Cancer-free or not. It was her heart that had made me fall in love with her and why I was still in love with her.

But I must have been looking at her in a way she didn't like because her brows furrowed and her lips dipped into a frown. "Don't look at me and see cancer-girl. Look at me and see Harlow ... please." That last word came out like her throat was in a chokehold. Her eyes pleaded with me.

My head bobbed. "I ... I do. You're all I ever want to see. Who I've seen in my dreams for eight fucking years."

"But ..." Her brow hitched.

"Breast cancer was what took my mother ... so ..." I glanced away but could see the sudden understanding on her face and the soft *O* of her mouth out of the corner of my eye.

She toyed with the back of my neck, twirling her finger in the short hair at the nape. "Hey."

I swallowed.

"Callum, look at me."

I dragged my gaze back to hers, reminded once again why I loved this woman so fucking much. What stared back at me was my whole world. Adoration, kindness, love, understanding, and thankfully *forgiveness*. Harlow was it. She was everything. *My* everything and no fucking way was I ever letting her go again.

"I'm okay. Truly," she said. "Cancer-free. I swear."

I nodded. "I know."

The pressure of her hands on my neck increased as she pulled my mouth toward hers. "Then show me. Fuck me like you mean it. Fuck me like you do in your dreams. Like I'm not some fragile piece of crystal you're going to break if you get a little rough." Her grin turned wicked. "Manhandle me like you used to. Like you know I love. Like we both love."

A new heat and need exploded in my belly and, like nothing more than a pesky fly, I swatted away the triggers and thoughts of losing Harlow the same way we lost my mom and crushed my mouth to hers again. Pushing her back against the wall of the pond, I fucked her again, this time even more unbridled than before, pouring my love and obsession with her out through my kisses. From my body into hers. I said everything I could without saying a word, told her how I felt, how I'd never see her as "cancer-girl."

She broke out of the kiss, tipped her head back and cried out as she came, digging her nails into my shoulders as she found her release and I found mine.

We stayed there, coming down once again from our high, quiet with chests heaving.

"You're not cancer-girl," I said after a moment. "You're Harlow. And you're mine."

Her inhale was sharp.

I tugged the nipple on her other breast and looked her square in the eye. "You're spending the day with me. I want to hear about everything that has happened in the last eight years. I want to hear about your diagnosis, your treatment, recovery. All of it."

She blinked spiked, wet lashes at me, and tilted her head to the side, pausing mid-way down my cock and squeezing around me until I saw stars.

I twitched my dick inside her in response to her fist-like pussy, and she giggled.

We used to do this on the daily, just stay together and see how many rounds we could go before I'd grow soft and need to recharge. I wasn't twenty-two anymore, but then again, I'd never been able to go so many rounds with anybody besides Harlow.

She made me harder than I ever got and kept me that way.

"Spend the day with me," I said again, enjoying the way we could turn any moment into a funny one—just like the old days. "I'm checking out all the family holdings. Come with me. Show me Winter Harbor."

If I wasn't already inside her, the smile that erupted on her face would have made me take her every which way from Sunday. But then that grin turned sassy, and she twisted her lips. "On one condition."

Sure, I'd play along. Lifting a brow, I twisted her nipple again. "Yeah? What's that?"

With fire swirling in the blue of her eyes, she sunk down to the hilt of my cock, squeezing as tight as she could the whole way down. I had to do some serious deep breathing not to blow my load right then and there.

She knew what she was doing too, the minx.

"You use that skilled tongue of yours again, and then you buy me lunch."

Growling, I lifted her off my cock, plunked her ass back on the rock and dove into her pussy, not caring one fucking bit that it was full of my cum—in fact, I loved it. I knew this turned her on, and it did me, too.

"I'll make you come *twice* more, at least. And then I'll buy lunch *and* dinner," I murmured before I sucked her clit, making her gasp. Then I ate Harlow properly—twice—until her cries drown out the birdsong around us and my world finally began to make sense again.

CHAPTER THIRTEEN

HARLOW

Call me crazy, but once Callum ate me out in that pond—three times, I might add—something changed between us. It unlocked a door that we'd both been pawing at, waiting for it to swing open. Maybe it's just the clarity—or insanity—of so many mind-blowing orgasms, but we couldn't go back from that. And I did not want to.

Then it only took four hours wandering Winter Harbor by his side to prove just how quickly we could revert to our personal *best of times.*

Callum didn't drop my hand unless it was to drive the car once we got started on the Winters Holdings Tour. And even then, he held my hand in his lap as he drove with one arm. I felt insane, sitting in the passenger's seat, wrapped up in this bizarre experience that was equal parts memory, fantasy, and wet dream. I felt like we'd been here before, in this strange Winter Harbor fantasy, even though it was impossible.

This was what I'd been waiting for ever since we broke up. And for how perfectly unlikely it was, I planned to enjoy every last second of it.

Because who knew when this reverie might end?

His snort drew my attention.

"What?"

Shaking his head, he glanced in the rearview mirror. "Nothing. I just noticed that *Best Chiropractic* sign earlier and again right now. A bit conceited, don't you think? I mean, isn't being the *best* at something objective? Unless, of course, you're an Olympic medalist?

I rolled my eyes. "It's owned by Dr. Raphael *Best*. His son, Travis, just joined the practice with him. Travis and I went to school together, right up from kindergarten to senior year." Though, with there only being one high school in Winter Harbor, it was impossible *not* to go to school with everyone your age.

Callum cleared his throat. "Yeah?" Even in his profile, I could see that green-eyed monster lurking beneath his calm veil.

"Yeah. We never dated, though. He was big into lacrosse, hung out with the sporty crowd. I liked my nerd crew. Travis got a scholarship and went off to Minneapolis for school."

"Know an awful lot about the guy, though."

I shoved Callum's arm. "It's hard not to when the town is so small. There's still a lot you need to learn about small-town living. Also, Dr. Best *senior* is my chiropractor, and he golfs with my dad. You feeling a jealous tickle there, Mr. Winters?"

His head shook. "Nope. No tickle. Not jealous, just getting the lay of the land and all that."

Hmmm. *The lay of the land and all that.* Did he mean the *former lays* of his *property*?

That thought made me equal parts giddy as it did infuriate the feminist inside me. I was nobody's property, obviously, but the idea of Callum getting jealous meant he cared, and that meant a lot.

We needed to get off the topic of Dr. Best and his very handsome, very successful son, Dr. Best. One of my favorite places in Winter Harbor came into view, and I leaped to action in my seat.

"Pull over here." I pointed to the asphalt road leading toward a popular pier along the coast of Winter Harbor. After a great lunch on the outskirts of town tucked into the side of the hills and visiting two of the family holdings—a strip mall and an abandoned office building—it seemed time for something blatantly touristy. After all, we were living in a Winter Harbor fantasy now, weren't we?

"Is this part of my newest possessions?" Callum asked with a mischievous grin on his face.

"No. And even if it was, you don't *legally* possess anything until you complete the required 365 nights at the mansion. And," I made a big display of checking my imaginary watch, "looks like you're on day fifteen."

"Only 350 more to go," he murmured, slowing the car as he navigated down the skinny road leading to a parking lot overlooking Hope Bay.

Small benches buttressed the lines of the pier, and a passenger ferry rocked gently along the western edge. The view from Winter Harbor pier was stunning, and one of the quintessential shots that formed the bulk of postcards sold in the area. To the north, across the bay: the stunning backdrop of the cliffs spanning the mouth of the harbor. To the west, the round arc of the shoreline, like a protective arm around the bay. And to the east, the quaint lines of the town itself, colorful and clapboard.

And now with Callum at my side, beholding my most special place, I felt like I might wake up at any second. Because this was certainly too wild to be reality. This was the reality that I'd stopped hoping for after he broke my heart senior year. Not just a love story in my hometown, but a love story with *him*.

When we parked, Callum looked over at me, something soft in his gaze. "You planning something that I should know about?"

"Why would you say that?"

He shrugged, pushing the door open. But he didn't get out. "Seems like you've got something up your sleeve with the way you've been staring at me."

"Nothing planned. Just can't believe we've been in the same breathing space for over four hours and ..."

"And ..."

"And I've yet to wake up."

He cracked a grin, the dimple in his cheek making my heart race. We both got out of the car and he came to my side, slinging his arm over my shoulders. We'd gone from barely able to look at each other because of our painful past, to publicly canoodling in the span of an afternoon.

And the weirdest part was that I wasn't just okay with it, I was relishing it.

"I still think you've got something planned," he murmured into my hairline as we started a slow walk toward the sidewalk wrapping around the pier.

"Just more sex later," I told him with a laugh.

"See? I was right." His arm dropped, fingertips trailing down my side until the heat of his palm found my ass. He gave it a squeeze, which made my pussy pulse weakly. I might have been technically sated, but Callum knew how to make me want more.

"But weren't you planning that, too?" I teased, bumping my hip into his.

He scoffed. "Of course. I'm planning it for the next 350 days, too."

"Thanks for the transparency," I said with a laugh. But it was relieving somehow. Knowing that he wanted to continue *this*. Whatever it was … whatever it might end up being.

People sat on the benches looking out over the bay, basking in the warm afternoon. He took my hand in his and we strolled slowly. I knew damn near everyone on the pier; I smiled and nodded at each acquaintance as I passed. Mrs. Moriarty from the supermarket. Mr. Randall, whose son did my taxes. Buck Wilhelm, who seemed to live on this pier with a fishing rod in his hand, even though he almost never caught anything.

But all the smiles I received in return quickly fell. More than one person openly glared at us. I thought that maybe it was my imagination, until Callum whispered, "Is it just me or is everyone a fucking grump on this pier?"

I laughed, but it faded quickly. "I'm sensing the same." A sick lotus blossom of dread unfurled inside my gut. All I could hear in my head as we walked was Ripley's voice, imploring me not to start a second history with this man. And here I was—indulging a second history for a day, at least.

But that's all this is. Just testing the waters. Reminiscing.
At least, that's what it *should* be. If I was being smart.
But who was ever smart when it came to Callum Winters?
Not me. That was for damn sure.

My legs wobbled. I couldn't decipher this nugget of foreboding in my gut, so I needed to sit and regroup. "Let's watch the water for a minute."

Callum eased onto the bench beside me, his arm draped casually along the back of the bench. We watched the water in easy silence, but I couldn't stop thinking about the quietly nasty welcome we'd received on this very normal walk to the water.

Sure, Callum's family had a history here. But that didn't mean everyone judged *him*, right?

"I saw that Carson has started working on the wrap-around porch of the house," I said, allowing my gaze to follow a seagull as it spread its wings and rode the breeze. "What have you and Colton been up to?"

"No idea what Colton's doing. He helped me with the fish tank, but he's gone most of the days. I'm tackling the inside. Room by room, I'm chucking shit out. I plan to start painting the living room and hallways in the next week or so. Not that I have any clue what the fuck I'm doing." He grinned down at me. "But I'm a fast learner."

I leaned into him, melting at the mischievous twinkle in his eye. "That you were."

He dropped his arm to the top of my back and his hand fell to my shoulder, pulling me closer to his side. I let my head rest on his bicep.

"I want every day to be like this, Harlow."

"You mean you want to stalk me on my run, ambush me in the hot spring, and make me come like five times?"

His grin grew wide and wolfish. "Among other things, but yes."

Warmth bloomed in my belly and my chest tightened. I wanted every day to be like this, too, but my heart, despite how happy it was right now, was still guarded. It had long scarred over cuts from eight years ago. It'd taken a long time to pick up all the shattered pieces and paste them back together.

"I think the future could be really bright for us if we—*I*—don't fuck up again, don't you think? A new beginning. Both of us successful. You with your name on the leaderboard, me heading a wildly successful tech start-up, but always home for dinner and to help the kids with their homework and put them to bed together."

Kids? Homework? I loved the direction he was heading in.

I swallowed and peered up at him, my chest tight but my damaged heart crying out saying that she was okay and ready for love again. Not that she'd ever stopped. Because I had never stopped loving Callum, even when I hated him. "You think we've got what it takes?"

He tugged me closer and pressed a kiss to the top of my head. "I think we've got everything we need to make this time go the distance."

I beamed up at him. "I think so, too."

While the waves lapped at the edge of the steel pier, I sank into my thoughts about what a future with Callum might look like so deeply that I hardly noticed when someone had approached.

"Ms. Jackson?"

Callum nudged me, and I turned quickly to find a local standing nearby—Mr. Gentry. He looked both hopeful and apologetic, his tired, blue eyes shifting between Callum and me. He was older but spry, yet always wore holey, worn-out clothes. Word in town was that Mr. Gentry had a stockpile of money in the multi-millions, which probably explained why he disappeared every winter and occasionally showed off pictures of places like Switzerland, the Chilean Patagonia, and the far reaches of Canada.

"I'm so sorry. I was lost in my thoughts. How are you, Mr. Gentry?"

He took a step away, indicating that he wanted me to follow. "Do you have a moment to talk?"

I was no stranger to being approached for on-the-fly legal advice pretty much whenever I set foot out of my condo. I assumed this was no different. "For you? Of course." I offered a smile and hopped to my feet.

Mr. Gentry stuffed his hands into his pockets, and we walked a little way down the pier. "How are you today?"

"Just fine, thank you. And yourself?"

"Enjoying the beautiful spring afternoon off."

His smile looked strained. When he stopped walking and turned to me, I could see the tension lining his gaze. "This will be quick. I noticed you're here with the Winters boy."

All the secret fears and dread that had been slowly accumulating in the periphery of my mind solidified into a giant rock in my gut. I swallowed hard. "I am. Is there a problem?"

"There is. And he's it." Mr. Gentry jabbed his finger toward the bench where Callum sat. "I know that it's none of my business, but I don't want to see a fine young lady like yourself get hurt, or swindled, by the Winters boys. I know your parents. They're good people. You're good people. But the Winters ..." he shook his head and clucked his tongue, "they're not good people. None of 'em."

"I'm in no danger of being hurt or swindled—"

"You have no idea what they're like," Mr. Gentry went on, his normally soft voice becoming harder, edged with passion. "What happened between his granddaddy and this town is something that people my age will never forget. I know you and your family weren't yet established here back then, but it was a big deal. They take everything you love and ... and ruin it. And I'll be god damned if that boy is creeping back in to take Winter Harbor through the ringer for a second time."

I rolled my lips in, unsure how to respond here. My gut reaction was to put on my lawyer cap, but this was outside the scope of my case with Callum. For now. "I hear you. And I appreciate you looking out for me. But—"

"No, there are no buts. That's all I had to say. You watch out around him. Because I don't trust him, or his brothers, as far as I can throw them. Which at this age, ain't far."

I smiled, but it faded quickly. "Thanks, Mr. Gentry."

He nodded and headed the other way down the pier. I watched him go before heading back to Callum, indecision rippling through me. But one thing was for sure. We needed to leave.

"Let's head out," I said, trying to sound lighthearted. I wasn't sure how much I should reveal to Callum yet. Part of me still couldn't believe that Callum, who'd never set foot in this town before two weeks ago, could cause such a quiet uproar with the older generation.

Callum was buried in his phone, rapidly typing out a text. When he didn't respond, I repeated myself.

"Callum. Let's go."

"Okay." He didn't move, still glued to his phone.

"Have I told you this is a topless pier? I think I'm going to take my shirt off. Ready? One, two—"

His head popped up, breaking whatever intense concentration had been holding him hostage. "What the fuck?"

I grinned at him and giggled. "Only when there's the possibility of boobs can I pry you away from that phone of yours, yeesh. Some things never change."

A growl rumbled in his chest, and the primal look in his eyes confirmed my notion. His love for me certainly hadn't changed. Not in eight years. Heat flooded my belly.

"What could be *so* important that I nearly flashed half of Winter Harbor just to get your attention?"

He looped his arm around my shoulder and shoved his phone into his pocket. "Just this startup in California that I'm investing in. A large chunk of what I got on the sale of my condo in New York is going into this. Just asking a few last-minute questions before I pull the plug on the transfer."

"Okay, well, I *guess* that's important."

"Not as important as keeping those nipples of yours all to myself." With another growl, he reached for my waist with his free hand and spun me around to face him, our chests knocking as he pulled me close. "Let's get out of here. I need to taste those nipples you were so close to showing the world."

My smile was so big it hurt my face. "Not yet, stud. We should finish visiting the holdings before we go on to that last meal you owe me."

"Owe?" We started walking again, his arm once more casually draped over my shoulder. "More like offered. And what about my next meal? I want you spread on my fucking dining room table so I can feast."

My cheeks were hotter than the surface of the sun. "Not so loud."

He did nothing but grin wider.

I swatted his shoulder. "No, you owe me caviar, lobster, wagyu beef, and really expensive wine after the way you treated me when you broke up with me."

He clamped his mouth shut but brought me closer by the elbow. "You don't want to get into this here, do you?"

His warm, gruff voice at my ear sent a shiver down my spine. "Only if it means you'll let me get the most expensive wine at dinner. I want all the surf and all the turf."

"Who says we're going anywhere that serves wine? I just said I'm taking you home and spreading you out on my dining room table. Need to at least have one meal there, otherwise I think it's bad luck."

I sent him a jaunty smile. I wanted to push aside the drama of Callum's family for now. At least so we could have this one lovely day together. And maybe never again. "No, your brothers could walk in mid-meal and how awkward would that be?" I bounced on my toes. "I know exactly where we're having dinner. Warm up that credit card, bud."

His grin told me everything I needed to know. Because I remembered that smile plenty well.

It told me that whatever fight he put up, it was just a front.

Because the man still loved me. He'd let it slip at the pond, but my heart had known all along. And if I was being brutally honest, I loved him just as much as ever. Which meant that I needed to figure out where Callum fit into the bigger picture. Where he and I fit into a town that I loved, but that hated him.

The way things were going, it looked like Winter Harbor might not be big enough for the last remaining heirs of the family who founded it.

Hours later, after visiting the last of the physical properties on the holdings list and enjoying a sumptuous salmon dinner at the fanciest restaurant in Winter Harbor, we were back to moony-eyed teenager status.

I'd drank half a bottle of wine with dinner in an effort to avoid thinking about all the tension between Callum and the town, so I was feeling equal parts wound up and dreamy. Because it had been easy to get lost in Callum's gaze over a gourmet dinner. A little too easy to get lost in the dreamy ideas of what might come next, now that he was back in town for a year and things seemed to be thawing between us.

Hand in hand, we wandered out of *Chez Hiver* and down the sidewalk. Once Callum had paid, I'd made the decision to move our party to my place.

"My car is this way," Callum said, pointing toward the parking lot.

"Yes, but my condo is right over there." I tipped my head toward the side street where my home sweet home lay. "And I think we should go there."

His handsome grin told me he knew exactly what I was getting at. We strolled under the amber lights illuminating the sidewalk, and when I shivered, Callum pulled me tighter into his arms. It was a dizzying blend of past and present. At our cores, we were still the versions of ourselves we'd fallen in love with, but also new and different, practically strangers meeting by chance.

Once we made it into the cozy nest of my condo, Callum had me backed up against the door, kissing my face off. His kisses were warm and thorough, tinged with red wine and lust. We broke for air after a few moments. The thick ridge of his cock pressed into my hip and I palmed it, lifting a brow.

He smirked. "Don't I at least get the grand tour before you tear my clothes off?"

"You were here earlier when I changed after my run."

"You made me wait on the patio."

I batted my eyelashes and led him by the hand deeper into my condo. It was true—I hadn't wanted him to see my place in less-than-perfect condition. But now that I was drunk and horny, I *did not care.*

It was an open floor plan, so it didn't take much leading around. I gestured broadly in front of me. "Here is the living room, kitchen, and dining room."

Callum nodded, stuffing his hands into his pockets. "Great."

"Want to see the bedroom?"

"Obviously."

I led him into my softly illuminated oasis, with the raised king bed, excessively soft mauve bedding, tasseled throw pillows that were a pain in the ass to move each night, even though I loved how they looked in the daytime.

An appreciative smile curled at his lips. "Nice."

"It's no inherited mansion, but it's home," I said, throwing my arms around his waist.

He smiled down at me, his fingers threading through my hair at the base of my neck. He tugged gently before pausing. Something vibrated between us.

"Shit. Hang on." He fished his phone out of his pocket and looked at the screen. A frown replaced his grin. "I gotta take this."

"Okay." I released him as he answered the call, following him back into the living room.

He paced along the far edge of the kitchen as he murmured softly to whoever it was on the phone. While he was busy, I did what I do best—check my email. I scanned a few new emails that I knew could wait until tomorrow. But one from the early evening caught my eye. It had come from Oregon Health and Science University Hospital in Portland. The only reason I got emails from the hospital was about my breast cancer follow-up.

I swallowed the familiar knot in my throat that accompanied any mention of my diagnosis. The knot cinched harder when I saw the contents. A secure message from my doctor awaited inside the medical portal. *I'd like to discuss the results of your last mammogram. Schedule ASAP.*

I set my phone aside, wishing I could set my anxiety aside as well. After how much uncertainty and fear I'd lived through during the first round of cancer, I wasn't sure I had it in me to weather the storm a second time if something proved worrisome again. And how would this trigger Callum? His mother had died of breast cancer, for Christ's sake. I couldn't just forget that look he gave me in the hot spring and the way my news cast a haunted look in his eyes.

This was why I needed to stop checking my emails during off-hours. I didn't want to ruin what had turned out to be a very lovely day, and showed promise to be a very lovely evening. I had to divert back to the fun times. No worrying about the future—*for now*. I rummaged through my wine rack, trying to select the perfect accompaniment to our first evening in my condo.

"Yeah, yeah," Callum said into the phone. "The idea is solid. Let's do it. I'm ready for the next step. Just let me know what you need from me."

The sharp enthusiasm in his tone made the hairs on my arm stand up. As I uncorked a bottle of merlot, I thought back to what both Ripley and Mr. Gentry had warned me about. It just didn't seem possible that Callum and his brothers were here to swindle me; to swindle *anybody*. The brothers could barely stay in the same room together, which meant that any collaboration between the three of them was a non-starter.

I listened to as much of his side of the conversation as I could, but he ended the call before I could make heads or tails of it. I poured two generous glasses and headed his way, passing one off cheerily.

"Here you go. Bottoms up." I lifted my glass, and he clinked his against mine. Before I took a sip, I asked, "Who was that?"

"An old partner of mine." He must have caught the curiosity on my face because he hurried to add, "Business partner."

I nodded, taking another sip of wine. Usually two glasses was my limit, but when Callum was in my condo, the rules flew out the window. In every possible sense. "Someone who's helping you with ... the holdings?"

"No. A buddy from college. Investment opportunity." He ran a hand through his hair, looking suddenly weary. "It's complicated. Nothing is set in stone yet, so I don't want to talk about it and jinx things. You know?"

I didn't, but I would respect his request for privacy.

There was so much I didn't know about his life since we'd broken up and parted ways. So much that I needed—and wanted—to discover. But if he could put up a roadblock, then I could simply exist in my happy, sexy bubble for another night. I'd leave the fact-finding for another day. I deserved to have this sexy night out with my former love, no strings attached.

Except I wondered if maybe there were now so many strings I was being knotted up tight without even realizing.

"So we didn't get to see everything on your holdings list," I said, taking another sip of wine.

"You're not playing my lawyer today, remember?" Callum guided me toward the big sectional facing the glass sliding doors looking out over my tiny backyard. "Let's relax."

I didn't know whether to take this as a clever side-stepping maneuver, or a simple pivot to sexy times. I hated that Ripley and Mr. Gentry were making me doubt this. I hated that I knew I had plenty of reasons to doubt Callum ... yet still wanted to just bask in the warmth of the love we'd once shared.

It had been so long since I'd felt anything like it. And honestly, I wasn't convinced I ever would again.

So I let him lead me to the couch.

"What did that old guy at the pier want to talk you about?" he asked, bringing my socked feet into his lap and massaging them like he used to. This alone could make me come, and he very much knew that.

I'd had a fair bit of wine tonight, so my lips were loose. "He warned me against you. Said all the Winters are swindlers and bad news. Said the town doesn't believe for a second that you guys aren't like your dad and grandfather. Ripley at The Grind has said the same thing."

He stopped massaging my feet. "Do you have that old codger's number?"

"Who? Mr. Gentry?"

"Is that the name of the guy at the pier?"

I nodded, then yawned. "Yeah. And no, I don't have his number. Why do you want it? To call him and tell him to stop bad-mouthing you to me?"

He shook his head. "No. You already know what kind of an asshole I can be."

"That's true."

He snorted and tugged on my pinky toe a little too hard. "But I'm digging into the family history and why the town hates us. We're not ignorant to the glares, murmurs, and sharpening of pitchforks."

"I don't think anybody in this town owns a pitchfork."

His lips pressed into a thin line. "You know what I mean."

"I do. And yeah, you're not liked in this town."

"And I'm trying to figure out why. Someone here knows who my mother was. They have to. I was at the library the other day and the librarian helped me look for anything on my family between 1984 and now. All we could find were my grandparents' obituaries and an engagement announcement for my dad and someone named Melody Summers. But nothing about my parents."

I tapped my chin. "That is odd."

"I need to talk to somebody old enough who would remember what happened. Who lived here when it all went down, and can tell me all the shady shit my grandfather and father did, and also what caused them to become estranged. Can you think of anybody?"

My brain was mostly wine at this point, and since he'd resumed massaging my feet, I was having a hard time *not* letting a foot massage induced orgasm take over my body. I shook my head. "I'll ask around."

His thumbs dug into my arches and I moaned. "Thank you."

For the remainder of the evening, we drank our wine, reminisced about old times, and laughed until my sides hurt. But eventually, the wine won, and I fell asleep snuggled up against his hard body, wrapped in his musky scent.

When I woke up, Callum was gone. I blinked, looking around. I was in my bed now. I stumbled out of the bedroom to find lights on, everything in its place, the dishwasher churning softly. My phone read 1AM. I yawned. Had I imagined the entire day with Callum? Or maybe Mr.

Gentry was right—this was Callum's first step in a long road of swindling me.

My stomach clenched as I double-checked the condo and the back patio. Callum was nowhere to be found. Not even a goodbye note. But the opened bottle of wine—half-drained—told me I hadn't imagined our unexpectedly perfect day together. And it looked like he'd even loaded the dishwasher before he left. Would a villain really load a dishwasher? I pulled up my messages and fired one off to him: *"Where did you go?"*

Delirious with drowsiness, I headed back into my bedroom, not expecting a response. I washed my face and shed my clothes, Mr. Gentry's warning still echoing in my head. By the time I was buried in my ultra-comfy bed, Callum's response had arrived.

I have to spend the night at the house, remember? Those are the rules, babe. But leaving you was the hardest thing I've had to do in a long time. So next time, we're coming to my place.

I drifted off to sleep, grinning to myself.

Callum couldn't be the villain when he loaded a dishwasher, much less when he obeyed the rules.

So maybe I needed to tweak the warnings from Mr. Gentry and Ripley. They worried about being swindled in bad business deals, but me?

I needed to worry about being swindled out of my heart.

CHAPTER FOURTEEN

HARLOW

Cue the summer romance montage, set to some upbeat tune like "Summer Lovin'" from *Grease*. As much as I didn't want to admit it, it was too easy to fall into a new routine with Callum. Coffee at his place on the wraparound porch in the morning? Check. Goodbye kiss at my car in the gravel cul-de-sac while the hummingbirds flitted past our heads? Check. Little check-in texts throughout my busy day, followed by late dinner, and bed at Hope Creek Manor?

Check. Check. Check.

This was the Callum I'd always felt in my heart; the future with Callum I'd mourned after our break-up. The only thing I hadn't expected or predicted was the way Winter Harbor would react to him.

It seemed wisest to retreat into our own bubble of bliss. Which wasn't hard, given the fact that I usually worked seventy hours a week and Callum was required to spend each night at the mansion.

A few weeks after Mr. Gentry had given me his stern warning on the pier, I left work early to head to Portland for my follow-up appointment with Dr. Reinberger. I hadn't told Callum about it, since I didn't want him to worry—or maybe because *I* didn't want to worry. Even though I worried terribly. If I acted like this was routine enough to warrant not mentioning it, then it would naturally become that innocuous ... right?

At any rate, as soon as my appointment ended, I'd be heading straight to Hope Creek Manor for a home-cooked meal with Callum. He loved to make dinner for me now, and I couldn't say no. I had no time for prepping and cooking food, much less the patience. And honestly, it felt nice to have a semblance of a personal life. I smiled as I strode toward the front doors of *Quick & Fairchild* around noon, determined to make this excursion to Portland as painless and worry-free as possible.

"You leaving early today?" My co-worker Ian's voice grated on me, causing my smile to droop.

I looked at him over my shoulder. He'd joined the firm a full three years later than me, but somehow thought he was three times as entitled to this promotion.

"It's noon. I could be going to lunch like everybody else in the world. Why do you care?"

He sauntered toward me, that smirk straining at his lips like he'd gotten a stroke mid-smile. It was his regular look; constantly analyzing, judging, scheming.

Resting prick face, I called it.

"I heard you weren't going to be in the office for the three o'clock meeting this afternoon." He tapped his knuckles on the wooden arm rest of one of the chairs in the foyer. "And that's not the first one you've missed."

I set my jaw, hoisting my purse higher. "What are you getting at, Ian? I need to go."

"Nothing." He raised his palms, his whole *minding my own business* air more annoying than I could tolerate. "Just thought it was a little out of character for someone who claims she prioritizes the firm to be shirking her duties to the firm *so frequently.*"

"Jesus Christ, Ian. Knock it off. I have this afternoon off for medical reasons. Okay? It's authorized. Dalton knows. Troy knows. And if you try to throw this in my face somehow, there will be consequences." My nostrils flared as I bit my tongue, trying to keep less savory words from flying out of my mouth next. But I couldn't add fuel to his fire. "You might practice estate law but don't act like you're ignorant to labor law."

"I'm not saying you're doing anything wrong. I'm just wondering if your priorities are aligned." The shit-eating grin on his face told me he was lapping up my frustration. He probably fed off it. Like a paranormal creature from the depths of hell. "That's not illegal. You can't sue me for wondering out loud."

I rolled my eyes as outrageously as possible and continued my trek toward the front door. "Ian, why don't you go back inside? You're late for your noon ass-kissing appointment with Dalton."

I didn't hear his reply as I pushed out the front door. A scowl accompanied me the entire walk from the office to the car. Ian had always been a shithead, but he'd been a special brand of insufferable since the name partner position came up for grabs. And though I hadn't thought it possible, Ian's meddling had gotten worse since I'd taken the Winters case. Part of me wondered if he somehow knew that Dalton had requested me for this case. Like maybe his Spidey senses alerted him that I was currently being favored for the promotion.

No matter the reason, Ian felt more and more like an adversary in the workplace, a thought that wouldn't shake me as I got in my car and started the drive to Portland. *I'm just wondering if your priorities are aligned.* His words didn't stop ringing in my head. Who was he to comment on my priorities? The more I combed through his words, I realized they reminded me of what Mr. Gentry had said the other week on the pier. And Ripley, at the coffee house.

Seemingly, every man in Winter Harbor, both friend and foe, had something to say about my life and the way I spent my time.

I arrived at OHSU Portland with time to spare before my appointment. I half-expected my doctor to comment on my relationship with Callum as well, but luckily, we only talked about my recent mammogram results.

There was an abnormality. He didn't want to sound the alarm, but he did want to schedule additional tests. He left me with some encouraging words, but I still left the office in a state of bewilderment. Feeling a strange sort of fury, helplessness, and resolve that almost scared me.

Because what if I had to go through the entire cancer process again? What if this time, it truly prevented me from living the life that I wanted? Now that Callum was back and things were going well, I still clung to that hope that we might be able to have the happy ending I'd always dreamt of. The one that included kids and a lifetime spent together.

Haven't I paid my dues? I drove back to Winter Harbor with tears in my eyes, alternating between cleansing yells and weepy intervals as I processed the news. *It could be nothing. Or it could be everything.*

And still, Ian's infuriating words returned to me. I did have my priorities straight. Health was my priority, followed by my job, and now rekindling the love that I'd had with Callum. My friends and family figured in there too, which meant that by all accounts I had achieved the trifecta that people loved to emblazon on their living room walls: *Live Laugh Love.*

I was living. I was laughing. And more recently, I was loving again.

I just didn't want this to be the end of all that. I had more living, laughing, and loving to do.

Determination cycled through me as I alternated between gripping the steering wheel so tightly my knuckles turned white and singing so loudly to the radio that my throat went hoarse. I touched base with Callum around six as I neared Winter Harbor. He texted that he was heading to the hardware store for some supplies.

A perfect place to intersect him and get our lovey-dovey reunion back underway.

I pulled into the slanted parking space just outside the front door of the hardware store, spotting Callum inside through the front window. I couldn't stop the smile that overcame me. Callum was my person; and now, he was my person in *my town*. Even amid the worries of a second round of breast cancer, everything felt right. Callum felt right. Our time together felt right.

I had to find a way to release my worries and enjoy the present.

I drew a deep breath of gorgeous, early-evening summer air, full of humidity and the distant scent of flowers, and strode inside the hardware store. Pete, the owner, didn't notice me as he attended a different customer at the wide hardware counter. It smelled of wood dust and rubber tires in here, a scent that was oddly comforting as this had been the place my father had brought me as a young girl whenever our house or car needed repairs.

"Excuse me, sir." I wrapped my arms around Callum from behind as I snuck up on him in the screwdriver aisle, relishing the warm steel of his body against mine.

He chuckled, turning to pull me into his arms. "Now, this is a surprise. You here to help me pick out tools?"

"I just couldn't wait to see you at the house. I needed to find you here." I propped my chin on his chest, smiling up at him. Questions danced in the back of my mind—should I tell him about the appointment? What if it was nothing? Was it so wrong to just want to be happy until I had the bad news in hand? I decided I'd say nothing—for now. Maybe this was my way of continuing to ensure it *wasn't* a big deal.

"Did you volunteer at the library this morning?" I asked, rubbing my hands down the muscular length of his back.

He smiled wide and inhaled deep. "I did. Do I still smell like old books?"

I pressed my nose to the front of his shirt and breathed in deep. "No, just Callum, and it's delicious."

His growl made my belly do a happy somersault and my nipples pebble beneath my blouse.

"You have a good day at work?" he murmured, his blue eyes drawing me in like they always did. The world around us shrank to encompass only us. Only this. Two lovebirds swaying gently in the screwdriver aisle.

"Fantastic. How was your day?"

"Just a few birds short of paradise."

My grin spread so wide my cheeks hurt. "Does that mean you picked up extra rescues? Or maybe you and your brothers had some sort of fight."

"No, no, nothing dramatic." His eyes crinkled at the edges as he returned my smile, smoothing his hand over the side of my head. "Winter Harbor takes some getting used to, you know?"

"It must. I wouldn't know—I've lived here my whole life."

"Well, let me tell you, from the mouth of the most recent arrival: this place surprises me every damn day."

I laughed, pulling back and grabbing his hand. He led me further down the aisle. His gaze was focused on the stock on the shelves, but my gaze was stuck on the dark-haired Adonis I called my man.

"Good surprise or bad surprise?"

"Let's say 'surprise' and leave it at that." He paused, checking his watch. "Speaking of surprises, I noticed you're off *extra* early today. How'd you finagle that?"

In so little time back together, Callum already knew the one steady truth about my existence: I worked all the fucking time. I appreciated that he didn't give me shit about it, though. He supported me instead. He optimized his schedule to complement my own, by cooking dinners for me, and allowing us to enjoy every bit of free time that I had before the next workday started.

And if there was anything that said *love* to me, it was that.

"I told them I had a very important date at the hardware store," I said, wiggling my brow. "They understood immediately."

Callum wet his bottom lip, drawing me close. "You keep looking at me like that and we're gonna get kicked out of this hardware store."

I giggled, wriggling against his tight grip. "Oh yeah? Why's that?"

"Because when you look at me like that, crazy things happen," he growled, nipping at my earlobe. Shivers raced down my spine. "Sex in the cupola, for starters. And then sex in a hot spring ..."

"I would never add sex at the hardware store to that list," I teased, swatting his chest. "Unless you know of a secret closet somewhere ..."

He squeezed my ass cheek, prompting a giggle from me, just as the front door bell rang with a new visitor. He looked over my shoulder, the expression on his face tightening.

"Hey, that's the guy from the pier," he said quietly.

I twisted to look. Mr. Gentry had come into the hardware store, pausing just inside the doorway to wipe at his forehead with a handkerchief.

"Hi, Mr. Gentry!" I called out, waving. He looked my way and nodded, but I swore I caught the traces of a scowl on his face. I turned back to Callum. "So, what are we shopping for today? Let me help, so we can move this party back to Hope Creek Manor."

But Callum's eyes were still fastened on Mr. Gentry. He blinked finally, then looked down at me. "Uh ... paint rollers and painting tape."

"Okay. Anything else?"

"Drill bits. But I'll get those."

"Perfect. I'll find the paint roller and tape and meet you at the front counter." I pushed onto my tiptoes to give him a kiss and we parted ways. I hummed to myself as I scoured the tightly packed aisles. There was about a one-and-a-half person berth in each aisle, which made for the occasional awkward encounter like in any centuries-old mom and pop shop.

The mixed chatter from different parts of the shop floated through the air. Pete at the front, ringing up a customer. Some other gentleman, the next aisle over. And then Mr. Gentry.

Shouting.

"I don't want your kind anywhere near me!" Mr. Gentry shouted. My stomach cinched into an acorn. I knew this had to involve Callum. *Had to.* Who else could Mr. Gentry be referring to by 'your kind'?

I raced out of my aisle, following the sounds of the commotion. I found Callum and Mr. Gentry along the back wall. Callum had his palms held up, like trying to convince Mr. Gentry to calm down.

"I thought we could have a chat," Callum said.

"Absolutely not! And don't you step any closer!" Mr. Gentry stumbled even though he used a cane, glancing around. He lunged for a nearby hammer out of the aisle, holding it up shakily. "I'll never forgive your grandfather for what he did, and I'll be damned if I'll be caught dead with you!"

"Mr. Gentry!" I ran up to the men, holding my hands up between them. I almost couldn't make sense of what I was seeing. "There's no need to make threats. What is going on here?"

"He's the one who threatened me first," Mr. Gentry said, still wielding the hammer like he planned to hit Callum with it.

Callum's mouth was a thin line. His gaze swung to me, dejected. "I just asked if we could get some coffee so I could pick his brain—"

"You're cornering me," Mr. Gentry sputtered.

"You knew my family," Callum countered. "I didn't. I'm just looking for information."

"And you're liable to poison my coffee if we meet somewhere," Mr. Gentry spat. He tuned in a huff, searing me with a glance as he headed out of the store. "Next thing you know, your life will be ruined, Harlow. Mark my words."

I watched, agape, as Mr. Gentry hurried toward the front door, dropping the hammer on the counter before he left the store. I looked back at Callum, who looked equally spooked.

"Well, that didn't exactly go as planned," Callum said.

"Did you come on a little too strong or something?" I said, only half-joking. I'd never known Mr. Gentry to be aggressive like that.

Pete's eyes were on us from the front counter as he wrapped up with a customer. And even though their confrontation had happened in a small store, with relatively few witnesses, it felt like everyone in Winter Harbor somehow knew what had happened.

Because everyone *would* know. Some way or another.

"Maybe that was it." Callum raked a hand through his hair. "Or maybe he's getting old and senile. Does he have a medical condition or something?"

"I don't know." I sighed heavily, ready to shake off the encounter. But Mr. Gentry's warning to me was just one more unsolicited opinion on top of too many others. "Let's just get what we need and head home. I'm ready for a glass of wine."

Callum cracked a grin. "Me too." He pressed a soft kiss to my mouth and gathered the items he'd set aside during the confrontation. I hurried to locate the paint roller and met Callum at the front counter, where the previous customer had just shuffled away.

"Anything else?" Pete asked curtly, not meeting my gaze.

"This is it," Callum said.

I stared at Pete, wondering if there was something else going on here. He was usually so friendly. Always ready to greet people with a big smile. The man could rope you into a conversation about logging season before you'd even had time to set your things down. And here we were without even one mention of pinewood or the latest updates on lumber.

"How are you, Pete?" I asked brightly, ready to re-establish the friendly baseline.

He glanced at me, nodding. But his gaze quickly returned to the items he scanned. "Just fine, Harlow. And yourself?"

"Busy as usual," I chirped. "We're getting ready to paint and—"

The front door opening cut me off, and Pete shouted out a greeting to the newcomer. I clamped my mouth shut. The difference in how he'd treated me was palpable. And it had everything to do with the man standing at my side.

I cleared my throat, waiting as Callum paid. When it was time to leave, I told Callum to head over without me.

"I just need a minute," I told him, forcing a grin. Really, my heart pounded in my chest and I was one sly, unsolicited comment away from passing out. "See you at the house."

Callum nodded, his gaze darting between me and Pete before he exited the store. I turned to Pete then.

"Pete. You'll be honest with me, won't you?"

He blinked a few times. "Of course."

"What happened over there with Mr. Gentry? Did you see it?"

Pete wilted visibly. He tugged at the green plastic visor he wore every day without fail. "I can't say for sure. But I know Mr. Gentry has a big heart. And he wouldn't react like that unless provoked."

I tapped my fingers against the wood counter, searching Pete's face for some kind of sign. An answer, maybe, as to why *he* was also acting strangely. "What did Callum ever do to this city?"

Pete's tired gaze found mine quickly. "It's not about him. It's about his family. He's cut from that same cloth, no matter how much he wants to deny it."

"But he's not the same as those people. I swear it."

Pete sighed heavily. "Harlow, you've always been a smart girl. But don't let love blind you, okay? Sometimes, wounds run too deep for healing. They just make scars. And those scars stick around for a lifetime."

A customer approached the counter then. When Pete gave me a sad smile and went to ring up the newcomer, I knew it was time to leave. Pete's words stung, no matter how much I didn't want them to be true. Because if wounds had turned into scars, then that meant Mr. Gentry was nursing old grudges against Callum's father, or maybe even grandfather.

But what could be so awful to make Mr. Gentry try, decades later, to attack Callum with a hammer?

The very town I'd grown up in and spent my whole life loving was changing before my very eyes.

And though I was very much an insider ... I hated that the one man I chose to be with might never be allowed to join my ranks.

CHAPTER FIFTEEN

HARLOW

Winter Harbor was not taking the presence of the Winters boys very well.

It was obvious to me, after our visit to the pier and the near-hammer-assault at Pete's, that people had big opinions and even bigger wounds.

And being that I had a big love for Callum, I didn't know how to reconcile these opposing forces. I just knew that I wanted to continue basking in the honeymoon period while I could.

After all, we had the perfect place to honeymoon: Hope Creek Manor. Between cupola sex and hot springs visitation and every manner of sprucing up the dilapidated mansion, Callum and I had a bustling honeymoon period. The only thing that stood in the way was work and, well, the blatant distaste Callum received every time he left the house.

But our love was stronger than that. I knew we would find a way forward. Winter Harbor just needed time to grapple with, and accept, the facts.

Callum and his brothers were here to stay.

It was a Friday evening at the office when Dalton tapped on my door. He stuck his head in, offering a tight smile. "You got a minute?"

"Sure. Just wrapping up some documentation." I gestured for him to take a seat.

Dalton sat in the armchair facing my desk, watching me for a moment with the studious, emotionless face he was known for. Finally, he said, "I just wanted to touch base on a couple of things."

"Sure." I abandoned my computer and interlaced my fingers, giving him my full attention. "Let's touch base."

"Ian told me you've started a romantic entanglement with a client."

My mouth parted as the words filtered through me, bulky and outrageous. I wasn't even sure where to begin with that bomb drop. "Wh—He ... Excuse me?"

"Not just an entanglement, but one that has gone sour and caught the attention of our community." Dalton frowned, lowering his chin. "Is this true?"

"Dalton, I don't even know where to begin with this."

"I'd just like to know where we're at. Because this ... this could affect your standing for the promotion. Not to mention the reputation of this firm."

There it was. Ian's plan laid clear. I cleared my throat, schooling my features so I didn't launch in the blood-hungry warrior princess I wanted to become when it came to Ian's not-so-subtle sabotage.

"I think Ian has taken creative liberties when it comes to reality. The Winters case involved an old flame of mine. We're currently dating again, yes. But there has been no souring. No scandal. No entangling. Just simply two consenting adults who enjoy spending time together."

Dalton eyed me for a moment, nodding slowly. "Good. Good."

"Furthermore," I went on, "Given the nature of our client/attorney relationship neither of us is in a vulnerable position to be taken advantage of and I have gone over the terms of employment for the firm and they do not state it is against company policy to date a client." I lifted a brow. "You wrote them, right, Dalton?" My smile was tight when I said that last bit. It was fairly common knowledge that Dalton's current wife had been a client of his. So I wasn't *saying* pot/kettle, but I was letting it hang unspoken between us.

"That's true," Dalton said slowly, catching my drift.

"Did Ian mention where he had sourced his information?"

"He said it had become common knowledge. Wanted to inform me since I do fall out of the loop sometimes, living in Summer Hills." He rapped his knuckles on my desk.

"Well, I trust you to know best. Because your work here does involve the community. And earning the trust of our community—that's what our business relies on."

"I live and breathe that every day," I reminded him with a big smile.

"Of course you do. Have a good weekend, Harlow." Dalton let himself out of my office and silence settled once more, thick and meaningful.

Ian was getting into Dalton's ear. He'd already found out about Callum and I—hell, maybe he'd simply caught wind of what had happened at Pete's last week—and now he was spinning it to our boss.

The boss we both wanted to become our partner in law.

I grumbled to myself as I finished up the documentation, equal parts irritated and angry about Ian's stunt. He was playing dirty. And he had ammunition now. I was officially vulnerable.

I just had to prove how irreplaceable I was. How much of an asset I could be.

But nothing could be done until next week. I was face-to-face with my weekend now, and it could not have come sooner. Callum had already acclimated to my long workhours, which meant we sucked every second of enjoyment out of the weekend that we could. Which, these days, was purely spent at Hope Creek Manor.

We had reduced our public outings to a minimum after what happened at Pete's. We hadn't made a decision to—it just unfolded naturally that way. It was easy to always stay in, with how much work the house needed. So it didn't seem like we were avoiding public life. Simply that we were choosing to focus our free time together on the house.

Even though part of me *was* avoiding public life.

I couldn't shake Dalton's surprise visit to my office as I drove back to Hope Creek Manor. But the further I got from work, the worse my anxiety drilled. And soon, it wasn't just Dalton's visit that gnawed at me, but Ian's confrontation, and the lingering words of my doctor, and the whole swirling tornado of *What if?*

The sight of Callum's recently-purchased black sedan calmed me slightly. I pushed back my shoulders and took a deep, cleansing breath as I walked up the gravel path to the wraparound porch. I was determined to leave that anxiety behind. I'd put on a happy face. It was time for the damn weekend.

I wasn't three feet inside the foyer before I spotted Callum at the end of the long hallway. He wore gray sweatpants—unfair, since he knew what those did to me—and a paint splattered tee. His handsome face lit up in a grin—until it faded slightly.

"Hey babe. What's wrong?"

So much for putting on a happy face. This man knew me too well to fool.

"Oh, nothing ..." I tried to fill in the blanks with some excuse or reasoning, but nothing came. Instead, my shoulders slumped and Callum immediately wrapped me in a hug.

"Good try, but you can't lie to me," he said with a laugh as his thick arms squeezed around me. Anxiety dissolved in his embrace. At least there was that. I heaved a deep sigh and nuzzled up against his chest.

"Why don't you tell me what's wrong?"

"Nothing, technically. I just—" My throat tightened. Okay, so maybe things were bothering me more than I wanted to admit. But did I want to get into *all of it*? I wasn't entirely sure if I wanted—or needed—to rope Callum into the worry pit.

But why wouldn't you tell him? This question had been weighing on me. It wasn't that I didn't trust him.

It's that I'd gotten used to shouldering the burden by myself.

I still had a chance to reduce my worries and keep this a one-woman show, but Callum stroked the side of my face so gently it prompted tears.

He cared about me. He *loved* me. And this second chance was really taking us somewhere.

"It's okay, babe," he murmured, swiping his thumb against my cheek to catch a tear I hadn't realized had fallen.

"Ian is trying to sabotage my promotion efforts," I said in a shaky voice. "And I might have cancer again."

The concern that slashed across Callum's face nearly brought tears to my eyes for a different reason.

"I don't know where to begin," Callum whispered into the side of my head, "except that I love you, and we'll get through this together."

I nodded, allowing him to press soft kisses to the various points of my face: my forehead, my cheeks to clean up tears, my lips.

The love that softened the hard edges of his face was all I needed to see to know that this man was in it for the long haul with me. That safety—that permanence—made the burden of the unknown somehow easier to bear.

It was what I'd been missing while we were apart. I'd always had the support of my parents, my brother, my best friend...but Callum was my rock in a way that nobody else was.

I drew a shaky breath and tried to compose myself. I hadn't planned on breaking down like that. But I hadn't planned on being bitchslapped by the truth either: that Callum was my rock and his presence in my life was non-negotiable already, after so little time.

"I've been working so hard for this promotion. After I got cancer the first time, I promised myself I wouldn't let any of my dreams go unfulfilled. Life was too short not to grab everything I wanted by the balls."

Callum smirked, so I added, "Figuratively, of course. Unless you have a bedroom request."

"Not at the moment," he said through a smile. "Why don't you finish what you're saying first, and *then* we'll get to my bedroom requests?"

I squeezed my arms tighter around his waist. "Ian stopped me the other day when I was on my way to an oncologist appointment in Portland and questioned my commitment to the firm. He also got in Dalton's ear about how I'm seeing a client."

"Wait, hold up." Callum pulled back to look me squarely in the eye. "When did you go to Portland?"

"The day I met you at Pete's. I didn't want to tell you, because I didn't think it would be a big deal. But apparently there's something concerning enough to warrant additional testing." Tears returned to my eyes. "I'm just so afraid the results will be bad again. I don't have the strength to do it a second time, Callum. And if Ian uses our relationship to get in the way—"

"Shh. Shh. Babe." Callum wrapped his arms around me again and we were rocking, ever so gently. "I can't predict the future, but I do know this. You don't have to worry about Ian. And whatever happens with this testing, I'll be by your side. I can promise you that. I want to go with you to your appointments. I want to be there for all of it."

I nodded, burying my face in his chest. It felt good to let it out. To speak the words I'd been bottling up inside.

"I am not above paying Ian a visit, either, to set him straight about whatever he thinks he knows about us," Callum added with a smirk.

I laughed through the tears that streamed down my face. "Ooh. Are you going to defend my honor?"

"Defend it *and* defile it. Though that's part of the bedroom request," he said with a wink.

My grin stretched ear to ear now. Callum had such a way of calming me. And now that he was back in my life—both calming *and* exciting me—I knew I wouldn't be able to go on without him for a second time. Cancer had taught me things. And one of the biggest lessons was not to squander the present moment.

"I'm so glad you're back in my life, Callum," I whispered, the tears returning to my eyes.

"You're not getting rid of me this time," he murmured.

"May I remind you that *you're* the one who got rid of me the first time around."

"Semantics. At any rate, I'm here and I'm yours." He pressed a kiss to my forehead. "No matter where life takes us."

"You mean right here, to this very spot, for the rest of our lives?" We'd started swaying again, that starry-eyed lightheartedness taking root within me.

"I think there are a few other exciting places life has in store for us," he said with a wink.

"Bali? Thailand? Easter Island?"

He cocked a grin, the kind that reduced me to a puddle, made me a pliable, willing victim to whatever he might suggest next. "Just promise me you're along for the ride."

"Promise."

Though the words were unnecessary. He knew as well as I did that what we had between us was the only thing worth committing to.

Callum had my heart. He had my word.

And he also had my future.

CHAPTER SIXTEEN

CALLUM

Summer whizzed onward, a blur of house upgrades, life upgrades and, well ... sex.

A whole lot of sex.

The house filled my days, and Harlow filled my nights. And all the time in between was spent on my quest for betterment.

I'd transferred forty thousand dollars—from the sale of my condo in New York—to the start-up in Silicon Valley to secure my share, and promised that once I got my inheritance, I'd put in more. Gary knew I was good for it, so he had no problem convincing the other partners to agree.

I just needed to make sure that the businesses my brothers and I owned were as profitable as possible when I went to sell off my shares. That way I could get the most bang for my buck.

Now that the plans for my future in Silicon Valley, post-Winter Harbor, were in place, I could breathe a little easier. It felt like things weren't just on track; they were thriving. *Finally.*

I had the girl. I had the career—or the promise of one. And I had a place I could call home—for now.

Harlow and I threw ourselves into Hope Creek Manor upgrades with abandon. Which is exactly what we were in the middle of on this too-hot-to-be-real Sunday afternoon in July. Even with paint on her arms and cheeks, she was the most beautiful thing I'd ever seen, and if my brother wasn't outside putting new soffits in the deck overhang, I'd have taken her right then and there on the drop sheets, among all the paint splatters.

When the furniture Carson ordered arrived, we moved all the stacks of newspapers, dusty books, and photo albums to the basement. Colton suggested we keep at least the newspapers, albums, and books in case there was something important about our parents and grandparents in them, which made sense. The rest of the crap we tossed. I would never in a million years need a garbage bag full of floral fabric squares for a quilt. That kind of shit went to the thrift store or into the incinerator.

We had music from her phone playing on a portable speaker, as Carson was making a terrible racket outside. A part of me thought he was making more noise than needed simply to be a dick, but I didn't say that out loud—more than twice—without getting a grumble, eye roll, and huff of a response from Harlow.

"It'd be nice if Colton helped out around here," I said, setting my roller brush into the paint pan and making my way over to where the big oscillating fan was set up. I cranked the fan to *max* and stood directly in front of it for a moment to cool off.

As quaint and intriguing as these old houses could be, their lack of a heat pump or central air was a bitch. We were in the middle of a heat wave and the sun was currently trying to broil Winter Harbor.

"You say that nearly every day," Harlow said with irritation in her tone. "Maybe *do* something about it and speak to your younger brother, find out what he's up to, and ask him to help." She was down to a pair of tight black running shorts and a gray sports bra. I didn't like the idea of her being in such skimpy clothing, particularly with Carson around, but it was too hot to argue. I'd taken off my shirt days ago and hadn't worn one since.

I rolled my eyes, took a sip of water and handed the bottle to her as she came to stand next to me, closed her eyes and took a deep breath. "I *have* tried talking to him. On numerous occasions and he blows me off."

"Then corner him, force him to talk." She was all teasing grins, sexy as hell even with paint on her arms and her hair up in a messy bun. The woman could be in a tattered old potato sac and she'd still be stunning. That smile and those sparkling eyes made her the most gorgeous creature on the planet, and for some crazy reason, she still wanted me. Except now she was even more gorgeous than ever, because I knew what she'd been through. How hard she'd fought to get—and stay—here.

"Fuck, it's hot," she murmured, squirting water into her mouth; droplets clung to her chin.

"Like Satan's balls," I replied.

She opened one eye and lifted a brow, giving me a curious look. "You've felt Satan's balls, have you?"

I grinned, nodded, and took the water bottle back from her. "He likes to have them tugged. That's how he gets his jollies."

"You and Satan have something in common, then." Her sassy smirk had me wanting to tug her ponytail, take her mouth, and tear off the rest of her clothes.

But it was too hot for sex.

It was too hot to touch another person.

"I'm not the best boyfriend, am I? I finally get an entire day with you and I have you painting." The sweat cooling made my body break out in gooseflesh.

"We're together, and that's what matters." Wandering over to the fish tank in the corner of the living room, she bent down. "Are you guys keeping Daddy company while I'm at work?" She glanced back at me with a sassy grin. "How're Jonas and Petra?"

A pleasant warmth filled my chest. "Jonas comes for breakfast every morning, brings more friends every day, and Petra brought a friend along this morning. I'm worried it's her boyfriend. She's too young to be dating."

Harlow snorted and wandered back over to me, looping her arms over my shoulders and around my neck. "Such a protective Daddy." Her face turned somber. "And how's our little Olivia?"

Ah, yes, Olivia. My latest rescue. *Our* latest rescue. After all, I'd been with Harlow this time when I found the poor little thing. We were on one of our evening runs and nearly stepped on a marmot on the side of the road. She'd been hit by a car but was still alive. She'd been living in my room for a little over a week, but things still seemed touch-and-go.

"She's better," I said, feeling my guts twisting at the thought of losing the fuzzy little buck-toothed beast. "Not eating much, but at least she's eating."

"She'll be right as rain in no time, Callum Doolittle." The smile on her lips faltered. "I'm sorry I'm working so much—"

Holding up my hand, I shook my head. "Don't apologize. Your tenacity is part of what I love about you. And I'm getting a lot done. Saving animals, sorting out the family businesses, doing a shoddy painting job in the house." I waved my hand around dramatically. "Might forgo the family fortune and start my own painting company. What do you think?"

With the smile on her face again, she released my shoulders and stepped away, turning around so the fan hit her back. "Thank you, and no. I'd say don't quit your day job and become a painter but ..."

"Don't exactly have a day job *to* quit," I finished. But not for long.

"You've got a lot on your plate here. And once the year is up, you'll have the inheritance and won't *need* to worry about the day job because *this* will be your day job. All of it. Plus, you have that startup you're investing in."

All I did was nod. I hadn't told her much about the start-up in Silicon Valley, since the entire enterprise was on the DL until we secured the rest of the investors and funding and could break digital ground.

She knew I was chatting with an old college buddy and had invested in his startup, but the fact that I planned to move to California when my year in Winter Harbor was up, was something that I hadn't told Harlow yet. Mostly because I was still trying to figure out a way *to* tell her and convince her to come with me.

"But back to Colton," she started. "I really think you should make more of an effort to get to know your brother. Don't let him blow you off. I mean, I think you should speak to *both* your brothers, but I understand why you're more reluctant to have a pajama and s'mores party with Carson."

"I've never had a pajama and s'mores party with anyone in my life, and Carson is not the person I want to pop that cherry with," I said blandly, following her train of thought and turning around so the fan hit my damp back. "What would I say to Colton?"

"I dunno, how about, *Hey, broski, how's about you help us on the house? Or the yard or something? We're in this together, brah, let's all pitch in.*" She'd dropped her voice down several octaves, scrunched her face and adopted some jock-like mannerisms that had her looking ridiculous.

"Is that how you think I sound?" I asked incredulously.

She nodded, her grin luminous. "Yep. I am an excellent impressionist." Returning to her paint roller, she ran it through the pan a few times, then went to work on the north wall of the living room. "Just find out what he's been up to all this time. Where he goes every day. What is the beef between you two, anyway?"

I'd picked up my own paint roller and was poised to continue my task and reply to her when a thunderous crash and an angry, manly "Fuck" just outside the window had us both saying "Shit" at the same time.

I dropped my paint roller. "Carson!"

"Did he fall?" Harlow asked, on my heels as I bolted from the living room, out the front door, and around the porch to where, sure enough, my little brother laid in a heap, a look of anguish on his face.

"Are you okay?" Harlow asked, bending down.

The wooden ladder he'd been on had snapped a rung and he'd taken a tumble, the ladder apparently eager to join him on the ground.

Harlow and I lifted the ladder off Carson, but my brother still hadn't sat up.

"I think I broke my arm," he said, struggling to get up while also cradling his left arm with his right hand.

Harlow's eyes snagged mine before we both looked down at Carson's arm.

"Shit," I muttered. Unlike Jonas, I didn't think I'd be able to splint Carson's arm with Q-tips and gauze.

With me on one side, Harlow on the other, we helped Carson to his feet.

"Can you walk?" Harlow asked him, wrapping her arm around his waist.

He grunted. "Arm's broken, not my legs."

"Don't be a dick," she warned, her tone stern. "We're trying to help you."

His sorry was a half-hearted mumble.

"You *are* limping," I added.

"Twisted my ankle in the fall, that's all."

Harlow pursed her lips together before she spoke. "If it's broken—"

"It is," Carson barked. "My arm, I mean. Leg is fine. Broke it a couple of years ago, know what it feels like. It's not broken."

Harlow rolled her eyes. "*If* your arm is broken, you'll need x-rays and a cast. We need to get you to the hospital."

"Fuck," Carson grumbled as we escorted his hobbling ass down the steps toward the vehicles parked in the circular driveway. "This is going to set back my progress so fucking much."

"I can take you to the hospital," Harlow said, attempting to steer us toward her vehicle.

I jerked us in the other direction. No fucking way was I going to let Harlow and Carson spend any alone time together. Not that I had any fear of history repeating itself, but my brother was an asshole and things between Harlow and I were good. I didn't need him poisoning what we were working to rebuild.

"*I'll* take him," I said reluctantly, not looking forward to sitting in a vehicle with my brother, let alone a hospital waiting room.

Harlow's blue eyes widened, but she didn't say anything, and let me take the lead.

She helped Carson into the passenger seat of my car, buckling his belt for him as he couldn't because of his arm.

I grabbed the T-shirt I'd tossed into the backseat days ago and pulled it over my torso before swinging behind the steering wheel.

"I'll just keep painting then?" Harlow asked, worry etched across her fine features.

I nodded, instantly nauseous and dripping in sweat sitting in my hot-as-Satan's-balls car. "We shouldn't be too long."

"Don't touch that ladder," Carson said through clenched teeth. "Don't want you falling, too."

Harlow's gaze softened, and she smiled at Carson, which only made fire ignite in my belly. I revved the engine and gunned it out of the driveway, stirring up gravel as I did.

CHAPTER SEVENTEEN

CALLUM

Three hours later, I pulled into the driveway and shut off my car. A mopey Carson sat in the passenger seat, holding his blue cast.

"Rest of the summer," he'd muttered under his breath at least five times on the drive. "What the fuck am I gonna do now?"

He had two hairline fractures in his ulna, and the doctors figured he'd need a cast for at least six weeks. Which took us right to the end of the summer. Thankfully, though, Carson was right-handed and he'd broken his left, so he wasn't going to be completely useless, just less efficient.

I opened my car door, walked around, and opened Carson's for him as well, but didn't wait for him to get out. I was about to head into the house when movement in the overgrown garden toward the tree line of the property drew my eye.

I hadn't given much thought to the yard, figured we could hire a landscaper as they come cheaper than tradespeople, so I hadn't bothered to really scope out the greenhouses or fenced and netted overgrown bushes. We needed to tackle one thing at a time. And the first thing was the house, the second was the businesses, the third … a very *distant* third could be the yard.

"Hello?" I called out, wandering through the ankle-deep, over-dry grass toward the fenced garden. "This is private property."

"I know, bro. I own it," came Colton's voice from inside.

Relief filled me and my body instantly relaxed.

"I'm in here, too," Harlow called, her head popping up from behind a big bunch of bushes inside the garden. "Come inside and see what we found."

Noise behind me had me glancing back at a sullen-faced Carson.

"Colton came home, and I mentioned the idea of him tackling the yard. Since Carson is doing the exterior of the house and Callum is doing the interior, it only makes sense if he pitches in and does the yard," Harlow went on, as Carson and I ducked our heads to enter the chicken-wire fenced and netted space. It was totally overgrown with weeds, some of them shoulder height, but upon further inspection, it appeared to house at least three rows of some leafy bush.

"Blueberries!" Harlow cheered, scrambling toward me and tripping over weeds. "These are all blueberry bushes and they are loaded." She opened her palm to reveal a mound of plump, blue little balls perfectly ripe and sure to be sweet and juicy.

I picked one out of her palm and popped it into my mouth.

Just as I suspected, it was like a burst of summer across my tongue.

"There's a raspberry patch behind that greenhouse with the red door," Colton said, joining us where we stood. "Not too many berries, as they haven't been properly maintained. But with some Googling and care, I might be able to bring them back to life." This was the most excited I'd seen my youngest brother since he arrived in Winter Harbor.

"And we found strawberry plants in one of the other greenhouses," Harlow added.

Colton crammed a handful of blueberries into his mouth. "G-rents had quite the produce garden. I'm looking forward to bringing it back to its original glory."

"Do you have a green thumb?" I asked him.

Colton lifted up both hands, making fists except for his thumbs, his gaze bouncing between them. "Nope. But I can learn."

"This yard is really overgrown, but it's got a lot of potential," Harlow added. "Rhodos and hydrangeas, butterfly bushes blooming all among the weeds. I bet with some elbow grease and a good pair of gardening gloves, we could really spruce this place up." She popped a few berries into her mouth and chewed as she spoke. "Your grandparents used to win awards for their gardens. My assistant was telling me about it. They were part of the annual garden tour. I thought for sure roses were a big thing here." She elbowed her way between Carson and I and stepped out of the blueberry patch. "Of course, by the time I was a kid, the garden was already forgotten, but I could have sworn I heard talk of the *Winters roses* growing up."

Like lemmings, we followed her out of the blueberry patch and through the yard as she hummed and tapped her finger to her lips in thought.

I didn't like that she was still in nothing more than those tight black shorts and a sports bra. There was nothing left to the imagination. Her taut ass tucked into those shorts, in front of my brothers' eyes did nothing but spike my blood pressure.

Growling, I picked up my pace and stepped behind her, blocking their view of her ass.

"Possessive much?" Carson said with a rude noise in his throat. "Nothing wrong with window shopping."

I resisted the urge to punch him, particularly considering he had a handicap and all.

Colton was in front of me and since this was the first time I'd ever seen him with his shirt off, it gave me the perfect opportunity to check out his tattoo. And it was bigger than I thought. Completely in grayscale, a beautiful compass with waves,

flowers, mandalas, and lotuses spanned from shoulder blade to shoulder blade and fell to the bottom of his ribs. It was big, but it was well done and I hoped that one day our relationship grew to a point where he would feel comfortable sharing the significance of the tattoo with me.

We came to an eight-foot-high brick wall with a small metal gate that squealed like a scared pig as Harlow pushed it open.

"Ah-ha!" she shouted, lifting her hand into the air and pointing her finger. "I knew they were here somewhere. Behold, brothers Winters, the roses of your ancestors."

Colton, Carson, and I all snorted. But we quickly smothered our amusement when we saw what Harlow was referring to.

A rose garden to rival all other rose gardens. Overgrown, of course, but beautiful nonetheless. Roses of nearly every shade of pink, red, and yellow. There were a few white ones, some peach-colored ones and one that caught my eye immediately. It was such a deep dark red, it was nearly black.

Several concrete statues wearing sweaters of moss dotted the weed-riddled, winding gravel path through the garden. There was also an archway and what was once probably a small open patch of grass but was now knee-high and full of weeds.

"This is cool," Colton said. "How come we're just now finding it now? You didn't see it from your sex cupola, big brother?"

I shot my baby brother a steely glare, which only amplified his grin.

"It's probably because everything is so overgrown, for one thing," Harlow said. "Another is that it's fenced in by the bricks with only two access points. This little side fence, and the big entranceway over there, but that gate is also closed as you can see and totally overgrown with ivy that you can't even see through the metal bars."

She was right. The place was so overgrown that from the cupola it'd just looked like a concrete pavilion with a gazebo surrounded by green bushes.

Perhaps I should have taken more time to thoroughly explore the property and not just the house and holdings. Well, now I would. I'd turn over every rock, open every gate and door, and walk under every archway until I knew all the secrets of Hope Creek Manor.

That reminded me, I still needed to check to see where that small hobbit-sized door on the side of the house went. So many secrets.

Luckily, I didn't have so little time.

I had an entire year.

"I could get into fixing this place up," Colton said, his hands in the pockets of his shorts as he wandered through the garden. "Saw a posting in town for a Gardening 101 class at the community center. I could sign up for that, get my diploma in roses and then make this place shine again." He glanced back at the rest of us with a cheeky smile curling his lips.

I really couldn't figure this guy out.

"Yeah, that'd be nice," I said, deciding to bite my tongue and not chastise him about his lack of helping out thus far. I knew how it made me feel when Carson called me a lazy bastard, and I didn't want to widen the gulf between Colton and I any further than it already was.

My attention was quickly drawn to Harlow, who was up on her tiptoes, her eyes closed, nose in the center of a rose.

"People used to get married in here, I was told. Small ceremonies, but I bet it was beautiful when everything was in bloom," she said, dropping back down to her heels and smiling placidly my way.

The distant sound of gravel crunching by what had to be at least two vehicles had us all pivoting to face the house. The high brick walls kept us from seeing who was there, so one by one, we filed out through the small gate. It squealed once again like a terrified swine when Colton closed it. "Need to get some WD-40 for that thing," he said with a painful wince.

By the time we made it through the tall grass, the bulky café owner, Ripley—a man I'd only met once and wasn't keen on meeting again given his frigid welcome when I grabbed an espresso at his café several weeks ago—was climbing out of a red pickup. Further down the driveway, my college buddy, Gary, stepped out of his rented BMW with his phone to his ear. We'd been planning to talk about the startup later this week, but I hadn't expected him to show up *in-person,* much less on the same schedule as old Mr. Clean-on-steroids.

"Ripley?" Harlow asked. When Gary started to approach, I held up my hand, a quiet signal for him to wait until whatever this was blew over. He nodded, leaned against his BMW, and started doing shit on his phone.

"Everything okay?" I asked.

Ripley's face was nearly as red as one of those roses back in the garden. "No! Everything is *not* okay." His glare hit me and my brothers like a sniper's laser. "What the fuck's the meaning of you guys selling my building? Is it for that Dunlop project like everyone's sayin'? Gonna tear down a building that's been there since before your daddy could even shoot sperm just to make a buck? Puttin' in a high rise, city boys?"

Carson, Colton, and I exchanged equally confused looks.

"What are you talkin' about, dude?" Colton asked. He turned to Carson. "Did he just call us *city boys?*"

Ripley sneered. "Like you don't know."

"Clearly, we don't, otherwise we wouldn't be looking at you like you're off your fucking rocker," Carson retorted. "What are you going on about?"

Harlow snapped her fingers and understanding flashed into her eyes, like she'd just found the last piece of a thousand-piece puzzle under the couch. "You guys own the building Ripley's coffee shop is in."

I nodded. "Yeah, but no plans on selling it."

"That's not what I fucking heard," Ripley said, waving a piece of paper in the air. "Not what this notice says."

I held out my hand calmly. "Can I see that, please?"

With a huff, he handed it to me.

"You guys also own Rothwell Marsh directly behind the spot where Ripley's café is," Harlow added.

"And you're selling it off to put in a fucking hotel, casino, and spa," Ripley spat out.

I held up my hand. "Hold on just a second. We haven't been asked by anybody to sell anything." I tipped my gaze down to the paper. Mother fuckers. Dunlop Holdings was applying for eminent domain on the marshland, which basically ran right up to Ripley's front door. They were putting in an offer to buy the land the building was on to expand their holdings.

I shook my head and looked back up at Ripley. "They're applying for eminent domain on the marsh. This has nothing to do with us. They're going through the government, trying to say that putting in the casino and spa will increase traffic and business for the town, turn Winter Harbor into more of a destination town."

"We already are a fucking destination town," Ripley said with a snarl. "Don't need no fucking casino and spa."

"I agree." I grabbed my phone out of my pocket, took a picture of the paper, then handed it back to Ripley. "I'll look into this more. But either way, we're not selling the building your coffee shop is in. Legally, we can't until probate is over, anyway."

"That marsh should be protected," Harlow added. "And if it's not, we should look into getting it protected land status. See what kind of birds or animals call it home." She turned to Carson and Colton. "I'm guessing whoever manages your LLC for you has been approached and word has gotten out."

I stepped toward Ripley, feeling everyone's eyes on me, beseeching me for answers. I didn't really have any, but I'd do my best to diffuse the situation, at least for now. "I'm sorry, I had no idea. I'm still reading through all the business reports and everything that is owned by the family. It seems like every day it's something new. This town, this house, it's been nothing but one surprise after another. Add in the fact that every time I try to talk to somebody and get some more answers, I'm being met with dirty looks and doors in my face."

"Been a frosty welcome from the locals, for sure," Carson murmured.

A muscle at the side of Ripley's head pulsed. "With good reason."

"And we'd love to hear it," I said.

"You say you know nothing about this, so then why did a suit come knocking on my door this morning telling me they're selling my building, and that I had four months to find somewhere else to go?"

Holding up my hands and pressing the air, I shook my head. "Wait what?"

Ripley scoffed. "Yeah. You heard me." He glanced away, his head shaking. "Shady and fucking liars, just like your dad and grandpa. Should have known you three coming to town was going to cause problems. It's in the fucking name."

"Just wait a fucking minute there, bud," Carson said, taking a step forward.

I held out my arm to stop him. "Ripley, I don't know who approached you. But if they work for us, I will get to the bottom of this. You absolutely do not have to move. We own the building you are in. It is a profitable piece of property, and we have no intention of selling it. We'll fight their claim for eminent domain on the marsh. But I need to do some more digging." I turned to my brothers. "If someone who worked for dad is making executive decisions without consulting us, we need to find out."

"What is the name of the LLC?" Colton asked.

"Three C Holdings," Ripley said, his gaze fierce. "Which makes it tough for me to believe you *three*, whose names all start with *C*, didn't know a damn thing about it."

"Fucking old man and his games," Carson said under his breath. "Probably managed by some shell corporation with one of Dad's suited stooges pulling the strings."

"It's probably something Dad bought and started on his own, after grandpa passed," Colton said. "I know he had more than just the import business. And grandpa didn't know us, so why would he name a company after us?"

Yeah, that was probably all true.

And the mysteries just kept coming.

"Look Mr.—" I paused. Was Ripley his first or last name? It didn't matter. "Look, Mr. Ripley, I'm not going to let this slide. I'll head into the house shortly and start making some calls and looking through the files. We'll figure this out."

The feral curl of Ripley's upper lip told me he didn't believe me as far as he could throw me. Which, given the guns for arms on the guy, might actually be a decent distance. Either way, he wasn't buying what I was lying on the table.

Gravel under shoes had Ripley turning around. Gary was finally off his phone, and in a pink polo shirt and chinos, he approached us wearing that classic nothing-gets-me-down Gary Buchanan smile. Pushing his Oakley shades up into his dark brown hair, he winked at Harlow before stepping forward to shake my hand. "Did I interrupt something, folks? I know it's a scorcher today, but the air right here seems extra hot."

Ripley made a bear-like noise in his throat. "I have rights too. I will fight you if you kick me out. The town will fight you."

"We don't want to fight anybody, dude," Colton said with wild, bewildered eyes. "We just said we're not selling or kicking you out. Chill. Just give my brother a couple of days. They're not gonna be bringing a wrecking ball to your front door tomorrow."

Ripley snorted. "You three are just like your old man. Arrogant. Born with silver spoons in your mouths."

"And he apparently pissed off nearly the entire town." Carson shook his head. "Don't know what the hell he did. But we're not him, and we shouldn't be blamed for his fuck ups."

"Or our grandfather's fuckups," I added.

"Then prove us wrong," Ripley said, before turning to go. "Get on the side of the town for once, Winters. Choose your neighbors over padding your bank account. Turn over a new leaf. Don't be like your grandfather and father—money-hungry and compassionless. Be better."

Money-hungry and compassionless.

Ripley obviously knew a great deal about what our dad and grandfather did to this town. When the dust settled and his complexion wasn't that of a tomato, I'd have to seek him out and try to get some answers.

My brothers and I exchanged more confused glances as we watched Ripley head across the driveway and climb back into his truck.

"I thought Mr. Clean was a happy guy." Gary smirked. "That guy must have bleached his favorite red shirt or something to be that angry." He slapped me on the back. "Good to see you, man."

I couldn't mistake the curiosity burning in Harlow and my brothers' eyes. It beat out the heat of the sizzling sun with no comparison. "You, too," I said warily.

"Had to come and see the place for myself. And since you can't be gone overnight, I thought I'd bring the contracts to you."

Harlow and my brothers exchanged looks, causing worry to prickle in my gut.

Gary and I had only spitballed the idea of him visiting Winter Harbor in the near future. I didn't think he meant so near that he planned to smash my cheek against it.

"Contracts?" Harlow finally asked. "What contracts?"

Gary, ever the oblivious optimist, smiled her way. "Why, for the tech startup company Callum's investing in with me."

Harlow nodded slowly. "Oh right ..."

Carson and Colton's brows lifted in skepticism at the same time.

Carson's scoff set my nerves on edge. "Yeah? And where's this taking place?"

"Down in Cali," Gary confirmed. "Silicon Valley. We're a bunch of finance geeks who are partnering with a tech company. They have this new algorithm and we're collaborating. It's going so fucking well." He jerked his chin toward me. "But this fucker can't join us in the flesh until his prison sentence is up. Your dad was some eccentric weirdo, making you live in this shithole for a year just to get your money. I keep seeing listings for condos with pools or backyards right on the golf course, and I'm just like, *Callum, haul your ass down here and snag this place, it's perfect.* But once you sell your shares of the house and company and get your inheritance, you'll be sitting pretty and can buy yourself a house with its own pool." All smiles, he plunked his hands on his hips and leaned back as he took in the entirety of the house, whistling. "Not my style, but I'm sure the land is worth a pretty penny. Bulldoze this gargoyle and re-zone it for a subdivision or commercial. A lot of potential in the land, for sure."

"We're not tearing down the house," Carson snapped. "I'm fixing it up."

"And then what?" Gary asked. "All three of you going to live here like one big happy family?"

I did not like where this conversation was going.

Not at all.

"Hadn't thought that far," Colton chimed in. "But the house has good bones and is a historical landmark, seeing as it's over a hundred years old. We can't just *bulldoze this gargoyle*, as you say. There are laws and regulations in place." The defensive tone in Colton's voice was surprising.

Gary had already lost interest in the conversation, as Gary was prone to do, and had turned back to face me. "Should we go grab a drink, buddy? Catch up and I can go over the contract with you?"

Harlow's face was a stony mask. A lone eyebrow twitched, but if I'd blinked, I would have missed it.

"You staying at a hotel?" I asked Gary. I needed time to explain things to the people around me. Time to set things right. "I just took my brother to the hospital and have been painting all day. I need to clean up."

Gary must have had some seriously strong muscles in his face to always be smiling like he was. Or he was a closet coke-addict. "I'm at the Hope Creek Motel. Only one night, though. Place was booked solid. So sure, I'll go check in and then message you later and we can meet up for drinks."

Later was better, but not ideal. I'd planned on telling Harlow about the deal. I just hadn't found the right time. I also wanted to make sure the ink was dry on the contract. I was sinking a shit ton of money from the sale of my condo into this deal. If it didn't work out, all I had left to fall back on was the inheritance. And I didn't want to do that. I didn't want to rely on "daddy's money" to make my mark on the world. I wanted to blaze my own trail.

Besides, with the way we were fast becoming the town pariahs, I was looking to get away from the Winters name as much as I could.

But of course, that came with a price.

One thing I knew for sure, though, when the three hundred and sixty-five-day mark was up, I was getting the hell out of Winter Harbor. Why stay in a town that hated you? My future was elsewhere. Somewhere where Harlow and I could start fresh and every other building wasn't owned by a Winters or bore my family's smeared name.

Gary glanced at his phone. "All right, buddy, I'll see you later. Gonna go take a dip in my hotel pool." He grinned at Harlow, Carson, and Colton as if nothing was wrong—because in his mind there wasn't—and headed for his car.

Once he was down the driveway, three curious, pissed-off people stared back at me.

"Care to explain?" Harlow asked, her hands on her hips, the afternoon sun catching on the sweat droplets on her chest and forehead and making her glow.

"He's getting the fuck outta Dodge," Carson said, shaking his head and turning to go. "Don't need any more explanation than that."

"A heads up would have been nice, bro," Colton said, his expression full of disappointment.

My mouth hung open in shock. "You barely talk to me. I've been trying to get to know you for weeks." I gave him an incredulous look. "You've done nothing but blow me off and accuse me of being your mother."

Colton rolled his eyes but didn't say anything.

"Hmm?" I probed. "I can't figure you out. You were all gung-ho about the house, wanting to spend the first night in it with a sleeping bag and have a slumber party with all the ghosts, and then you did a complete one-eighty. We hardly see you. You're gone all day and seem to want nothing to do with the house *or* us."

Colton's nostrils flared and heat filled his eyes. Eyes nearly identical in color to mine.

"I'm interested in knowing where you're going every day, too," Carson said, stopping on the middle step to the house. "Got some secret lover you're keeping from us, baby brother?"

I could tell Colton was clenching his molars. The muscles on either side of his jaw were ticking.

Was he going to snap?

Not that I knew my youngest brother very well, but he'd never been a hothead.

Colton took a deep breath in through his nose, appeared to hold it for a moment, then released it slowly through thinly parted lips. He unclenched his teeth and shook his head. He seemed to relax almost instantly. Then came the smile and the shrug. "You're right. I haven't been home much. But now that I've agreed to take care of the yard, I'll be around more. No girlfriend." He pinned his gaze on Carson. "*Or* boyfriend. Just ..." He shrugged again. "Exploring the new place we're forced to call home."

That didn't answer a damn question, it just created more. He still hadn't answered me about why he was blowing me off.

Colton turned to go, planting one foot on the bottom step leading to the house.

"I want to know," I called after him, causing him to pause and turn around to face me.

"Know what?" he asked, now appearing bored.

"Why you've been blowing me off."

He shrugged again. His shrugs were beginning to bug me. "Why *now*, after all this time, do you want to get to know me, Callum? Is it because Dad *told* you to? Or because you actually *want* to?"

Couldn't it be both?

"Not one of your questions to me since we moved here has been about *my life*, or about *me*. You don't want to get to know me. You just want to keep tabs on me." Colton glanced away and shook his head, his gaze focused on the horizon.

My face fell.

That wasn't true at all.

"But you just said ..."

Colton scoffed and did another shrug. A sadness that tugged painfully at my own heart flashed behind his eyes, but it was only for a moment. Then the edge was back and his expression hardened. "You've never wanted anything to do with me, not even when we were kids. And we all know why."

We do?

183

"It's just as well, you leaving," he continued. "One less person to look at me like I killed his mother." Colton swallowed hard, turned, and headed up the stairs and into the house, passing Carson on the steps whose shocked expression mimicked my own.

Suddenly, it was like the rift between Carson and I no longer existed.

Our little brother was hurting more than any of us knew. And he had been hurting for a really long time.

A boulder dropped heavy in my gut and it was like someone—Colton—had reached into my chest and yanked out my heart.

He thought we blamed him for our mother's death.

Had he thought that all this time? All these years? Did he think our father blamed him, too?

He was a baby. Our mother *chose* not to go through any more chemotherapy during her pregnancy. She did what she could, but when the cancer wasn't going away, and she wasn't getting any better, the choice came down to continuing with treatment and aborting Colton or ending treatment and having her baby. She chose to have her baby, but that meant she just got sicker and sicker. She barely made it through delivering Colton and died less than a year after he was born.

But not once did the thought that Colton killed our mother ever enter my mind. And as much of an asshole as Carson could be, I knew well enough that he'd never thought anything like that either.

Bile threatened to rise up my throat and my feet itched and shifted on the gravel. I needed to tell him that I didn't blame him for our mother's death. That I never had and I never would. He was just as innocent in all of this as the rest of us.

Raw emotion streaked across Carson's face and a muscle ticked in his tightly clenched jaw. "I'll go talk to him," he said with a solemn nod at me, before climbing the rest of the stairs and heading into the house.

I nodded in return, my throat tight and the backs of my eyes burning.

I waited until they were both inside the house and Carson closed the door before I turned my attention to Harlow.

"Is that what Colton thinks?" she asked, pain and empathy etched across her face as she stared at the door my brothers had just walked through. "Oh my God. He must be hurting so much. I can't even imagine."

"Carson's going to talk to him."

"And then you will, but not before I get some answers." Her throat moved on a hard swallow as she pivoted her gaze to me and plopped her hands on her hips. "Is what Gary said true? Are you selling off your shares, taking your inheritance, and moving down to California when this is all over?"

Running my fingers through my damp hair, I avoided her heated gaze. It bore right into me, hit my soul, made me question everything I was working toward, everything I was trying to rebuild. So much had come out in a very short span of time. I was struggling to make sense of it all, to process the information.

Ripley's accusations, and the Dunlop Group seeking eminent domain on our marsh, Gary showing up in his pink polo and letting the Silicon Valley cat out of its Louis Vuitton bag, and then Colton's gut-wrenching bomb drop. I knew it was hot out, and the sun was directly in my eyes, but that wasn't why my head felt like it was in a vice and some sadist was slowly turning the handle to make it tighter.

"Answer me, Callum."

With hesitation, I lifted my head and found her eyes with mine, studied her like the goddess that she was. "I plan to, yes," I finally said. "But I want you to come with me."

CHAPTER EIGHTEEN

CALLUM

"Let me get this straight," Harlow said, tossing her hands up into the air before slamming them back against the sides of her thighs, pacing the driveway in front of me. "You want me to give up my condo, my job, my *life* in Winter Harbor and move down to California with you?"

I clenched my teeth for a moment but nodded. "Yes."

Her laugh was brittle. "After I've been working my ass off to become partner? Which you have known all *fucking* along. Even offered to pay to put my face on a bus bench."

When I didn't answer right away, she glanced off and up toward the sky, shaking her head. "Which one of us has a job right now, Callum?"

Well, that was a low fucking blow.

I didn't necessarily have a *job* in the traditional sense, but I was working to change that. I was also working my ass off at the house and with the businesses. I wasn't sitting around with my finger up my ass and counting the clouds.

She swiveled her gaze back to me and hit me hard with a look that had me immediately bracing myself for what was about to come next. "Which one of us has roots? Has a mortgage. A *life*. Friends. A community of people who would give the shirt off their back to help a neighbor?"

"And those neighbors have shunned you since we got back together," I pointed out. "Doesn't seem like the kind of community you can depend on. Where's the loyalty? As soon as you start dating someone *the townsfolk* don't like, you're chopped liver? Forgive me if I'm not chomping at the bit to set down my own roots here when the neighbors are keen to dump acid on those roots before they even start to grow."

"But once they see all the good you guys plan to do ..."

I shook my head. "We're guilty without trial. And you're guilty by association. So no thanks. Not the kind of place I want to raise a family and call home. Sorry. Besides, you can have the community, the neighbors, the name partner in California. We can blaze our own trails together. I told you I was investing in a tech start-up in California. I thought you knew this was in the wind? I haven't been secretive about this."

She rolled her eyes. And scoffed. "*I* thought you were going to be a silent investor. A financial contributor but not an active member of the company."

I shook my head. "No. That was never the plan. I want to be a part of it. Build it from the ground up. I need to be there, and I want you to come with me."

A noise very close to a growl rumbled through her. "You're delusional. I can't just walk away from being name partner in the firm and you know it." Her head shook again, this time as if she was startled. "No, wait, sorry. *I'm* the delusional one. I thought you being back here meant the start of something for us. Meant *we* were starting over. Giving what we had—what we still have—a real shot. But all along you've been playing me."

"I haven't been playing you. I want a life with you. We are starting over, but based on the welcome—or lack thereof—from this town, Winter Harbor is not where I'm meant to settle down. You have to understand that. Would you want to put down roots in a place that hated you the moment you moved there?" I stepped toward her, reached for her, but she backed away and shook me off like an irritating mosquito.

"You're basing all of this on a gamble. You're gambling on this start up project. And you want me to gamble too. Meanwhile, my job is secure. I am months if not *weeks* away from making name partner. And you want me to walk away from that?" Her eyes held a level of hurt I felt deep in my marrow. To know that I was once again causing her agony gutted me to the point where I felt like I might double-over. I lifted a shoulder. "Everything has risk. But I can't stay in a town that hates me. Particularly one this small."

I didn't want my mark on the world to be one first made by my grandfather and father. I didn't want to follow in their footsteps, putting my shoeprint over top of theirs. I wanted to make a fresh print. Build my own legacy, my own empire, without the Errol and Elliot Winters names tainting my success.

"I need to make something of myself, Harlow. I had it all in New York, but then a business deal went sour. I got fired. I have nothing left. No place to call home. This is my last shot to prove—"

"To who? Who are you trying to prove yourself to?"

"To myself." The world. My father. My grandfather. My brothers. Everyone. "I've been angry for so long, I just—I want to feel that rush of success. Feel the joy that comes along with doing something right. I feel like I've been treading water with ankle weights for so fucking long, I'm drowning."

I hung my head. Even though being with Harlow these last weeks made me happier than I'd been in ages, the anger that I harbored toward myself and my father lingered in the back of my mind like a faceless figure in the dark.

Haunting me.

Following my every move.

Infiltrating my dreams, my memories, and all my thoughts.

"I can't be who I'm meant to be in Winter Harbor," I said.

"And who are you meant to be?"

"*Not* the hated, screw-up, Wallstreet washup bastard that everybody thinks I am."

"Nobody thinks that." Her tone softened.

"They do." I closed my eyes for a second, then opened them, shoving down the pain in my chest that was threatening to send me doubled over. "If my brothers decide to stay, that's on them. But one less Winters in Winter Harbor won't be missed."

"That's where you're wrong," she whispered, her eyes turning watery. "I'd miss you. Just like I've missed you every day for the last eight years."

I bridged the gap between us and cupped her face. This time, she didn't pull away. "Then come with me. We'll start a new life down in California. You can start up your own practice. I'll have more than enough money to help you out once I get my inheritance. We can build our own empire. Start fresh. We don't need Winter Harbor." I bent my knees and pressed my forehead against hers. "We need each other."

We stood there for a moment, our breaths mingling, the sun beating down on us. I went in for a kiss, but she tore away, her head shaking, pain in her cornflower-blue eyes. "You're asking a lot from me, Callum. We've been back together for all of a minute and you're already asking me to move to California with you. Give up my job, my house, my life. I have family here. My parents. My brother. My friends."

"But it's not for a year. We'll be back to where we were eight years ago by then. Solid as ever. And you won't be losing everyone. You'll still have me." I stepped toward her again, but she backed up, her hand up telling me to stop. Warning me.

Her head shook. "I know that might be enough for you. But a lot of the people I love—the people who helped me pick up the pieces after you left the first time—are here, and I can't just leave them."

I didn't understand. How could she not see that all we needed was each other? Parents weren't everything. Brothers weren't everything. Hell, even friends weren't everything. I'd been in Oregon for two months now and not one friend from New York had reached out to see how I was doing. Not one. What mattered, what we needed, was each other. All I needed was Harlow.

"I think we want different things," she whispered. The sexy line of her throat bobbed and her bottom lip trembled.

My head shook frantically as the thought of losing her *again* crashed into me like an out-of-control train. "No, we don't. I want you, and you want me. We want a future together. You said you were down for the adventure. Remember?"

Anguish that this was the beginning of the end hung like a painful spike in my throat. I tried to swallow it down but struggled. I wanted her so fucking badly. Needed her. But I also needed to get out of Winter Harbor. The town held no future for me, and I needed to figure out a way to show Harlow that California was the future—for both of us.

Her head shook. "It's not that simple and you know it. I want an adventure, but I meant the adventure of a life spent together. Not *moving*. I don't want to move. I want to live in Winter Harbor. I want the small-town life."

"Then we'll move to a small town near Silicon Valley," I blurted. "Someplace that we can start fresh, and we can both get what we want."

She headed toward the front door of the house, climbed the steps and ducked inside. I was about to follow her when she reappeared with her purse and phone in her hand. "I think we need a few days apart, okay? I just need some time to think, process everything I've heard today. Go talk to your brother. Colton needs you."

The summer had only just started and already the montage was ending.

I stood there like an idiot, watching as my world came crashing down around me for the second time that year. First, when the Raven Corp deal tanked, and now again, as Harlow walked away from me. The first time she walked away from me, I'd stupidly, vainly told her to go. She'd left with tears in her eyes, begging me to listen and give our love a chance, but I'd been too consumed with anger to listen. Too hurt to consider that what she was saying was true. So I let her leave. I forced her to leave.

Now she was leaving of her own choice—walking away from me because I couldn't see a life for us in Winter Harbor. I was still pushing her away this time, too.

I wanted to chase after her, take her keys, and throw them into the grass, but what could I say?

We were both stubborn. And normally, her stubbornness, her conviction and passion were what I loved most about her. But not when she wanted Winter Harbor, and I wanted success.

"I need some time to think," she said, tears in her eyes as she opened her car door. Her sniffles tugged at my heart. I needed to run to her, take her in my arms, and absorb the hurt I knew I'd caused.

With my hands in my pockets, I walked with long strides to the side of her car. She was inside but rolled down the window. "We can figure something out," I said, the burn of unshed tears making my throat grow tight. I pulled my hands from my pockets and held on to the top of her car door. "Don't end this ... please. Let me figure something out."

A plump tear slid down the crease of her nose. "I'll call you in a few days." She turned over the ignition, put the car in reverse, gave me one last look that tossed a stick of dynamite onto my heart, and she left.

My temper flared, and I picked up the closest object I could find—a rock the size of a navel orange—and heaved it toward the moss-covered concrete birdbath in the center of the circular driveway. It made contact, and the cherub in the center of the bath went flying off into the tall grass.

My plans were beginning to derail before they'd even been finalized. Before the ink was even dry on the contract.

California.

Silicon Valley.

That was where my future was. Where *our* future was.

Now I just had to convince Harlow to join me.

Because as much as she was my future, Winter Harbor was not, and I was not leaving Oregon again without her.

CHAPTER NINETEEN

HARLOW

I asked for a few days.

Callum gave me a few hours.

I was crying on my sofa, sticky but cooled off after our marathon day in the summer heat. I figured if I started mourning the loss of him now, then it would hurt less when we actually broke up.

Because how could this work out?

He saw a life for us—had been fantasizing a life for us—in Silicon Valley. A place that I have thought about approximately zero times as my ideal life destination.

The suggestion was so insulting that I could hardly explain *how* insulting it truly was. And I still wasn't ready to explain it by the time Callum came pounding on my door.

"Harlow." His gruff voice sent a shiver up my spine. "You in there?"

I covered my face with my hands, one last sob wracking my body. I didn't want to face him yet. I'd told him a few days for a reason because I needed the time, but more important, the space.

Being around Callum would only make me crumple into his arms. Push me closer to the ledge of saying YES to his insane and ridiculous idea that we leave Winter Harbor behind and start fresh in Silicon Valley.

193

"Harlow."

I sniffed, wiping at my face. I could wait him out. Feigning the type of silence that only an empty house could convey.

"I know you're in there," he said. "Your car is out front."

I sighed, head dropping to the back of the couch. "Yeah, well, maybe I went for a walk!"

"Open up."

"No."

Something thudded against my door—a palm, or perhaps his forehead. "Harlow. Let's talk about this."

I pushed up off the couch, storming to the door so he wouldn't miss a single, angry word I was about to shout at him. "I told you I wanted a few days. You need to give me a few days."

He sighed. "I just had a beer with Gary and I want to talk to you. I'm sorry I didn't tell you about my plan sooner. That was wrong. But will you just listen to me? Please?"

The vicious knot in my belly returned. I pressed my forehead to the cool metal of the door as more tears rolled down my cheeks. "Did you sign the contract?"

It sounded like a question, but really it was a test. I wanted there to be some loophole that our conversation had activated.

"Yes. Of course I did. I've already put down forty grand on this project. I can't back out now. And Gary flew here from California, and this is a project we've been working on for months. Ever since I got fired in New York, I've been chasing after a new version of success. You know that."

Did he have any more secrets he was keeping from me? There could be a lovechild or a surprise ex-wife waiting in the wings at this point. Sighing, I pressed my forehead to the door. "Then what do you want to talk to me about?"

A heavy pause emerged on the other side of the door. "I need you to know I'm serious about us."

"So serious that you're going to move away as soon as the inheritance is through," I replied, my throat tightening again.

"The town hates my family. Would you want to live here if everywhere you went, people looked at you like you were a piece of garbage? Where you had to worry if your food was tainted because of something one of your relatives did to somebody's relative here sixty years ago? I can't live like that. Nobody should have to."

"And we're trying to figure out *why* the town hates you, so you can fix it. But even an impatient person like me knows that it's not a quick fix and will take time." But the truth was plain to me now. This was the rift that had been here all along. I'd viewed it as something to build a bridge over. He'd viewed it as an obstacle to avoid altogether. He didn't want to move past it. He wanted to move *away* from it.

He exhaled loudly through the door. "You could have gone into intellectual property and contract law like your parents, but you didn't. You're blazing your own trail. Why is it so wrong that I want to do the same thing? I want to create my own success without the Winters name following me around like dogshit on my shoe, stinking up the joint no matter where I go."

"Using the inheritance money and the money you get from selling off your shares to help fund your new life?" I asked, unable—no matter how hard I tried—to keep the snark from my tone.

He was quiet for a moment. "Yeah ..."

"So even though you're going in a different direction, you're not going to be self-made. Self-made is starting from nothing and building something. And you're starting with a big chunk of money—your *family's* money—to help you reach your goal faster."

Another long pause. "What are you getting at, Harlow?"

Emotion hung like a ball of razor blades in the back of my throat. "Getting a helping hand is nothing to be ashamed of. But you and your brothers were handed an amazing opportunity here. An opportunity to undo two generations' worth of town destruction. To rebuild and create your own legacy. Rebrand the Winters name and have it mean something good. But you're throwing that opportunity away on a gamble."

"I'm not throwing anything away," he snapped back. "I have a life. A plan. I know you've got everything all made for you here, but I don't have that. I *want* that. Can't you at least understand?"

"Yeah, sure. I understand." The man hadn't listened to a word I'd just said.

Every word from him dripped with insensitivity, with condescension. Because Winter Harbor could never be that place for him. So the only way to have Callum was to accept his plans, which could only take us away from here.

I squeezed my eyes shut. "Long-distance will work super well. I'm sure seeing each other once a month will be fun. Can't wait."

The pounding against the door returned. "Just open the door."

"No. I told you a few days. I meant it."

"I want you to get excited about this project. As excited as I am."

"Oh, trust me." I wiped away a few more tears. "I'm excited for you. I'm just not excited about the consequences."

"Me signing the papers doesn't mean anything about us. Okay?" His voice sounded grittier, more forceful. Like he just wanted to shout it into truthfulness and be done with it. "Do you hear me, Harlow?"

I steadied myself, palms pressed to the door.

"*Harlow*, I can't let this opportunity slip away."

I swayed as another wave of emotion pummeled me. He would sign, which meant he would leave. And then our lives would once more resemble the past eight years: Pining for the other. Deeply in love. But ultimately...apart.

I knew Callum for what he was, which was a time bomb. He created a time bomb inside of me, one that was destined to explode—it was only a matter of when. The process had already started. Now it was up to me to untangle the wires before the explosion occurred.

And maybe this heightened state of emotion actually gave me some clarity. I'd asked for a few days, but maybe I only *needed* a few hours. Maybe Callum knew that, and I was the one who wanted to sit on the fence. Regardless, I could now see the truth.

We were destined to fail a second time. And if we kept dragging on for ten more months till he received his inheritance and then bolted for Silicon Valley, I wouldn't just explode when the bomb went off. I would be pulverized. I would be reduced to nothing.

That truth led to only one choice.

"We need to end this now," I said, my voice eerily steady. I swiped away a few more tears that had fallen.

"Harlow—"

"Don't argue with me. Ending us is the smartest choice, and you know it. We aren't going to work out. Not when you and I want such different things."

"But we want to be *together*," he insisted.

"No." Even if unwittingly, Callum had helped me trudge through the muck of my desires. "I want to be with someone who's ready to build a life with me in this part of the world." I continued slowly, clarity washing over me in thick waves. "I told you cancer taught me hard lessons. This is one of them. We all need to move toward our goals and dreams because tomorrow isn't guaranteed."

I had no time to waste. Once again I needed to grab life by the balls. Which meant investing my time finding a partner who wanted to head in the same direction as me.

And in the grand scale of lovers and heartbreak, Callum had revealed he wasn't destined to be my forever man. He might forever stain my heart, but it was time to get used to the truth that he wouldn't—*couldn't*—be the man who stood by my side in Winter Harbor.

I was a fool for ever thinking he was up for anything so grand.

I could still have my happy ending, the family and the life that I'd secretly dreamed of during my months of radiation. But it just wouldn't be with Callum. The thought sent shock waves of grief through me.

"I want to build a life with you." Callum's tone was rougher now. Another *slam* hit the other side of the door. "Why isn't that enough?"

"Because you and I don't want to build the *same* life." My voice finally wavered. "You told me so yourself today. Now leave me alone, *please*."

Callum let loose a string of curse words and slammed the door again. "This is fucking ridiculous, Harlow. You're being ridiculous, and you know it. Just remember, when you think back on our second chance, that *you* were the one who didn't want to fight for us."

Tears rolled down my cheeks as I listened to him stomp away. I keep listening until I heard his car start and its tires squeal away. Only then could I haul myself to my couch and burrow back into its comfort.

Previously, I'd wanted a few days to get used to the idea of breaking up with Callum, but now that I'd done it like ripping off a Band-Aid, I needed to cope with the pain. And the only way I could cope with anything right now was with moral support from my best friend.

Jayne was in Winter Harbor by seven p.m. for an Emergency Girls' Night. These were the rules of our friendship, and Jayne wasn't one to shirk her duties.

"Hello, my gorgeous gal," she said in her typical singsong voice as she sailed through my condo's front door. Her arms were full of tote bags and from the way bottles clanked, I could tell she'd brought wine. She set the bags down and we shared a long, warm embrace. Her dark ringlets were a comforting place to temporarily rest my worries.

I released a deep breath. "Please tell me I'm not an idiot."

Jayne pulled back dramatically, the sheer shock on her face distracted me from my misery. Jayne never let an opportunity for histrionics go unused. "Excuse me? An idiot? My bestie is *never* an idiot, and I don't appreciate you using that word when referencing her."

I snickered despite my sadness. "Okay. Thanks."

"What happened, girl?" We drifted into the kitchen where Jayne began arranging bottles and pulling out wine glasses.

I heaved a sigh. "I broke up with Callum."

The long silence that stretched between us made me nervous. Jayne wasn't one for deliberating over her response.

Finally, she said, "Are you sure?"

"Of course I'm sure. I mean, maybe I'm not. That's what you're here for!"

"Well, let's start with the *why* first." She uncorked a bottle, poured two generous glasses, and led me to my couch.

A half-assed charcuterie board sat on my coffee table, with a sleeve of crackers, and about ten tiny cubes of cheddar. And that was it. I'd started gathering snacks in advance of our night, but I hadn't got far.

"After all our reconnecting ... he wants to sell his inheritance and move to Silicon Valley after his year in Winter Harbor is up."

Jayne gasped, which only cemented how right I was.

"He expects me to go with him. Has no interest in Winter Harbor. Could never live here. Can't wait to escape. Need I say more?"

"Yikes," she muttered with a grimace. "And also yikes to this snack tray. Girl, let me fix this."

I covered my face with my hands, laughing at how inept in the kitchen I was. I could boil water wrong, Callum had always said. The reminder of him made me sad all over again.

"Ooh, grapes," Jayne said from the kitchen. She returned a few moments later with a new and improved snack tray—aesthetically pleasing rows of cheese cubes and all. "Okay, now we can continue." She popped a grape in her mouth as she settled on the couch next to me.

"Winter Harbor hasn't taken kindly to Callum and his brothers showing up. Which I know is hard. But his solution is to relocate to California, even though I might literally have nightmares about it. I think he can fix the bridges his family burned. But maybe I'm just blinded by my own desires. Am I so wrong for being a small-town girl?"

"Not wrong at all," Jayne said. "I just wonder if you'll be able to stay away from him while he's here."

I heaved a sigh. This was the crux of the matter. If Callum didn't agree with my decision, then it was only a matter of time before I crumbled. One drunken night at the condo. A week later, another drunken night up in the cupola. Come fall, we'd be back to where we'd been in the summer. Maybe it was a fool's hope to think I could resist him when he was a mere mile away from me at any given time.

"I don't like that he kept his plans from me, and I don't think it's fair for him to ask me to uproot everything because of some plan he started three months ago," I said. "Callum is chasing money. He's chasing success. And if that's what he wants, then I want it for him, too. But I'm realizing that although our love is deep, it might not mean that we work out in the long run. I want the promotion and the family I've always dreamt of, in the small town that I love. He wants success anywhere as long as it's not here."

"Awww, honey." Jayne tutted, stroking my hair. "It's hard to fall in love with a town that hates you. Even harder when you fall in love with a man that your town hates."

"I know. I know." I grabbed my wine glass and took a big sip. "But he just needs to give it time. The town will come around, I'm sure of it. Once everyone sees that the Winters brothers *aren't* like their father and grandfather."

"And maybe this year *is* that time. Nothing is instant." Except for my love for Callum. "He's making an instant decision to leave here in a year, no matter the outcome, though. He's acting rash. Not even thinking about me or his brothers or anyone but himself."

She petted my head again. "Says the woman who just dumped him through a door without hearing him out."

I scowled at Jayne and grumbled, which only pulled a sassy grin to her lips. "I just don't want to *waste* a year and hurt my heart even more when he doesn't change his mind. A clean break is better than pretending for a year and winding up a shattered mess, drunk on my bathroom floor while you mop up my tears." I was saying this from experience, since that's exactly what had happened the last time Callum walked away from me.

I'd been living with heartbreak for the past eight years. It was as familiar to me as my morning coffee. If I could survive the past eight years, then I could surely survive this.

Except I was sick of just surviving. I wanted the passion and excitement that came from *thriving*, and there had only been one man to inspire it in me.

"We need more wine," Jayne said, getting up from the couch to grab another bottle from my kitchen counter. "We can't solve the world's problems, or your boy troubles, with only a buzz."

I buried my face in a cushion. "Take my phone, Jayne. If I have too much, I'll definitely drunk dial Callum."

My friend grabbed my phone off the counter and stuffed it into her back pocket. "I promise to be the voice of reason tonight. All we're allowed to do is guzzle wine and play *Cards Against Humanity.* Until we're totally hammered and then *I* start drunk dialing him from your phone, pretending to be you."

I laughed helplessly into the couch cushion. "Is this how people recover from heartbreak these days?"

"I don't know, but it's the best shot we've got." She poured two *very* generous glasses of merlot.

"If you say so." I reached for the glass she held out to me.

"I do say so. Because here's what's gonna happen. After your prerequisite one-evening moping period is completed tonight, you're going to wake up ready to tackle anything. After the hangover, that is. But the point is, you are your best guide, Harlow. You always have been. I trust you'll know exactly what to do from here."

We clinked glasses, but the smile that strained at my lips felt false.

I did know best. But what was I supposed to do when I wanted Callum as much as I wanted to see through the life of my dreams in this corner of the world?

Callum was *part* of the life of my dreams.

Unless this mess was a sign that I needed to pick a new dream.

Maybe Callum wasn't part of the future.

Maybe he needed to stay in my past.

CHAPTER TWENTY

HARLOW

I must have pissed Callum off real good with the breaking-up-through-the-door trick because he didn't show up or reach out to me at all.

Not during girls' night with Jayne. Not for the rest of the weekend. And not even through the first part of the following week.

When I was having coffee at Ripley's on Wednesday morning and my parents called me, as they had done most weeks during their extended European vacation, we chatted about the newest goings-on in their life. They had visited the Louvre, which marked their sixth visit of all time. They had bought train tickets to Belgium because Mom had it in her head that Belgian waffles were not all they were cracked up to be since she last tried them twenty years prior, so she needed the proof to update her decision. And, a particular doozy: they had found a husband for me.

I nearly spit out my coffee when my mom delivered this little nugget. I started coughing, and Ripley sent me a concerned look from across the café. I waved him off.

"It's the strangest thing," Mom gushed. "He lives in Portland, but he's being assigned to a new post in Summer Hills."

Summer Hills was where Jayne was and just a forty-five minute hop, skip, and a jump south from Winter Harbor.

"And you met him in Europe?"

"Last Wednesday, after we talked to you, we met him at dinner! He headed back to Oregon the next day. He's probably less than sixty miles from you right now!"

"Okay, and why does this make him my husband?" My heart started pounding simply from saying the words. I looked around, wondering if somehow Callum had overheard. Even though that was impossible. The whole conversation seemed wrong, on a cellular level. Because my heart and tender parts had not gotten the message. They still foolishly believe that I was supposed to end up with Callum, and we were supposed to live happily ever after in Winter Harbor.

"We think you're going to *love* him," Mom oozed. "He's handsome. Tall. Oh! Oh! I almost forgot!" A delighted peal of laughter erupted from her.

In the background, I heard my dad say, "Jesus, Hannah, you're going to break an eardrum."

I couldn't avoid being swept away by her excitement. "What did you forget, Mom?"

"He's a *lawyer*!"

I nodded, drawing a deep breath. Of course, my parents would love the lawyer. Having their two children become lawyers was a long-held fantasy. Adding a lawyer son-in-law to the mix would probably make them ascend to heaven on the spot.

A year ago, this might have sounded like a light at the end of the tunnel. After my breast cancer recovery, I prayed for the man of my dreams to show up. At the time, I'd never imagined it would be Callum, so I contented myself with imagining some generally attractive lawyer type. But hearing about this mythical dream man now, after finding—and losing—Callum a second time, felt like a cruel joke

"He sounds lovely—"

My dad's voice appeared on the phone next. "Harley, listen. Your mom's not cutting to the chase fast enough. She set you two up on a blind date."

My mom squealed in the background.

I could just imagine the way she was hitting my dad's arm in a loving reprimand.

"A blind date?"

"I told her it was insane," my dad said. To my mom he said, "See? She thinks it's insane."

"It's not that I think it's *insane*—" I started. The phone rustled and then my mom's voice appeared.

"Is your phone on speaker?"

"How the hell am I supposed to know?" Dad asked.

"It's on speakerphone," I told them, unable to contain my grin. For all their bickering and squawking, they were the best couple I'd ever met in my life. I wanted their tenacity, their lifelong love. And for a brief, psychotic period this summer, I thought that Callum and I might have had a shot at something like that.

"So will you do it?" Mom asked, short of begging. "Will you meet him?"

My gut reaction was *hell no*. I shouldn't do it. I didn't *want* to meet another man. I didn't *want* anyone but Callum.

But my kneejerk reaction wasn't always the smartest. After all, I'd drawn the line in the sand with Callum. I told him what I wanted. What I knew my future should be. And Mr. Maybe-Handsome Lawyer seemed like a harmless way to get myself used to creating the future I wanted.

It wouldn't mean anything. It would be friendly. I couldn't stomach the thought of doing anything beyond chatting with someone new. So where was the harm?

"Well," I finally said. "I'll think about it. Just make sure he knows I'm not really looking for a relationship right now."

"What?" my mom demanded.

"I'm so busy working on my promotion." That was true, but it wasn't the whole truth.

My parents had no idea that Callum and I had crossed paths again, and I didn't plan on updating them until they were home. After all, what would I say? The recap sounded disappointing at best, depressing at worst: *My first and only love turned out to be the prodigal son of my hometown, moved back, hated it and everyone, won me over again, and now wants to bolt with all the money he'll get from selling off the town.*

It was too much to get into when they were six thousand miles away, and besides, I knew my mom would ask a million questions—probably half of which I couldn't answer.

"Sure, sure. No expectations," Mom said. "Nothing but a nice night out in beautiful Winter Harbor! After all, honey, you need it! You've been working so much."

"Well, I'm gunning for the promotion," I reminded her. "I can't hit that bull's-eye if I don't work my ass off."

"You'll be the best damn partner that firm has had," Dad rumbled from the background. "Even though *Quick, Fairchild & Jackson* doesn't sound quite as elegant as *Jackson, Jackson, Jackson & Jackson.*"

"Just remember to make time for other things once you get that promotion," my mom cut in. "Like, you know...finding *the one.*"

I squeezed my eyes shut. I'd been avoiding love and romance through working so much, yet I'd still managed to fall back in love, which only ignited my secret desire to start a family. My plan was both succeeding and failing miserably.

"It'll happen when it's meant to," I told her, only half-meaning it. It had already happened, and I was screwed. But it was the only platitude that would get her off my back for now.

"How is everything else? Anything we should know?"

My mind went back to Callum, but that wound was too fresh and raw to dive into. I considered catching them up on my oncology updates—but again, that only reminded me of Callum and the other big pulsating thing I wanted to stop thinking about.

My follow-up appointment at OHSC was in a week. Callum wanted to accompany me. But I couldn't let him be a part of that if he wasn't with me for the long haul.

I was back to shouldering this burden alone.

"Everything's great," I finally forced out. There was no sense worrying them before I knew for sure. They would cut their vacation short to come be with me, and I'd feel terrible that they had to miss out on the beaches in Croatia.

My mom had been gushing over them for months before their trip.

We chatted for a bit longer about their upcoming plans—they had three weeks left abroad—before we said goodbye. An email arrived soon after from my mom with the contact details of my purported future husband.

Mr. Clinton Delametre.

By name alone, he sounded like a lawyer or an eighty-year-old man with plenty of stories about the wars he lived through. I guess I was of that age that I qualified for blind dates set up by my parents, so why not? Let's bring on the potential octogenarian.

Once I'd replied only to Clinton with a polite yet distant greeting, I immediately texted Jayne.

HARLOW: My parents set me up on a blind date...while they're in Europe...and I'm considering it. Am I crazy?

Jayne worked from home as a freelance graphic designer, so I knew she'd message me back immediately. And she did, in classic Jayne fashion.

JAYNE: Verifiably crazy. But this is one soap opera I'm tuning into.

Because that's what my life was. A freaking soap opera. I finished my coffee, added extra money to Ripley's tip jar because I was feeling so weird on the inside, and then headed to work. The summer breeze, richly scented with pine and salt water, was a temporary balm. By the time I reached my office, I was feeling even stranger.

Probably aided by the fact that Mr. Clinton Delametre had written back:

Hey Harlow!

So weird, but I feel like I know you already? Your parents talked nonstop about you when we were in Nice. They are so sweet, and so in love after so many years. Not trying to make this weird—this blind date was their suggestion, and not really looking for anything serious right now. But I'll be near Winter Harbor tomorrow, so if it works for you, let's grab dinner tomorrow night? We can make it casual, nothing wild. What do you think?

Not only was Clinton hip to rapid emailing (making him *probably not* eighty years old), he was also on the same page as me. Meeting the following night seemed fast, especially since I only learned of him a few hours ago, but why not?

This was modern blind dating. *Casual, nothing wild.*

So why did it feel so wrong?

I avoided responding to him for a few hours, reminding myself of all the important tasks I needed to finish before I could orchestrate a potential date. But really, I needed to let my thoughts percolate.

This was my chance to prove to myself I was serious about moving toward the future I claimed I wanted.

This could be your chance to date the lawyer, start a family, and forget Callum once and for all.

I clicked 'reply' and started to write my response.

CHAPTER TWENTY-ONE

CALLUM

To Harlow, we might be broken up, but to me, we were far from over.

I needed to do this strategically. I needed to be smart about things and not push her away like I had once before. I was an idiot then. I'd like to think I was older and wiser, and had learned from my mistakes.

So I was giving her time to cool off, and me time to create a game plan on how to win her back.

I realized that I did some of my best thinking while doing mindless shit, like painting the banister and crown molding. I'd been cooped up in the house all damn day, high on paint fumes, that by the time the dinner hour rolled around I was not only hungry as fuck, but sweaty as fuck and despite all the *thinking* I'd done, still confused ... as fuck.

The music Carson insisted upon playing as he attempted to work on the exterior of the house with his arm in a cast did very little to tune out the thoughts in my head. I was reluctant to admit I shared my brother's taste in music and caught myself humming along to more than one Arkell's song. But that was a secret I would keep to myself. The last thing I needed was for my brother to find out something else I enjoyed and then sabotage it for me just for his own jollies.

But, no matter how much I sang along to *Leather Jacket* and *Knocking at the Door*, the last encounter I had with Harlow was ten times louder inside my head.

She hadn't even given me a fucking chance to explain my side of the story. She walked away from me, kept the door closed, and then eventually just stopped responding to me all together. She shut me out.

As a lawyer, you'd think the woman would want *all* the facts before reaching a verdict, but it would appear this lawyer didn't give a shit about the facts or hearing the defendant's side of things. She convicted me, labeled me guilty of plotting against her, against *us,* and intent on ripping her from the only world she knew of. I was guilty on all counts and she was giving me zero opportunity to appeal.

But she had her facts wrong. At least some of them. The important ones.

I didn't want to *rip* Harlow from anything. I wanted us to go on a journey, on an adventure together, and build a new life. Our own life. Not a life tainted with rumors and scandal in a town where everyone knows your business even sometimes before you know it yourself. Would half of Winter Harbor know Harlow was pregnant—if that fateful day ever came—before I even did because a local gossip saw her buying a pregnancy test at the town's one and only pharmacy? I hated that kind of privacy invasion. I missed the anonymity of New York. Where my business was my own and I could go days without seeing anybody I knew.

I needed to blow off some steam. Much like Forrest Gump, I left the property, not even bothering to change out of my painting clothes, and I just started walking. Before too long, I found myself walking the boardwalk along the bay. It was flooded with people, mostly couples or families, and it was easy for me to pick out the tourists from the locals. The tourists paid me no mind, and the locals glared at me like a pariah as they licked their ice cream and munched on their fish tacos.

You'd think I had a big scarlet letter on my chest or made a habit of swindling widows and drowning kittens in the river the way their stares grew heated in an attempt to burn my already sweaty forehead.

After living here for two months, I should be used to this. But in a small town when you saw the same faces over and over again and those faces had murder in their eyes, it started to fuck with your head just a wee bit.

The town's hatred for my brothers and I only intensified my need to get to the bottom of this scandal and find out why my father broke off his marriage to Melody Summers and why he and my mother left Winter Harbor. And even more importantly, find out who my mother was. Somebody in this town knew something. I couldn't start a new life in California until I found out the truth about my past.

The shipping container turned to-go restaurant came into view and, as if on cue, my belly rumbled.

Harlow had dragged me there a few times and the fish tacos at El Pez Dispenser were the best I'd ever had. Maybe that's why my feet led me there. I had ten dollars in the back pocket of my painting pants, change from when I'd run to the hardware store for more painting tape. That was enough money to buy a couple of filling Pacific cod chipotle tacos. Enough to take away the nauseating hunger pangs and burning anger.

Careful not to catch the wary-eyed glares of anybody on the boardwalk—even though I felt them like laser beams on my forehead—I raised my gaze and scanned the second-story buildings that stood on stilts over the walkway and came face-to-face with blue eyes I imagined every night before I went to sleep. Blue eyes I had fallen in love with and never fallen out of love with. Blue eyes that looked at me, even now, with so much love. More love than I knew I was worth.

Her attention was zeroed in on me, but then, for a brief moment, it darted to the person she sat with—a man. A good-looking man. And he was smiling and laughing and looking at her like she was his ticket to a happily fucking ever after with the picket fence, babies, and matching rocking chairs on the porch.

Suddenly, I no longer felt hungry—at least not for fish tacos.

My first instinct was to march right up those steps into the restaurant and demand to know what was going on. But I liked to think that during the short time I lived in Winter Harbor, tending to my wild animal family, rekindling the passion with Harlow, and navigating the rocky terrain that is the relationship with my brothers, that I'd grown.

I've learned a lot about myself and how my actions and my *re*actions had consequences. Had I not reacted the way I did eight years ago, perhaps Harlow and I would be married with kids, blissfully happy and running our empire. But instead, I'd allowed my pride and arrogance to get the better of me and I tossed her aside, rather than hear her out.

That wasn't the man I was now.

I didn't want to be that man anymore.

I wasn't hungry for food or revenge.

I was hungry for Harlow.

For the life we could have had, the life we could still have.

I glanced up at her once more, and she was staring at me again. I offered her a grim smile, but it felt like the higher I lifted the corners of lips, the tighter the strings of my heart became, and I struggled to breathe.

She looked away again and smiled at the man across from her.

Was she on a date?

Who was he?

Don't assume, Callum.

I continued down the boardwalk, my heart heavy, throat tight and laden with razor blades. I'd walked all this way for tacos, and now all I wanted to do was go home and talk to my brothers.

Things with Colton and me were still tenuous. After the afternoon, where he told us he thought we blamed him for our mother's death, he'd opened up a bit to Carson. But even Carson said trying to get information out of Colton was like trying to move a dead hippo without a forklift.

Colton was just plain avoiding me, and I had to say, it really hurt.

A soft, melodic female voice interrupted my thoughts. "Do you have a minute to sign this petition?"

"Hmm?" The weight of seeing Harlow on a date made my chest feel like it had caved in. My mind was fuzzy from the lack of oxygen getting to my lungs.

I took a deep breath and blinked a few times to clear my head and my vision.

In front of me stood a doe-eyed blonde holding a clipboard. "This is a petition to stop Dunlop Holdings from claiming eminent domain on the Rothwell Marsh. We're organizing a protest." With her hair fixed in plaits down either side of her face, she was cute. She was dressed in denim shorts, a wide-brimmed Tilley hat, and an army-green T-shirt. Her name badge said *Lily Summers*.

Summers.

Could she be from the infamous rival family?

The family my family scorned and went to war with, turning Winter Harbor into a battleground.

I accepted the clipboard that she offered. It held a lot of names. Names I recognized. Names of townspeople I was slowly getting to know—or at least trying to.

Ripley. Still no last name. Who did he think he was? *Bono?*

Maribel Malone was on there, too. So was Janice Rambo from the grocery store. Pete from the Hardware store and even Mr. Gentry, or should I say *Thor?*

"Not only is this project harmful to the environment, what with all the wildlife habitat it would destroy being put in, but it's going to mean the demolishing of several Winter Harbor historical landmarks. We can't let that happen. We don't *need* a casino or a luxury hotel. That's not what Winter Harbor is about. Did you know the land Dunlop Holdings wants to bulldoze the home of the rare Red Crossbill? They breed year-round, so Dunlop would be destroying nests with eggs and fledglings."

I immediately thought of Jonas. He visited me earlier this morning. What if his nest was in that marsh? Jonas would never forgive me if I let some asshole with a bulldozer take out his nest. Also, I fucking owned the place.

"Gimme the pen," I said, practically snatching it from her. I signed my name.

"Thank you." With a big smile, Lily retrieved her pen and clipboard. "We're holding a town hall meeting about it next week if you're interested in attending." She handed me a flyer with the date time and location for the meeting. She glanced at my name. "Callum Winters." The same intrigue I'd had at learning her name flashed into her eyes. But she stowed it and tossed her shoulders back. "Wait, you own the marsh."

I nodded. "Not yet, *technically*. Probate and all that. But my brothers and I will soon. And we're going to do everything in our power to save it."

Her head bobbed enthusiastically. "A man with your power could have a lot of sway on this project. You could be just the key to saving the marsh... and the town."

If you choose to be better than your predecessors. She didn't say this out loud. But it hung in the air, thick enough to touch.

"I'll be at your town hall meeting," I said with a curt nod, my mood slightly bolstered at the idea of helping. The weight on my chest was lifting too, and I attempted another deep breath. "I'm already trying to save the building that houses *The Grind*, but I want to do more. I *need* to do more. Winter Harbor is our home, and we can't let it be destroyed by those who don't give two shits about it."

Holy shit. What did I just say?

Winter Harbor is our home.

Those words came out of my mouth, and they didn't taste bitter at all.

I was home.

I'd been fighting this for months, determined to get out of a place where I didn't feel welcome, meanwhile, I'd come to feel more at home here than New York had been for the eight years I lived there—despite the hate this town harbored for me. My family had a legacy here, and although it wasn't a great one, it wasn't a lost cause either.

There were Winters in Winter Harbor again, and we could change the way the town saw us. Carson, Colton, and I could put the Winters back in Winter Harbor and right the wrongs of our father and grandfather.

And the first step was the Dunlop Holdings Project.

"I'd like to know what else I can do to help. If there is any board that needs a body or you guys need someone to draft up a letter, just let me know," I said with a smile that hurt my cheeks and a lightness in my chest I hadn't felt in possibly forever.

Lily's gentle brown eyes lit up, and she smiled, but it was a smile that held a knowing, a secret. Was she a missing piece to the puzzle? I needed to talk to her more. I needed to find out if she was related to Roger Summers and if she knew anything about my mother and father.

Anticipation made my body tingle. Could it really be that easy? That I just stumble into a Summers? Maybe we could form our own alliance and mend the decades-old rift between the two families. Start a new dynasty built on respect, collaboration, and a goal to preserve the heritage of the town.

Or maybe this was just the insane ramblings of a drifting, inspired, heartbroken man, looking for an easy fix to at least one problem in his life.

Her smile widened. "We can always use more bodies for the cause. Come to the meeting next week, and we'll put you to work ... *Mr. Winters.*"

I nodded. "Will do."

I opened my mouth, prepared to ask her all the questions that were cannoning around inside my head, but another person who was collecting signatures approached and Lily quickly excused herself.

"Are you the animal guy?"

I glanced around for the voice, but had to look down to find it.

A boy, no more than about seven, with blue eyes and blond hair, stood in front of me. He had a chipmunk in a small box. A kitchen cloth acted as bedding.

"Mrs. Rambo at the grocery store said one of the Winters boys was taking in hurt animals. My mom said you are a Winters. Are you the one that helps

News traveled fast in a small town.

I glanced up to find a woman roughly my age, standing ten feet away. She eyed me cautiously. Another Winters boy hater?

I smiled at her and waved.

She didn't wave back.

Okay then.

I focused on the little boy. His eyes were hopeful. He held no preconceived hatred toward me. He only saw me as the man who might help hurt animals. Not the man whose father and grandfather had hurt this town and a lot of the people in it. If I couldn't win over my own generation, or the generations before me, the least I could do was try to make it right in the eyes of the next generation.

I reached for the box. "I am the Winters man who helps hurt animals."

Relief fell across the little boy's face. "Oh good. My mom said we can't keep him or help him. She told me to bring him to you."

Crouching to one knee, I made sure to give the little boy my full attention. "What happened?"

The kid shook his head. "Not sure. Think he might have fallen out of a tree, or been catched by a bird. But he looks real hurt."

That wasn't a lie. The chipmunk had talon marks in his torso, and they were bleeding. My guess was he'd been nabbed by a bird of prey but then accidentally dropped.

"Can you save him?" The boy's lip wobbled. He looked on the verge of tears.

"I'll take him home right now, and get him cleaned up and fed. Then we'll just have to wait and see."

The little boy nodded. "Please save him."

I glanced at his mother. "I'll try."

She nodded, then held out her hand for her son to join her again.

"Thanks, Mister," the boy called back.

"Thanks for bringing him to me."

The kid waved and then he and his mother continued on down the boardwalk.

I glanced into the box at the injured chipmunk. "Let's get you home, buddy."

CHAPTER TWENTY-TWO

CALLUM

"Dude, you're turning this place into a fucking zoo," Carson said, though it seemed to be mostly in jest, as he followed me into the kitchen where I kept my animal repair kit.

"All temporary," I said. "Jonas only comes by for breakfast, the same with Petra. Olivia is doing much better and shouldn't be here much longer."

The kitchen door swung open, and Colton stepped inside. "Who's on the operating table now? Ferdie the Frog? Tessa the Turtle?"

I set the box on the table and started cleaning the chipmunk's wound with a cotton swab. "Would you care to name this little guy? He's a chipmunk ... at least I think it's a *he*."

Colton grabbed a beer from the fridge and sat down across from me. "Doesn't look like a boy." He took a pull on his beer.

"You can sex chipmunks?" Carson asked.

Colton grinned as he leaned over the table to get a closer look at the little rodent. "She looks like a Simone."

"Simone the chipmunk?" Carson asked with a snort.

Colton gave Carson a hurt look. "You don't like the name Simone? What would you call her?"

Carson lifted a shoulder. "I dunno ... Chippy?"

"Hope you're more creative with carpentry than animal names," Colton quipped. "Or names for your own kids. God forbid my niece or nephew winds up with the name *Kiddo* on their birth certificate. I'd report you to child services."

I finished bandaging Simone, then went to the sink to fill the tiny plastic syringe I had to deliver water to her mouth.

"I can do that," Carson offered, taking the full syringe from me and offered it to the chipmunk.

"What do they eat?" Colton started opening cupboards. "Nuts and berries and seeds?"

I nodded. "Yeah. Insects too." I'd rescued a chipmunk back in college and researched their diet.

Colton plopped a bag of trail mix on the table before opening the fridge and bringing out blueberries and raspberries.

Before I knew it, we had Simone fed, bandaged, and sleeping soundly in the sun room next to Olivia.

Colton handed me a beer—an olive branch, so to speak—and jerked his chin toward the front door. I followed him and joined Carson, already sitting in a deck chair, nursing a beer and cradling his cast.

Colton made a noise you typically only hear from men over forty as he reclined into his chair. "You and Harlow over?"

I stared at my shoes. "I have no idea. She was on a date today. Saw her when I was walking the boardwalk."

"Do you *know* it was a date?" Colton asked, lifting his right brow that I think had at one time been pierced. It had small holes on either side of the narrowest point.

"No. And I don't want to assume, but ..."

"It's hard not to let your head go places." Colton was talking about more than mine and Harlow's relationship.

I raised my gaze and focused on my youngest brother. Intense pain glittered in his eyes. Eyes as blue as mine.

"You know I never blamed you for Mom's death, right? Not ever. Not for one fucking minute."

"Me neither," Carson said, sipping his beer. "It wasn't your fault, our fault, or even Dad's fault. He's at fault for a lot, but not Mom dying."

Colton scraped at the label on his beer with his thumbnail. "Hard not to think those things when your dad ships you off to boarding school at the age of two. Like he can't stand the sight of you because it just reminds him of his dead wife. And then you two did your own things. We might have been at the same school—until I got expelled, that is—but I hardly saw you guys."

"We were *all* grieving and confused. I was six and Carson was four when Dad shipped us off to Switzerland. We were even younger when Mom died. We didn't understand."

"And then the confusion just turned into anger," Carson said. "At least it did for me. Add in my dyslexia diagnosis and the way I just felt shunned by Dad for having a learning disability ..."

"I didn't know you were dyslexic," Colton said to Carson, understanding, and curiosity in his gaze. "When did you find that out?"

Carson lifted one shoulder. "About six, I think."

I nodded. "I remember that. Dad just hired you extra tutors and told you to figure it out."

Carson's expression turned dark. "Yep."

I glanced back at Colton. "My anger was at Dad, the universe and Dad even more." I tipped my head toward Carson. "And this asshole, but never at you. But I'm your big brother, and I should have been there for you more. Stepped in when we were shipped off and helped raise you, protect you. I should have seen that you were struggling, by the way you were constantly acting out. But I was too caught up in my own grief, confusion, and anger to see that had the three of us stuck together, we might not all be as fucked up as we are now." My gaze fell to Carson. "I should have been there to help you with your learning disability, too. I'm sorry."

"You were just a kid, too," Colton said softly.

"We were all just kids," Carson agreed. "Babies when Mom died, babies when Dad shipped us off."

"Who the fuck sends a two-year-old to boarding school?" I shook my head as I stared at Colton. "You were still in diapers."

219

"And I didn't speak until I was almost five," Colton murmured. "They had countless specialists examine me. They were writing and calling Dad constantly. They thought I was going to be a mute forever."

Holy shit.

My jaw dropped and my heart rate picked up. "I had no idea."

"Me either." Carson's shocked and concerned expression mirroring my own.

"I mean, I'm not a mute," Colton said, his tone slightly jovial in an attempt to lighten the mood. "I'm fine. But I think I *chose* not to speak because it was one of the few things I could control. Everything else was decided for me. Clamming up was how I dealt with my grief and confusion." He scoffed. "At least that's what my therapist and I determined."

"Got one of those, too," Carson said blandly.

I nodded. "Me too."

The three of us exchanged grim smiles.

I rested my hand on Colton's knee. "I'm sorry I didn't reach out to you, that I wasn't a better brother. But I want to do that now. I want us to be better than the shitty family Dad built. We can remake the Winters family legacy in this town, reinvent the name, and make it something to be proud of."

Carson's expression was skeptical, as was Colton's.

"But you're leaving," Colton finally said. "You plan to do all of that in less than a year and then dick off and start a new life in California?"

I shook my head and took a long pull on my beer. "Been doing a lot of thinking, and I don't think I can leave. With or without Harlow in my life, this all happened for a reason."

"Yeah, the senile inclinations of a desperate man on his deathbed." Carson huffed. "I'd stare up at the heavens and shake my fist at our old man and his old man, but after the rude welcome this town gave us, we need to shake our fists at the ground. Those guys—especially Errol—are not playing racquetball with angels and Mother Teresa right now."

Colton snorted, as did I.

"Errol, for sure, is tapdancing on hot coals with Napoleon while trying not to get a pitchfork crammed up his ass." Carson reached for the chopstick on the deck railing and shoved it down his cast to scratch his arm.

Colton and I both shook our heads.

Kicking my feet up onto the railing, I surveyed our yard. Colton was making decent headway in his landscaping endeavors. "I hope Dad is with Mom, and that he's finally happy. I honestly don't think he was happy for even one day after she died."

"Agreed," Carson said.

Colton nodded. "So, does all this mean you're really staying?"

I sipped my beer. "I have to. Too much to do in a year. Have that Dunlop Holdings thing to sort out. Need to get this house and yard in tiptop shape, uncover the family secrets, find out who our mother was ,and what happened with Dad and Melody Summers."

Both my brothers' dark brows rose.

"I'll dig into the Summers family more." Colton's expression turned wily, and he gave me some serious side-eye. "On one condition."

I returned his side-eye. "And what's that?"

"That you get off your ass right now and go talk to Harlow. You know she's the best thing that's ever fucking happened to you, and unless she ran out and married the guy from the restaurant, you still have a chance. Even if you've decided to stay with her by your side or not, you'll never forgive yourself if you don't try."

Carson clinked his beer bottle with Colton's. "Agreed."

I looked at my brothers.

"She's fucking perfect for you, you dipshit. And if you're too stubborn or stupid to see that, then that's on you." Carson cracked a smile. "But I doubt there's any other woman out there who will love you for the fucked up bastard that you are the way that Harlow does."

Colton tipped his beer to his lips but spoke before taking a sip. "I mean, we *have* to love you. But she's choosing to."

Emotion clung hard and heavy in my throat.

Colton said he loved me.

It was a bizarre feeling for sure. Particularly since I'm pretty sure none of us had ever said that to each other. And not because we were guys, and guys generally didn't express their feelings that way, but because we'd never been given the opportunity to be a family and *love* each other the way a family usually did.

Our father took that from us.

Too stricken with his own grief and greed, Elliot Winters sent his sons away to be raised by strangers. He never taught me how to love my brothers. Never taught me how to be a big brother who protects his younger brothers, cares for them, loves them.

I had friends, but none who I would consider like a brother to me.

And now, I had my actual brothers, and we were forced to live together, to be a family, and that forced proximity was giving us something more than just the inheritance money we craved. It was giving us hope, love, and a new beginning.

Now, more than ever, I knew I was where I was supposed to be. Where I was meant to be, and that was in Winter Harbor with the Winters boys. Even if Harlow tossed me out on my ass because she was busy celebrating her honeymoon with the man from the restaurant, I wasn't leaving Winter Harbor. The Winters brothers had too many fences to mend, too many stones to turn over, and secrets to uncover for me to leave the job to just Colton and Carson.

"I think he's having a stroke because you said you loved him." Carson's guffaw brought me out of my thoughts, and I rolled my eyes at him.

"He can have a stroke later," Colton said. "First, he needs to go to Harlow and figure out if she'll take his flat ass back."

"Flat ass?" I stood up and glanced behind me at my butt. "I think I got the lion's share of the derriere genes, bro. Harlow used to say I had two well-done steaks in my back pockets. Any woman ever told you that?"

That made both of my brothers toss their heads back and laugh.

"And a Vienna sausage in the front pocket, hmm?" Carson said through continued laughter.

I shot him a look, but smiled after a moment.

"Don't need well-done steaks in the back when I have a foot-long kielbasa in the front." Colton grabbed his crotch and grinned.

I rolled my eyes. "Someone's overcompensating with that loud-ass bike. Maybe a *slice* of kielbasa."

Carson chuckled, but then something serious flashed in his eyes. My smile dropped and my gaze narrowed.

"I'm sorry for the stunt I pulled eight years ago," he said. "It wasn't cool, and I never should have done it. I knew you had a big interview, and that Harlow was waiting to tell you afterward. But I am ... *was* ... an asshole, and I'm trying to change."

Emotion hung thick and jagged in my throat. I'd been waiting to hear these words for eight fucking years. All the time we'd lost being angry and hating each other ...

It was futile to focus on the past and what could have been. We'd been given a rare and unorthodox opportunity to make things right. Because I doubt that if our father hadn't put that term in his will, we'd ever see each other again. So, as angry as I was at the delusions of my dead father, I was also grateful to him. He knew he fucked up as a dad and was trying to right some of his wrongs, even if it was posthumously.

"You been quiet for a while," Colton said, lifting his brow at me. "Gonna say anything?"

I snorted and grinned. "Only that I accept Carson's apology and want to do nothing but move forward and past the past." I stuck my hand out toward Carson, waiting for him to take it so we could shake it out like the emotionally crippled but still privileged white men that we were.

He stared at my hand for a moment, then lifted his gaze to mine, took my hand and we shook until we smiled and started laughing. He started to squeeze my hand, then I started to squeeze his back and soon we were in a hand crushing challenge that left us both with sore kinked fingers, smiles on our faces, and warmth in my heart.

"All right, enough of that shit." Colton jerked his chin toward our driveway. "Get the fuck out of here and over to Harlow's before she elopes with the guy from the restaurant."

The twist in my gut reminded me of the task ahead. I needed to go get my woman. I glanced at my phone. It was eight o'clock.

Before I headed to Harlow's to win her back, I had one stop to make first.

CHAPTER TWENTY-THREE

CALLUM

It was eight-fifteen. *The Grind* closed at eight on Sundays, so I was hoping that Ripley would still be there cleaning up. I also hoped that he'd cooled off since he came waving that eviction notice in our faces, threatening a thousand paper cuts to all who challenged him.

The temperature outside certainly hadn't dropped, but the café had air conditioning so my fingers were crossed the Mr. Clean lookalike's mood was a pleasant seventy-three degrees, unlike his triple-digit temperature from earlier in the week.

Cupping my hands against *The Grind's* glass door like some creepy voyeur, I searched for movement inside.

Nothing.

Shit.

"Here with good news?" Ripley's low voice behind me nearly made me jump clear out of my skin.

"Jesus, fuck."

With a smirk, Ripley heaved two gigantic black plastic garbage bags into the metal bin by the road. "Let me guess. You're here to tell me you ain't gonna sell."

"That and more. I'm here to tell you I've joined the petition to stop Dunlop Holdings from claiming eminent domain. I'm attending the town hall meeting and told Lily

Summers that I'd be on any board she needed me to be on. I'm going to do everything I can to make things better. But I'd like to ask you about my dad and granddad, and why everyone here seems to hate us. What did they do to piss off an entire town?"

Ripley's bushy white brows lifted. He pursed his lips as he studied me. "You really don't know?"

I shook my head. "Until two months ago, I didn't even know this town existed. Never met my grandparents, was estranged from my dad. We showed up to collect our inheritance only to find out we owned half the town and the other half hates us."

Ripley snorted. "That about sums it up."

"I've tried asking people to fill in the blanks, but Winter Harbor treats me—*us*—like we've got contagious halitosis or something."

Ripley snorted. "Yeah, I've heard mutterings that you cornered old Phil Gentry at the hardware store, asking if you could take him for coffee and pick his brain."

"The man grabbed a goddamn hammer and wielded it like a weapon to get me to stop. Accused me of wanting to poison his coffee. Said I was ruining Harlow's life."

Ripley's lip twitched. "Oh, I've heard all the stories."

"Which means you probably have some stories to tell , right?"

"Perhaps."

"Can I hear some of them?" I pleaded.

"Come inside." Ripley jerked his head toward the door. "I still have some cleaning to do."

Relief hit me in the chest like a gust of wind and I exhaled, nodding, and thanking him as I followed him around the back.

He pulled out a worn wooden chair and indicated that I should sit.

"Put me to work." I wanted to prove to this man that I was willing to earn my answers with a little elbow grease.

He handed me a broom.

"Your great-great-great grandparents founded Winter Harbor." He started wiping down tables. "Came over from Europe and settled here. Still have ties to France and

226

England, I think. Winery money, shipping money, real estate money."

"Yes, we discovered a bottle from that winery in the cellar, and I located the paperwork indicating our shares in the vineyard."

He grunted. "Town grew through the generations. But your family always owned most of it. Always had sway. Some sat on the city council. I think an uncle or two were mayors for a time. Kind of like royalty except, you know, in a democracy. This was before my time, so I can't be certain."

He set the cloth on the table, headed to a fridge in the corner, and grabbed two bottles of kombucha. He planted one on a table in front of me and grunted.

I thanked him, opened it, took a sip, and continued to sweep.

"I went to school with your daddy."

"What was he like back then?" I barely knew my dad, so to hear what he was like *back in the day* intrigued me to no end.

Ripley sneered. "Ambitious. Arrogant. Aloof. Mouthy."

Besides the ambitious part, aloof, arrogant, and mouthy didn't describe the Elliot Winters I knew at all. Though it described his sons. I was ambitious, Colton was aloof, and Carson was mouthy. And we were all arrogant.

"A few towns over, another wealthy family—the Summers, if you can believe it—had a daughter."

"Yes! I found their engagement announcement in an old newspaper article at the library. And I met Lily Summers today on the boardwalk. She's spearheading the petition and protest."

Ripley nodded. "Yeah, I signed that, too. Lily's mama was the one your daddy was engaged to."

My mouth dropped open. I was right. She was the key. Or at least *a* key to uncovering this family mystery.

"Her name was Melody. Pretty girl. Sweet and kind. Your grandparents and Melody's parents owned a lot of shit between the two of them. They thought they could rule this part of the coast if they merged the families. Set up a marriage between your daddy and Melody."

"An arranged marriage in Oregon in the eighties?" Something wasn't adding up.

Ripley shrugged. "Not common, but not unheard of when it comes to business." He took a sip of his kombucha before he continued. "Elliot married Melody, but then a month later, vanished. Some say he only married her because another woman he loved—some *nobody*, as they say—was paid off and sent away by your grandparents. But then your daddy ran off to find this other woman. Other rumors say she was pregnant, came back, told your daddy, and they ran off together." Ripley's gaze narrowed. "How old are you?"

I swallowed, tamping down the rage bubbling inside of me at Ripley calling my mother a *nobody*. "Thirty-one."

He nodded. "Timeline fits. Was about thirty-two years ago this all went down. That would make you the bastard lovechild that tore apart the Winters family. And quite possibly the Winters-Summers alliance, 'cause things certainly turned sour between the two families after that. Like a new world War of the Roses—but without all the beheadings." He snorted a laugh at his own joke.

I didn't find it funny. I was still focused on what he'd called me—*a bastard*—my grip on the broom handle tightened until my knuckles ached.

Ripley focused on my hands. "You wanna hit me with that, son?"

I released the broom like it'd caught fire, causing it to crash to the floor. I stepped back, my nerves shot, body trembling as I suppressed the urge to scream, throw things, and punch the wall.

My mother was not a nobody.

I wasn't a bastard lovechild.

And I certainly hadn't torn the entire family apart or caused a decades-long feud between two prominent families.

I didn't even know Winter Harbor or my grandparents existed a few months ago.

"Take a couple deep breaths," Ripley said softly, his voice smooth and relaxed. "Breathe."

I did as I was told. Squeezed my eyes shut, sucked in air through my nose and released it through my mouth. I did this ten times before I felt even slightly in control.

"Feel better?" he asked.

Nodding, I opened my eyes. My throat was no longer full of razor blades, and the spots in my vision had faded. "Thank you."

"Anger is a powerful thing."

Walking toward the window, I showed him my back and stared at the cloudless blue sky. "I ... I've always been hyper-sensitive to anybody calling me a bastard. I could never figure out why. But anytime anybody calls me a bastard, I just see red. And my mother wasn't a *nobody*. She was my mother. Camille Winters was my mother."

"Shows deep compassion."

Huh? I spun around to face him.

His expression was impatient for a moment before softening. "Anger is a form of care. It shows us what we care about. What we wish to protect. What we're willing to risk ourselves for."

Did the Mr. Clean doppelganger moonlight as a psychotherapist?

He must have recognized my complete confusion because he fished his hand into the collar of his crisp white T-shirt and pulled out a set of dog tags. "I served. Marines. Was angry when I was honorably discharged after I lost my leg."

He lifted his pant leg where, lo and behold, he had a prosthetic from the knee down.

He didn't walk with any kind of limp. Had he not shown me, I never would have known. Made me wonder how many people were privy to the knowledge.

"I was a broken, angry man when I got home. Wasn't even mad about losin' my leg. I came back alive, which is more than I can say for a lot of my brothers. I saw shit. Shit that still haunts me. Saw friends die, children blown up, families slaughtered and there wasn't a damn thing I could do about it. Rage was my only constant for a good long time. The only thing I knew I would feel when I woke in the morning and still feel when I laid my head down at night."

"Jesus, fuck," I murmured.

He grunted. "Met a woman—a therapist—and she said that anger is the deepest form of compassion for another, for the world, for ourselves, our lives and body. What we name as anger is actually only our incoherent physical incapacity to sustain this deep form of care in our outer daily life. The unwillingness to be large enough and generous enough to hold what we love helplessly in our bodies and minds with the clarity and breadth of our whole being."

My mouth opened. My eyes didn't blink.

Ripley shrugged. "Married that woman. That therapist. She saw me for the fucked-up mess that I am, gave me clarity and perspective. Made me somewhat whole again. Been with her twenty-eight years this October."

"I ..."

His eyes rolled and his head shook. "You're angry because you care. You loved your mama—and your daddy—and the label *bastard* is a mark on them, not just you. And I'm sorry I called your mother a *nobody*, she wasn't. Just nobody knew who she was."

Therapist wife or not, I wasn't sure I was buying the psychobabble. He'd pegged me as angry and that was no lie. But as far as caring about all those I was angry with—I wasn't ready to go there yet.

He lifted his shoulder. "In this day and age, when you're born, nobody cares if your parents are married or not. Weren't all of Brangelina's kids little bastards? Nobody gives a shit. Out of wedlock, in wedlock. Who the fuck cares as long as your kids don't grow up to be pricks? So definitely don't let that word trip you up. Life's too fuckin' short."

It wouldn't be like snapping my fingers and suddenly that word was no longer a trigger, but what Ripley said carried some weight. Marriage was different now. So was having children. I might have been a "bastard" back then, but I wasn't now.

Either way, I needed to steer the conversation back to my parents. To my family and why the town hated its namesake.

"So my dad and my mom ran off together, tore apart the Winters-Summers alliance, and then what?"

"Then your granddaddy and grandma went a bit squirrely. Errol and old Mr. Summers just started doing everything and anything they could to stick it to the other. Didn't care who got caught in the crossfire. Bid on land and properties and jacked up the housing prices to nearly impossibly rates that nobody but the super-rich could afford. Drove a lot of good people out of town because they couldn't afford to live here. Families that had been here for generations. The Winters and Summers were the landlords from hell. Raised rent, showed no compassion, no leniency. Bulldozed treasured buildings to make room for new strip malls and office buildings. Your grandpa Errol blamed Roger Summers for their kids' marriage not working, and Roger blamed Errol. It was an ugly competition between them. Who could own the most? Who could have the most? Who could be the biggest prick? Not a neighborly bone in either man's body."

"Had there been before?"

He finished his kombucha. "Dunno much about Roger. Errol was never a super friendly guy, but he wasn't mean either. Your daddy leavin' messed up Errol Winters something fierce. Nail in that man's coffin however, at least when it came to the town, was when he tore down the low-income housing complex full of single parents and elderly and put in a big shopping complex. There was no need for it. He just wanted more money, didn't care that he put three hundred and fifty people on assisted living out on the street."

I pushed my fingers into my hair and shook my head. Jesus Christ, my grandfather became a monster. "What about my grandmother?" I hoped she had at least kept even a piece of her heart when my dad left.

"Peggy?" He clucked his tongue and shook his head in pity. "After her son left, she was never the same either. Almost became a recluse. Poured her heart into her garden, rarely left the property. Then when she and your granddaddy died, everything went to your daddy, but we never saw him around town. My understanding is that he never set foot back in Winter Harbor after he left with your mom. Not sure if the divorce with Melody Summers was ever finalized or you and your brothers are all little bastards."

Heat prickled along my arms at that word, but I took a few more deep breaths and pushed past it.

"Sorry," Ripley said." He'd noticed the way that word still affected me.

I dismissed his apology with a wave. "Do you know who my mother was?"

He shook his head. "Just know her name was Camille. But you already knew that. Don't even got a last name for her."

The café owner had taken me on a rocky, pothole-riddled trip through the past, only to wind up at another dead end. I had more questions than I'd shown up with, and there wasn't a hidden path with more answers in sight.

"Your mother's gone then?" he asked.

"Cancer. She was diagnosed while pregnant with my brother Colton. Refused treatment during her pregnancy. It spread rapidly, and she died shortly after Colton was born." I didn't tell him Colton had figured we blamed him for her death.

Even though I'd only known my mother for a few years when I was a child, I'd learned that if Camille Winters set her mind to something, there was very little anyone could do to sway her differently. And her sons had certainly inherited her stubborn streak.

Ripley's lips formed a grim line, and he closed his eyes for a moment. "I'm truly sorry."

"My dad shipped us off to boarding school a few years later. Said we were too wild for him or nannies."

Ripley clucked his tongue again. "That's a shame. Never had kids, but wish I had. Wouldn't have shipped 'em off to boarding school, that's for damn sure. Don't have kids if you're not going to be the one to raise them."

"Can you think of anybody in town who might be willing to share more about my mother? Anybody who would talk to me. I've hit so many dead-ends. Had a lot of doors slammed in my face."

Fuck, I didn't even know my own mother's maiden name. What did that say about me? My birth certificate listed my mother as Camille Winters. But if they weren't married when I was born, then ...

I needed to learn more. I needed to hear it from as close to the horse's mouth as I could who my mother was, how she met my dad, and why he ran out on Melody Summers.

Ripley's nose wrinkled. "Maybe find Maribel Malone. She's the oldest person in this town. Knows everyone and everything—if she can remember it." He grinned. "Memory is starting to go, but when you catch her on a good day, she can tell you the flavor her fifth birthday cake. Smart as a whip, that lady."

"Where can I find her?"

"You don't find Maribel; she finds you."

What the fuck did that mean?

More secrets and games. This town was fucking riddled with them.

"Finish sweepin'," Ripley ordered, picking up his rag and continuing to wipe tables. "That's all I know about your ancestors. Your granddaddy was a miserable fucker who had no problem selling his soul to the devil as long as the price was right, and your daddy was a selfish jackass who stepped out on Melody Summers and broke her and his parents' hearts—which broke this town. Then he became a money-hungry, compassionless landlord. Once your granddaddy died, Elliot pulled all the strings from wherever he sat on his throne. Made sure to double the rent as soon as he could. The one month I was late on my payment—by only two days—about fifteen years ago, he had a lawyer at the front door the next day with an eviction notice. Took a hell of a lot of wrangling to keep this spot. Your daddy didn't care about his tenants. Not a lick." Ripley sent me a severe look.

"You think my brothers and I are the same?"

Ripley lifted a shoulder. "You haven't proved us wrong."

"What happened to innocent until proven guilty? Isn't that the American way? Or is Winter Harbor some sovereign nation with its own set of rules?"

Ripley's grin was so white it was blinding. "All the history and bad blood with your family. You own too much to not get nervous. And when you're out of towners with no connection or love for Winter Harbor, what's to stop you from selling everything, tearing this town apart, and walking away?"

While I had planned to sell my shares, I hadn't planned to tear the town apart, but maybe selling would be the gunshot to start that avalanche.

Another reason not to leave.

The reasons to stay were really stacking up.

Harlow.

Rebuilding the legacy.

Rebuilding the town.

Changing the way people in this town viewed the Winters family.

And once again, Harlow.

"We all do damage. Our character, however, is determined by how we repair it. And in the eyes of this town, you three come waltzin' in here with the last name Winters, and that damage was your doing, whether you lifted a finger or not."

"What can we do to repair it?"

"You help me keep my café. Give back to this town instead of just taking from it like your granddaddy and daddy did, and people's opinions will change. It's a small community. News—good and bad—travels fast."

I finished sweeping, scooped up the dirt in the dustpan, and dumped it into the garbage can. "Thank you for not turning me away. I appreciate everything you've told me."

Ripley grunted.

"I'll do my best to help you and the town. I promise." I held out my hand in the hopes he'd shake it.

The man had allowed me into his place of business, answered my questions, and offered me a drink, but he was still prickly. He still didn't trust me or my brothers, and I needed to figure out a way to get him to do that. Or at the very least, trust that we weren't going to fuck up Winter Harbor any more than our predecessors did.

He eyed my offered hand like it was a snake that might bite him, but after a moment's consideration, he took it. "Glad I could shed some light. Still don't trust you boys, but I'd like to." The man nearly crushed my hand. "However, you hurt Harlow Jackson and even if you are innocent, more than half this town will be at your front door with torches and pitchforks, you hear me? You break that girl's heart and no amount of reparations will earn you this town's forgiveness."

"Harlow said nobody in town owned a pitchfork," I said, determined not to let him see me wince as he attempted to grind the bones in my hand to dust.

Just when I thought my knuckles were going to shatter, he released my hand and his chest shook with a chuckle. His grin was so big, so fake it was downright scary. He knew I was in pain, even if it took every ounce of willpower inside of me not to let it show on my face.

"We good?" he asked, wiping the last table.

I nodded, wishing I could massage my aching hand but knowing he'd probably judge me for it. "We're good. Heard you loud and clear."

Another massive smile. "All right then. I look forward to running my café here, in this building, for many more years to come. But today, if you don't mind, I'd like to finish up and head home to my wife."

That was polite townsperson for *"get the fuck out."*

I drained my kombucha, put it in the recycling box, and nodded. "Thanks, Ripley."

All I got was another grunt as I headed back outside into the blistering heat of the day, massaging my hand, when what I really needed was an aspirin before my head exploded.

My to-do list just kept growing.

Keep on Ripley's good side.

Find Maribel Malone.

Find out more about my mother.

Make things right with Winter Harbor. But the most urgent item on the to-do list?

Make things right with Harlow.

235

CHAPTER TWENTY-FOUR

HARLOW

My life post-Callum was quiet.

Quietly sad.

I drifted between my condo and work for a couple of weeks, trying to remind myself this was enough. Just as it had been before, he and his brothers showed up. Just as I'd been content with, before he won me back.

My life without Callum was enough.

So why couldn't I actually believe that?

Jayne had started coming up every couple of days under the guise of fun girls' nights, but really she was keeping an eye on me. I could tell. My vim and vigor had been replaced with apathy and overworking. These were warning signs.

I just had to stay the course.

Because with Callum, I knew it had to be all or nothing. There was no hope of being friends in our future, much less "let's be together until Callum moves." One look from that man could unravel me—as evidenced by what had happened after eight years apart. I stood no chance against casual sightings or, worse yet, casual hook-ups.

This was a tall order for a place like Winter Harbor.

Which meant there was no other option but working myself to death. It was the only place I was guaranteed safety from running into Callum in tiny Winter Harbor.

I'd even stopped going to Ripley's in the morning for coffee. Hello, made-at-home coffee with flavored creamer! It wasn't great, but it got the job done.

Except one afternoon I had a downtown meeting with a client—and they wanted to meet at El Pez Dispenser for lunch. I'd chosen to walk because it was so close, even though this exposed me to ample opportunity for spotting Callum. My heels clicked the cement sidewalk as I headed south away from the bay. The tang of summer was still rich in the air, and my brisk pace made perspiration gather under my silk blouse. I took a deep breath, forcing myself to clear my head and disconnect from my worries and sadness, which was becoming increasingly harder.

I turned the corner onto the street where the restaurant sat—and almost barreled into somebody.

"Oh—wh—" I stammered as I wobbled and pitched face-first toward the sidewalk.

Carson lunged to grab my arm, rescuing me from a near disaster with a sewer grate.

"Jesus! Harlow!" He helped steady me on my own two feet again, his brows drawn together. "I didn't even see you there. I'm sorry."

"It's fine, it's fine." I laughed a little, smoothing down the front of my skirt. My heart raced as I grappled with how to carry this unexpected run-in from here. Carson must have known what went down between Callum and me. Small talk seemed absurd. "What are you doing today?"

Something unreadable wrenched at his face, and I could tell within seconds that something was seriously not right with Carson. He ran a hand through his short dark hair, gaze stuck on the ground.

"I, uh..." His throat bobbed and he let out a humorless laugh. "I just went to the hardware store, but I forgot everything is freaking closed on Tuesdays."

"Ugh. Yeah. One of the quirks of Winter Harbor. Though, not our office." I chuckled, but when Carson didn't join in, I glanced toward the pier and grimaced. Could this get any more uncomfortable?

He nodded, his gaze still stuck on the ground. Whatever was going on with Carson overrode my own awkwardness.

"You okay?" I tapped his elbow, and his gaze jerked up to mine as though startled.

"Yeah. Well..." He shook his head, glancing behind him, back toward where he'd come from. "I just had the craziest blast from the past."

"Crazier than finding out your ex-boyfriend, ex-other boyfriend, and their family own the town you grew up in?" I teased, which finally earned me a laugh.

"Almost as crazy as that," he conceded. "But pretty high up there on the list of improbable bullshit."

"Hm. Who was it?"

Carson studied me for a moment, as though weighing whether or not to trust me. Then he blurted, "An ex. But not just any ex. I really thought she was someone special. Possibly *the one*. Then she ghosted me."

My brows shot up. In the months of sharing space with Carson, I hadn't seen one love interest cross that threshold. Not that Callum or I had expected him to be particularly open with us about his love life, but we'd wondered plenty about what Carson did on the sidelines.

"Wow. She lives here?"

"No," he said with a disbelieving laugh. "She doesn't. She lives in Portland, where I used to live."

I could tell Carson was shaken up but getting a little looser, and I wanted to keep this conversation away from anything resembling my relationship with Callum. "Maybe she's a ghost then? A ghost who ghosts. Ghosts can be jerks, too, right?"

Again, a laugh. Then he shook his head. "I've never heard of a ghost with a boyfriend before."

His admission crashed through me, and I grimaced. It was one thing to run into an ex unexpectedly—and entirely different to run into an ex that had moved on so blatantly.

"Shit. I'm sorry."

"She's the reason I haven't been seeing anyone in months and months and..." He trailed off, shaking his head. "I don't know. I guess I'm a sap."

"A sap? The Carson Winters I remember was definitely not a sap. He used to laugh at saps."

He stared at me, pain filling his eyes. There was something striking in this moment with Carson. He was more vulnerable than I'd ever seen him. Shaken, raw, and wondering. I squeezed his shoulder.

"I'm here if you ever want to talk," I told him. "Honestly. I have some experience with grappling with the long-term effects of strange decisions made by people I loved. Don't be a stranger if you need an ear, okay? I'm here, even if Callum and I aren't..." I faltered, unable to find the right word.

He rubbed at his forehead, a sad smile on his face. "Thanks. And that's kind of what I wanted to bring up."

My entire insides went tight, expectant. "What?"

"I owe you an apology. A long over-due one. I'm sorry for the way I fucked things up eight years ago. I never should have threatened to tell Callum about the fact that you and I hooked up a few times during our freshman year. But when you told me he had that big interview and that you'd tell him the truth *after* that, the devil on my shoulder took over."

I grimaced as the memories returned to me.

"I wanted to fuck with his head. I wanted to hurt him." He paused, as though he might have more to add, and then nodded. "I'm really fucked up. Have a lot of hate and anger, and even though not much of it is toward Callum, he bore the brunt of it, which wasn't fair to either of you."

"Anger toward your dad?"

"Yeah. And grandfather ..." He scratched the back of his head and wrinkled his nose. "Though that anger is new."

"Anger is powerful, but it can also be damaging. Might be time to let some of it go. Your dad is dead, so is Errol. Let the anger die with them ... maybe?"

His head bobbed in another nod. "Yeah, you're probably right. And I'm trying. Things with Colton and Callum are better than they've ever been, but we all know we've got a long road to go before we wrap our arms around each other in front of a campfire and sing Kumbaya."

My lip twitched. "When it happens, be sure to take a picture, otherwise nobody will believe you."

That got a real smile from him. And when Carson Winters smiled, it was really something beautiful. "I just want you and my brother to be happy. I really do. You belong together. Anybody with eyes can see that."

I stared at him, blinking, for what felt like minutes. "Thank you, Carson," I finally blurted out. "I accept your apology. But Callum and I ... we're not ... "

"No, no, I know what happened. But that doesn't change the facts, you know?" He expelled a breath of air. "You guys will work it out. You have to, you know? Because I don't want to know what Callum would do if he sees you carrying another man's child."

I opened my mouth to tell him he didn't have to worry about that ever happening, since I'd be hung up on Callum until the day I died, but instead I threw my arms around Carson for a quick hug.

"I have to run to work now. Maybe I'll see you around sometime." I backed away slowly, trying to force some words through the jumble of my brain. "I'll always love Callum, though. I just know better than to force a man to share my future."

Carson looked at me like he knew a secret, nodding. "Okay. Yeah. So I'll be seeing you sooner rather than later."

Sooner rather than later. His words hung strangely inside me as I headed for the lunch meeting. Once I entered the bright, clamorous warehouse-style seafood restaurant, it was difficult for me to return to work mode. My curiosity had been piqued in a major way. Because what the fuck did Carson mean by that?

The pieces refused to click together. And this was one puzzle I was desperate to solve.

I faked my way through a salmon salad and sparkling water, and practically ran back to my office. But for what? I didn't know. I just knew that I needed time alone in the quiet sanctuary of my office. Something big felt like it was coming, except I had no idea if I needed to hunker down or not.

The tall glass doors of *Quick & Fairchild* were a welcome relief as I hurried back to the office. I could only force a tight grin at the receptionist as I barreled down the hallway and took the corner fast.

"Wh—" All the air left me as I connected with something—or rather, *someone*—tall and made of warm steel. Arms shot out to steady me. My mouth parted as I beheld the tall, dark, and handsome man before me.

Who looked, smelled, and acted exactly like Callum.

Except it couldn't be Callum. This had to be a mirage.

"Harlow! You're just who I was looking for." Callum's warm smile nearly toppled me. Thankfully, he still clutched my forearms, steadying me.

I blinked rapidly, trying to make sense of this. "Wh—"

"Harlow!" Dalton appeared next, his voice jovial. "Don't want to keep you from your meeting." To Callum, he said, "She's such a hard worker. You know I couldn't have imagined anyone more perfect for the partner position. Like there was any choice."

"*What?*" My voice came out a squeak, and Dalton's grin grew from ear to ear.

"It's not officially announced yet," he said in a lower voice, squeezing my shoulder. "But the news will be coming soon. And I thought you should be prepared."

Tears came to my eyes, but I couldn't tell if it was from finally laying eyes on Callum again or obtaining the promotion I'd worked my ass off for. Or maybe it was both. Maybe it was everything. "Thank you," I finally managed to say.

"I should be thanking *you*," Dalton said. "You've picked up the slack in a major way since Leonard left. And you work to *build* bridges, not burn them, like someone we all know."

He could only be talking about Ian. And he confirmed as much when his eyes drifted to Ian's closed office door down the hall.

"We're a team here at Quick, Fairchild *and* Jackson, but some people conveniently choose to forget that." Dalton smiled at me before heading for the front door.

Callum's gaze swept over me, both appreciative and curious. "Congratulations, unofficially." A smile quirked his lips, promising more. "Can we go into your office?"

I nodded, still unable to form complex sentences. I stumbled toward my door, trying but failing to act like the news and Callum's appearance hadn't rendered me useless.

I cleared my throat as I headed for my desk, the familiar surroundings of my office calming me slightly.

The door clicked shut, and then it was just Callum and me.

Breathing the same air.

Staring at each other.

Seconds away from something agonizing or maybe amazing.

I crossed my arms like this might somehow steel me against the man who now sauntered my way, hands stuffed inside the dark pockets of his business casual attire. The navy-blue slacks, the button-up with the rolled-up sleeves. It was almost like he was trying to give me a heart attack on top of everything else.

"What ... do you want?" My speech was returning. Slowly, but surely. "Why are you here?"

"I had a meeting with Dalton."

My brows shot up. "What on earth did you need to meet with him about?"

A smile stretched across his gorgeous mouth, slow and purposeful. The way his icy blue gaze trekked up and down my body only lit me up, pushed me off balance. Thank God I had my arms crossed or else he might see just how good it felt to be observed by him again.

"I had to get some things straight before I came here begging you to take me back." His jaw flexed, his gaze never leaving me. "Just so you'd know how serious I was."

"Oh, is that—" My voice disappeared before I could finish my thought. Relief had started a hot, desperate trickle through me.

Carson had been right. This was a strange fucking day. One made of fever dreams and best-case scenarios and all the most wonderful things a person could hope to hear.

Callum's grin grew wider. "I've been trying to figure out my next steps since you broke up with me through your front door."

I opened my mouth to object, but nothing came out. What was there to say?

"I really didn't think I could stay here," he said, rapping his knuckles on the desk. "Not after the year was up. Not after the frigid welcome and chilly disposition of the town toward me and my brothers. Not after seeing that you've moved on." His eyes had drifted down to where his hand rested on the desk, but he glanced up at me beneath his lashes, hopeful.

My brows narrowed. "Moved on ...?"

His nod was slow since his shoulders appeared tight. He was back to not looking at me. "Yeah. You were at dinner with some guy downtown."

"That wasn't a date," I said quickly. "That guy was Jayne's husband. Jayne was just in the bathroom. They took me out to dinner to cheer me up because I was moping around about you and it was starting to drive Jayne nuts." The chuckle that emerged from my throat wasn't real and left a bitter taste in my mouth. "However, my parents *did* set me up on a blind date with someone ..."

His gaze shot up, panic in his deep blue eyes.

"But I canceled last minute because I just couldn't go through with it. I'm not ready to start dating ... not when my heart ..."

Still belongs to another.

The tension in his shoulders seemed to disappear as he took a deep breath and released it. "My brothers told me not to assume it was a date, so ... I'm glad I listened to them ... sort of." His shrug and lopsided smile were cute.

"Definitely not a date. Jayne and her hubby are disgustingly in love and perfect for each other. I gagged a few times at how adoringly they were looking into each other's eyes. It was like I wasn't even there." And it just made me miss Callum and how disgustingly in love I thought we'd been all the more.

That earned me a bigger smile. "I got to talking to some locals...started doing some research...and realized that if I wanted to make headway, I needed to start fighting for Winter Harbor. That fighting for this town was the first step in fighting for you ... for us."

Tears were coming to my eyes now. All I could do was nod.

"I wanted to help the person closest to your heart, to start with. Ripley. So I looked into the marsh preservation initiative. Not only did I join the board, I'm assembling a legal team to help fight Dunlop Holdings if, or when, they come claiming eminent domain. They're not taking our marsh, and they're certainly not depriving my woman of her favorite coffee spot."

I opened my mouth again, but any coherent response flew out the window when the first tear fell. I rolled my lips inward, nodding harder, struggling to keep my shit together, but it was a losing battle. A sob hitched my chest—the good kind. I just didn't want to break down before Callum had finished talking.

"Don't cry, babe," he said softly, coming around the desk.

A moment later, I was in his arms, clutching the front of his shirt, feeling like I could explode from the happiness inside me.

"Keep talking," I said between sniffles. "I want to hear it all."

Callum rubbed my back as he went on. "A few people told me I needed to reach out to Dalton. Because even though he specializes in estate law, he knows the right people for me to contact."

I wiped at my eyes, trying to stop the tears. "That's true."

"So now I've got the contacts. I'm assembling my legal team. And those assholes aren't gonna steal the best parts of the town I call home."

More tears returned, dammit. Composure was impossible while this man was in front of me, dispensing good news like it was candy.

"Yeah?" I sniffled again, dabbing at my eyes. "Home?"

"It's my home until you decide otherwise." He captured my chin between his thumb and forefinger.

"How are you gonna afford that legal team? Dunlop Holdings is ... big. They've got resources."

"And so do I. I funneled some of my start-up money into this. An advance until the inheritance is mine and I can reinvest even more in Winter Harbor. Gary is okay if I operate as a silent partner in the start-up. From the sidelines, here in Winter Harbor."

"Are you sure?" It was all I could do not to disintegrate from excitement. "Because I want you to go after what you want. I want you to be successful."

He squeezed me tighter and looked into my eyes with so much goddamn love I could burst. "I *am* going after what I want." With the rough pad of his thumb, he wiped a tear from my cheek. But it was a futile endeavor; the tears just kept coming. "I learned my lesson, babe," he said. "Success doesn't matter if you're not at my side. I don't want to spend another eight years apart, only to be a multimillionaire in California with a broken, useless heart."

I got lost in the icy swirl of his blue eyes. "It would be much better if you stuck around in Winter Harbor to become a multimillionaire. With a full heart."

"Very full," he whispered.

Every inch of my body tingled from his nearness. Waiting for *more*.

"I'll take mean stares in my family's hometown over blank stares in a city that means nothing to me."

I dragged my fingertips back and forth over the smooth fabric of his button-up. "What will Winter Harbor think now that you plan to stay longer than a year?"

"Winter Harbor might hate my brothers and I now because of what our dad and granddad did, but we have an opportunity to change that. The town will love my children and grandchildren because of what I do. You can't change history, but you can change the course of the future." He paused, a grin overtaking his lips. "Besides, I'm sure the excessive amounts of money I'm spending to ensure nothing changes downtown will win over a few hard hearts."

"Except Mr. Gentry," I added. "He might be a lost cause."

A lopsided grin pulled at the corner of his mouth. "I'm not giving up on ol' Thor. He knows something, and I'll pry it out of him eventually." Something serious overcame Callum's face, his gaze locking onto mine. "Are we a lost cause?"

"Is that even a question?" I asked through more tears and some laughter. "I don't work without you, Callum. I knew it before, and I know it again. You've always been right here. In my heart."

He pulled me into a deep, warm hug, one that both soothed and excited me. He'd always had a way of pushing me to the edge. Cracking me open in ways I couldn't plan for.

And here we were again. Right at the edge. And I wasn't falling alone. Because we'd opted to hold hands and jump together. That was what made the two of us, together, both explosive and powerful.

When he pulled back, I saw tears shining in his eyes, too. I pushed onto my tiptoes and captured his lips in a kiss. But it wasn't just any kiss. It was the type of kiss that consumed oxygen. Started fires. The type of kiss that heralded new beginnings, made toes curl, and paired *exceptionally* well with the rest of our lives.

"God, I fucking love you," he murmured when our kiss broke.

"I love you more," I whispered.

"Untrue," he said, squeezing my hips. "I love you more. Because you made an unhappy bastard love life again."

Tears came to my eyes, and I pushed at his chest. "All right. Maybe I can't top that."

His grin was equal parts devilish and sweet. "You can't. Now go finish your workday, new name partner. I'll be waiting at your condo with a home-cooked meal and a bottle of wine to celebrate, and then we'll make love until the strike of eleven-thirty at which point this prince must return to his castle lest he turn into a pumpkin."

I couldn't argue with that plan.

My phone buzzed and even though I shouldn't have, since I didn't want to ruin the moment, something told me to look at it anyway. I picked it up from my desk to see an email from my doctor.

I showed it to Callum and his infectious smile dropped, but he tugged me closer. "Whatever the outcome, we'll face it together, babe. I'm not going anywhere."

With my stomach in my throat, I brought up the email, keeping my phone out so he could see it. My test results were in.

"Here," Callum said, taking my phone from me when my hand began to tremble so badly that we couldn't see anything on the screen. He held it for the both of us as we read the forwarded biopsy results.

Negative for cancerous growth.

Thank God.

Relief flooded me, and I sank into his arms as the tears of joy burst forth from my eyes.

He set my phone down and pulled me into his arms tighter, his chin resting on my head, his muscles strong and reassuring around me. We didn't say anything, because we didn't have to. I'm not sure how long we stood there because when I was with Callum, time seemed to stand still. We'd almost picked up right where we left off eight years ago, with a couple of minor hiccups along the way. And I knew that even if I spent every waking moment with this man for the rest of my life, it would still never feel like enough time.

I lifted my head from his chest and looked into his soul-piercing blue eyes, mesmerized and overwhelmed by how much love looked back at me.

Using his thumb, he wiped away the last evidence of my tears, and I smiled up at him, and then, for some reason, I started laughing. And it wasn't just a fleeting giggle. It was the kind of delirious laughter that happens when things are so right, it almost feels surreal. But Callum seemed to know why, and soon we were laughing together until new tears sprang from my eyes and my mouth hurt from smiling so much.

He wrapped me back up in his arms and pressed a kiss to my forehead, our bodies still shaking with mirth. "Let's go home, babe. You deserve to take the rest of the day off."

Nodding, I looped my arm around his waist, and he looped his around mine, and side by side we went home, our new life, bright and beautiful unfolding unchecked in front of us.

CHAPTER TWENTY-FIVE

CALLUM

Harlow and I stopped off at the liquor store attached to Beer & Moor and grabbed a twelve-pack of beer to bring home to Hope Creek Manor. Today was a day for celebration. I'd suggested we get some champagne, but she simply shook her head, smiled, and grabbed a cold pack of brewskies.

Fuck, I loved this woman.

We were just climbing out of our respective vehicles when two sweaty-faced men who looked an awful lot like me came sprinting down the driveway.

Colton tossed his arms up in the air in victory as he crossed what I imagine was an invisible finish line first—but only by half a step—and grinned wide and cocky at a heavily panting Carson. "Better luck next time, bro. Good jog though."

Carson shot our younger brother a look, but there was no venom in it.

Their knowing smiles landed on Harlow, then the twelve-pack of beer in my hand.

"Looks like there is going to be some celebrating," Carson said, his chest still heaving.

"So much celebration is in order," I replied.

Colton had wandered into the shade of the house and collapsed on the grass. We followed him since it was a warm day and beer in the shade seemed like an exceptional idea.

"I take it you two have kissed and made up?" Colton asked, his chest lifting and falling rapidly while he shielded his eyes with his forearm.

I caught the eye of my love and we beamed at each other, our bodies seeming to be made of magnets and drawn together until I looped my free arm over her shoulder and kissed the side of her head. "We've kissed, but I've still got a lot of *apologizing* and *making up* to do," I said, watching her cheeks grow pink as she glanced up at me from under her lashes.

We settled onto the grass next to Colton.

"But we're also celebrating," I said, passing out a beer to each of my brothers. "Not *only* has Harlow been officially promoted to name partner at Quick, Fairchild and what will soon be Jackson, but ..." my throat grew tight, but I pushed the words past the hard spikey lump, "she's also cancer-free."

"It was just a scare," Harlow said quickly. "Just some dense tissue."

Colton bolted straight up to sitting again, and Carson's mouth dropped open like a codfish.

"You had cancer?" Carson asked.

"Did I forget to tell you guys that?" I glanced at Harlow and grimacing with guilt. "Whoops."

She merely smiled.

"Uh, yeah, bro. Maybe start sharing some of the important shit in your life if you're trying to mend fences." Colton shook his head and glared at me for a hot minute, but his ire faded fast.

"Well, that's amazing news. On both accounts," Carson said. "We're happy that you're getting a promotion—which you totally deserve—and even happier that you're cancer-free."

"And that you're back together, which I hope is for good this time," Colton added. "Because a mopey Callum is an unbearable Callum, and I was getting close to breaking the terms of the will just to get the fuck away from him."

Harlow snorted beside me and I bumped her shoulder with mine. "She's stuck with me forever, this one. I'm not going anywhere. And don't you fucking dare break the terms of the will." My words held no edge to them, though. We were past all of that. Or at least we were working to get past the animosity that had lingered between us all like a toxic cloud for so long.

My brothers' expressions turned avid and their brows lifted on their sweaty foreheads.

"You're putting the Winters back in Winter Harbor?" Carson asked, a sly smile tugging his lips.

I shrugged. "I was hoping that *we all* could put the Winters back in Winter Harbor."

Without saying anything, the four of us twisted the caps off our beers.

"Well, then, to Harlow." Colton lifted his beer into the air. "A name partner, cancer-free, and undoubtedly the most patient woman in the fucking world if she's willing to put up with my big brother."

We all clinked our bottles against his.

"To Harlow," Carson echoed. "And burying the hatchet." His gaze met Harlow's and then mine, and we all nodded at each other in understanding.

"To Harlow," I said, locking eyes with my woman as I brought the mouth of the bottle to my mouth. "My everything."

She grinned as she took a sip, her blue eyes glittering and filling with unshed tears. "To us and the amazing life that we're going to build together here in Winter Harbor."

"I can definitely drink to that." I tapped my bottle against hers again before taking another swig. "I could drink all fucking day to that."

My brothers sipped their beer as well, but then Carson set his bottle in the grass and stood up. "All right, this thing has been taunting me for weeks." He went to the hobbit door.

"You have a broken arm, dude. Don't be heaving on that." Colton joined Carson on the step in front of the five-foot-high door. "Let the man with the real muscles give it a try."

Harlow and I both snorted as we watched Colton rub his hands together, then spit on his palms, and rub them together again. He gripped the knob and started ramming his shoulder into the door.

"I don't need two invalid housemates," I called after him. "It's bad enough Carson makes me wipe his ass. I'd rather not have to wipe yours, too."

Carson flipped me the bird. "I got one perfectly good hand, bro. You *offered* to wipe my ass. Sick fetish or some shit."

I grinned at him while Colton just kept ramming his shoulder into the door.

"You know, they say *insanity* is doing the same thing over and over again and expecting a different result," Harlow quipped, bringing her beer bottle to her mouth. The sexy line of her throat moved as she swallowed, and I pushed down a groan. She caught me watching her and winked. "I think you just need to call Sal, the locksmith."

"We'll call Sal only after we've exhausted all other options," Carson said, which I actually agreed with. "Who knows what's behind this door? And with the way this town gossips, we can't trust anybody with whatever secret is in here." He tilted his head at her. "So no watercooler gossiping, lady."

Harlow snickered. "Lawyer-client confidentiality. Your secrets are safe with me. Just keep me on retainer after the year is up, and we should be fine."

"Callum's taking care of that," Carson shot back. "In bed, I assume."

Harlow's cheeks grew pink again, but I just laughed.

"I'm not sure I can keep her *quiet*," I said, "but I'll keep her from talking if you know what I mean."

Harlow swatted me, her face had to be on fire now. I tugged her from her seat beside me, so that she was now in front of me, between my legs and with her back to my chest. She sighed into my embrace, resting her elbows on my bent knees.

Planting a kiss on her neck, I settled into a perfect afternoon with my woman and my *insane* brother ramming his shoulder into the hobbit door, and my other brother, who I no longer called my enemy.

We were all on our second beer by the time Colton decided to throw in the towel and stop bruising his shoulder.

Using the hem of his shirt to wipe his face, showing off his youthfully toned stomach, he returned to his spot in the grass and poured a long swallow of beer down his throat before flashing me a grin.

"Time to call Sal?" Harlow asked, her voice sleepy and serene.

"Not a chance," Colton said with a headshake. "But I'm obviously the only one who can do it. Carson is an invalid, and Callum is a flabby old man, so it's up to the young buck with all the muscles to get 'er done."

"Flabby old man?" I shook my head. I lifted my own shirt to expose the abs I did crunches every morning to keep. "Fuck off."

His grin just grew wider.

My heart swelled at the easy and carefree ribbing my brothers and I dished out at each other. This was how it was always supposed to be. This was what we'd been deprived of and were now building.

The sound of tires onn the long gravel driveway drew our attention, but none of us got up from where we sat. When the car came into view, I didn't recognize it.

"Another Winter Harborite coming to tell us that dear old dad was planning to sell off their business, too?" Colton's expression was sarcastic but curious.

"No." Carson jumped up, clearly distracted. His posture was stiff. "That's not a local." His gaze fixed on the driver of the car and when she parked, he was just standing there by the corner of the house, clutching his beer bottle until his knuckles went white, watching her.

Harlow, Colton, and I pivoted where we sat, but didn't get up.

The car door slammed shut and a pretty redheaded woman walked toward us.

Colton and I exchanged glances, and I'm sure my eyes were as wide as his, but when I looked at Harlow, her knowing expression gave me pause.

"Do you know who that is?" I whispered to her.

"I have an idea." She pressed the side of her index finger to her lips. "I'll tell you more later."

Before I could demand that she tell me everything right then and there, the red-haired woman approached, and that's when I noticed her enormous, very pregnant belly.

My gaze flew to Carson, but his attention was glued to the belly. So I flicked my focus to Colton and wasn't disappointed. His mouth hung open in shock. We exchanged a wordless conversation with our eyes. Both of us asking the same thing.

Was that Carson's baby?

"Hi, Carson." Our visitor twisted her fingers around themselves overtop her stomach.

"Amaya," my brother said, his tone clipped, but not altogether unkind or assholish.

Her green eyes flicked to each of us for a moment, and a grim smile barely lifted the corners of her mouth. Returning her focus to Carson, she smiled a little harder. "Could we go somewhere to talk?"

Carson jerked his head toward the rose garden. "Over there."

With a small nod, she walked past us toward a set of lounge chairs and an umbrella on a silver of mowed grass amongst the roses. It was where Colton took his *siestas* in between all of his gardening.

Carson started to follow, but as he passed me, I tapped his leg and said, "Hey."

He paused.

"Whatever it is, don't keep it to yourself. We'll figure it out together, okay?"

Carson glanced at Colton, who nodded, then back at me.

"We're a family," I added.

Carson nodded. "We are, aren't we?"

"A fucked up one, but we're doing the best we can."

My brother's smile was dour, but his eyes held a glimmer of hope and love that made my chest tight. "Thanks," he murmured before heading in the direction of the garden.

Colton's beer bottle paused midway to his mouth, and he winked at me. "Dude, I think we're going to be uncles."

And the Winters in Winter Harbor just kept growing.

EPILOGUE

A few months later ...
CALLUM

The day was closing in on dusk. The sun hung low in the sky, and shadows danced across the field as I laid out my plan. Harlow had texted an hour ago to say she planned to be home by seven. I glanced at my watch. Six fifty-seven.

The crunch of gravel in the long driveway had me putting the finishing touches on everything, swatting at a spiderweb that was in my way, and heading back toward the main house.

I stepped onto the driveway just as she shut her car door. Glancing down at her shoes, I made sure she wasn't in the heels she'd left the house with that morning but had changed into her practical tennis shoes like she often did after a long day in those neck-breakers.

"Tough day at the office, Ms. Jackson?" I asked, approaching my woman and taking her bag from her.

The dramatic sigh that accompanied her smile and tired eyes said she was wishing today was Friday and not Wednesday.

Oh well, there were certainly ways we could make *Hump Day* bearable.

I wrapped my arm around her waist, and her head immediately fell to my shoulder.

"I'll tell you one thing, it ain't easy having my name on the side of the building." She smirked. "But somebody's gotta do it."

"I'm sure it's just as hard as having your name over all the benches in downtown Winter Harbor," I teased her.

"Definitely. Thanks for buying those, by the way. You didn't have to."

"But I wanted to." I pressed a kiss to her forehead.

"What other celebratory acts do you have up your sleeve?" she asked with a twinkle in her eyes.

For a split second, I wondered if she somehow *knew* what I had planned for right now. But no. There was no way she could. My brothers had been sworn to secrecy, and they wouldn't betray me. Not after everything we'd been through and how far we'd come.

"I'm curious to see what you'll do when we have a baby or something."

I loved it when she talked about our future family, it meant she was in this just as much as I was. I guided her away from the house and back into the field where I'd been.

"There's no telling what I'll do when you finally make me a dad." We wound a lazy path through the grass of the side yard.

A weighted sigh made her shoulders slump. "God, it's nice to be home."

I lifted a brow at her, secretly loving that she called this place her home, even though she still had her condo and—now that I'd finished my one year of having to end every day at Hope Creek Manor—we slept there most nights. But I'd told her to meet me here after work, and she'd obliged with no questions.

"You know what I mean," she said. "Where you are is where my home is."

I tugged her close. "I feel the same way, babe."

"Hey." Her head popped off my shoulder. "Where are you taking me? This isn't the way to the hot spring, and I'm not in the mood to go digging for buried family treasure, hidden gardens, or mausoleums."

"It's a surprise." I tightened my grip around her as I continued leading her toward a small copse of trees in the field.

It was a bit of a trek and the high grass tickled our ankles and knees, but it was no longer shorts season, so I barely felt it against my jeans. Harlow was in dark tapered pants and a sexy red silk blouse. I glanced behind us at her car, wondering if I should run back and get her coat.

No. We'd be fine. I'd planned for everything, including the dropping temperature.

After about five minutes of walking, we neared the trees, and I paused, guided her in front of me, and put my hands over her eyes.

"This is very *un*-Callum Winters," she said with a chuckle, her hands hovering midair and her feet stumbling as I encouraged her forward. "What has gotten into you?"

Smiling, I kept us moving, the daylight having already receded enough that I could see the flicker of light and flame up ahead.

"Callum, what's going on?"

"Just a little further," I said, steering us around a rodent hole. "Do you not remember what today is?"

"Oh, Callum," she said with exhaustion in her tone, "I can barely remember what I had for breakfast today. I'm so tired. Today was the hearing for the Winslow estate as well as the arbitration for the Glover estate."

"At least the Winters are one less feuding family you have to deal with now, right?"

Her head turned as if she intended to give me the side-eye. "You three still have a long way to go, but yes, I'm glad to no longer be dealing with the War of the Winters."

"Okay, we won't stay long. I'll get you into bed before you can say 'Callum Winters is the sexiest, smartest, most well-hung man alive.'"

That earned me a big snort. "You never were a modest man."

"No reason to be when I'm the whole damn package."

I barely dodged her elbow as it swung back in an attempt to nail me in the gut.

Chuckling, I applied pressure to where I still covered her eyes so she would stop walking. We were in a small clearing—a clearing I'd cleared—and I dropped my hands from her eyes.

Harlow's gasp had me smiling and moving around her so I could see her face.

I'd hauled out the lawnmower and weed whacker and cleared a huge chunk of the tall grass. Then I'd outlined the perimeter with LED Tiki torches and in the center set up a picnic blanket, LED candles, blankets to cuddle up in, an electric fondue pot, bread, champagne on ice, and fresh fruit. All of Harlow's favorite things.

"Callum ..." she breathed, glancing up at me with wide-eyes and an open mouth. "What ... is this?"

"Ten years ago today, I told an angel I loved her, and she said it back. Changing my world—my heart—forever."

Color bloomed in her cheeks, and she cast her gaze down for a moment, her lashes fluttering closed. "Callum ..."

"Harlow, you are honestly the best thing that ever happened to me, and I thank God every day that I had the balls to talk to you. I just fucked things up along the way for a bit, but—"

"But we're together now, and that's what counts."

"Now and forever." I took her hands and led her to the center of the cleared grass and then down onto the blanket. "I figured we could have dinner, watch the stars come out, and make plans for the future."

"For the future ..." She nestled onto the blanket, and I immediately draped another one over her shoulders and legs.

"Better?" I asked, turning up the heat on the fondue pot with the delicious melted cheese inside.

A closed-mouth smile drifted across her face. "Perfect."

"Just give it a minute to heat up and then we can dive in. Are you hungry?"

"Starved. Forgot to eat lunch. I was so busy running from one place to another."

She reached for a grape on the plate and popped it in her mouth, humming in delight as she crushed it between her teeth. "Damn, that's good."

"Eat up."

"I'm more interested in *drinking* up. You find that champagne in the depths of that dungeon you boys insist upon calling a wine cellar?" She selected a strawberry this time and took a bite, the pink juice trickling down her chin. I quickly leaned over and kissed her where the juice ran, savoring the sweet flavor of the berry and the even sweeter flavor of Harlow. "No, I picked this up special at the liquor store attached to Beer & Moor," I murmured against her skin.

Cupping my chin before I could pull away, she pressed her lips against mine and I took the opening and kissed her properly. I would never, ever get tired of kissing this woman. Her lips parted, and I dove in, tasting the fruit she'd just eaten on her tongue as she tangled it with mine. Her body melted into mine and before I could stop myself, I had her on her back.

"Make love to me, Callum. Right here, right now," she said, breaking the kiss and trailing her fingers down my back to tug at the hem of my shirt.

With a groan, I sat back up and pulled her with me. "I will, but not yet."

Her grumble of frustration and the pout that accompanied it were adorable. "Then crack open that bottle. If you're going to deprive me of dick, the least you can do is give me a drink."

Laughing at her bluntness, I handed her another strawberry. "Not yet." Standing back up, I offered her my hand and with a grumble and some mutterings of *"lures me out here, makes me sit, makes me stand, flaunts his body and yet I can't even get a drink ..."* I pulled her over to a corner of the cleared grass. "I figure we could put a mudroom here." Tugging her gently to the left, we stood in front of a Tiki torch. "If we clear a few of these trees, we'll have an amazing view of the creek. Could put the living room here with a big bay window. Just imagine a huge ten-foot Christmas tree in front of this window."

Harlow's head began to shake. "Wha—what?"

I continued on through the clearing. "And here, we'll put an office with matching his and hers desks, of course. Facing

261

each other so we can look lovingly across at each other as we conquer the world."

I made to pull her to the other corner, but glue had filled her feet and she didn't move. "Callum, what are you talking about?"

"Our house. I want something new, that is all ours. From start to finish. And your condo is too small for a family. There's nothing like this property in all of Winter Harbor—believe me, I've looked. I want to stay here. I know Carson wants to stay, too. And hopefully, Colton will choose to stick around. The land is already zoned for multiple houses, so we'll subdivide. We'll have to run a new sewer line, but I've talked to the sewage department and it won't be as big of a deal as we think. Errol had already started that process before he died, but obviously my dad never finished it."

"You want to live here? Build a house?" Her eyes were saucer-sized and darting around the clearing wildly.

"Yeah. I've walked every inch of this property and besides where the main house is, this is the best plot of land. I've called dibs and have already started talking to an architect Carson recommended to draw up some plans. We can break ground in the spring."

"Callum ..."

"Harlow, I'm in this. One hundred and fifty million percent." I continued wandering the clearing. "We'll make it a two-story, or a three-story, or even a four-story. We can put in a basement with a wine cellar and cold storage."

She was back beside me. "Don't forget the cupola off the master bedroom." Her fingers linked with mine. "A replica of the one at the main house."

Grinning, I turned to her. "Abso-fucking-lutely. A little pre-breakfast delight, each morning?"

Her coy side-eye and seductive hum made my dick twitch. "And how many bedrooms?"

My lips twisted. "I figured four upstairs and two on the main level. Or we can put four upstairs and then a futon in our office and one in the rec room. What do you think?"

Her smile turned wry, but the sparkle in her eyes intensified. "How many children do you want?"

I shrugged and looked skyward for a moment. "I dunno, a baker's dozen?" I focused back on her face, not wanting to miss the shock and fear in her expression.

I wasn't disappointed.

Lifting her and twirling her around, causing the blanket on her shoulders to fan out like a cape, I laughed. "As many as you'll give me. One? Two? Three? Ten? I just want to be with you and have a family, no matter how big or small that may end up being."

I set Harlow back on her feet, and she gazed up at me with damp eyes and a brilliant, beautiful smile. "I want what you want. I want this. All of it."

That was my cue.

Keeping our hands clasped, I dropped to one knee, reached into my back pocket, and brought out the box.

Another gasp escaped her lips before her hands covered her mouth and her breathing grew rattled. "Callum ..."

"Harlow Jackson, you are it. You are the one. The only woman for me. None compare and none ever will. I must have done something right in a past life to have a woman like you love my angry, fucked up bastard ass in this life."

She hiccupped a laugh and tears brimmed her eyes, spilling over when I opened the box to reveal the ring that I designed myself. I'd be lying if I said I didn't order the diamond and start sketching a band design the night Harlow and I officially got back together for good.

I needed it to be perfect. Perfect for her. And nothing I found online said *Harlow*, so I decided to create one that did.

A rose gold band twisted into an elegant lover's knot with white shoulder diamonds, and a halo of black diamonds encircling the main marquis-cut white center diamond. The jeweler who made it said I had superb taste and an eye for creating something breathtaking and original. He even asked me if I'd be willing to design more rings for him on commission. I was mulling it over, but a part of me liked that Harlow's ring was a true original.

"I want to marry you," I went on. "I want to be your husband. The father of your children, grandfather of your grandchildren, and your plot neighbor in the Winter

Harbor Cemetery—though, I'd rather have my ashes sprinkled at *our* creek and not take up any more space on Earth once I'm gone."

That earned me another laugh. Followed by a, "You can be so morbid."

I brought her knuckles to my lips. "I've spoken with your parents, and we have their blessing. They think it was a touch early, but they know how much I love you and how we're meant to be, so they're on board. I think your mom is super stocked to wedding plan."

Harlow's bottom lip trembled, and she sniffled, laughing again through the now free-flowing tears.

"Marry me, Harlow. Save me once and for all from this miserable life I've been living for so many years because with you, it's not miserable. It's ... It's fucking fantastic. I'm a better man because I'm with you, and you make me want to be an ever better one. I will strive to be the man you deserve each and every day of our lives, I promise. I'm not going to fuck this up again."

Breathing out slowly through thinly parted lips, her chest shook. But it was her head's subtle nod that had my heart rate skyrocketing and my happiness meter going berserk. "Yes," she croaked. "Yes, I'll marry you."

I slid the ring onto her finger—and of course it fit like a glove. She hauled me to my feet, and I took her in my arms, spinning us around the grass under the now indigo sky. The first stars of the evening were beginning to wink and the last remaining crickets of the season were singing their swan song.

I set her back down, took her face in mine, and kissed her soundly. Kissed her completely. Kissed her truly. Kissed her because she was mine.

When we finally came up for air, we were both panting but smiling like idiots.

She held her hand out to the side of our smashed together bodies and studied the ring in the light of the nearby Tiki torch. "It's beautiful, Callum. I've never seen anything like it."

"And I've never met anybody like you. One of a kind for one of a kind."

Her gaze grounded me and I held on tight, absorbing her love and the overwhelming joy I felt just knowing my life was finally beginning to make sense. I had a plan. I had a good woman by my side, a favorite patch of land, a growing business, and a future to look forward to. And my brothers and I were working on our relationship.

Wrapping an arm around her waist, I steered us back to the picnic. "Now we can pop that champagne."

We settled down on the blanket, and I deployed the cork like a veteran sommelier, pouring us each a glass.

Harlow snuggled into me and lifted her glass. "A toast."

"A toast," I repeated.

"To third-times-the-charm, new beginnings, and happily ever afters."

"To all of those things. To you. To us. To Winter Harbor and my weird family and their secrecy. Without that fucked up will, I'm not sure I ever would have found my way back to you."

"To fucked up wills." She tapped her glass against mine, and we both took sips of the bubbly.

"We need to come up with a name for our new house," she said, settling against me where we sat snuggled up in the blankets.

"Hmmm ..."

"What about ... *Sunrise Manor*? Because every sunrise is a new beginning, and that's what we are, a new beginning. Starting over, doing it right this time."

I squeezed her tight and kissed her neck. "Doing it right this time, and every time hereafter. You, Harlow, are my forever, and I can't wait to watch every sunrise in our cupola with you."

Harlow's hum of a response was soothing, and I squeezed her tighter against me, kissed her neck once more and settled into my new forever with the woman of my dreams.

For the first time in a long time, I finally knew I was where I belonged.

I was home.

TO FIND OUT IF THE BABY IS CARSON'S GO HERE TO
GET YOUR COPY OF THE ASSHOLE HEIR—> https://
mybook.to/the-asshole-heir
FOR A DELETED BONUS SCENE OF
THE BASTARD HEIR GO HERE—>-
https://dl.bookfunnel.com/i7l3swmqeg

SNEAK PEEK

~ THE ASSHOLE HEIR ~
CHAPTER ONE

CARSON

"Need more screws."

I also need to get screwed.

Fuck, when was the lasttime I got laid?

I gave that thought the ol' heave ho before it had a chance to take root in my brain. Because when I thought too hard about the last time I got laid, or who the last person I got laid *by* was, the heat from my fury was enough to burn my cheeks. And it was already hot as fucking balls outside, so I didn't need to get any hotter.

"Grab me another paint roller while you're there," Callum called from inside the house. The door was open and he was busy painting the foyer while I struggled with my one good arm—the left was in a cast from a fall a few weeks ago—to finish fixing the deck railings. Colton, our other brother was off in the garden pulling weeds and making friends with ladybugs.

"And see if they have a big wheelbarrow," Colton said, his head poking out from the dilapidated, overgrown greenhouse. "The one I found in here is rusted through."

I muffled my frustrated grumble. I wasn't their damn errand boy. And why couldn't they go get the stuff? They had each had two working arms.

Because you're the contractor. You're the one with a carpentry ticket and either one of them would inevitably get the wrong kind of screws forcing you to go back and get the right ones anyway. Also, you're trying to mend fences with your brothers, not stir up more shit.

Right.

I was all about trying to be a better person. Learn from my mistakes and not let my past transgressions or our family's past transgressions affect my future. At least that was the mantra I was attempting to live by. Baby steps of course.

"Beer, too," Colton added. "And maybe ice cream."

"I'm only going to the fucking hardware store. I'm not making fifty stops." Ugh. What was going to be a twenty-minute trip into town and back for screws was turning into a full day of grocery shopping.

"They're all beside each other in the strip mall—that we own," Colton retorted. "Pull your panties out of your ass crack."

Fuck, it was hot out. And when it was hot my mood took a turn.

"I'll see what I can do," I said, rolling my eyes.

I grabbed my keys from where they rested next to my empty can of ginger ale on the deck railing, pocketed my phone, and headed down the porch steps. The middle one creaked beneath my weight.

I'd need to get to that at some point, even though Callum told me not to touch it as he said the creak was quaint.

The man is naïve. The creak meant something was loose or worn or rotten.

It needed to be fixed.

I opened the door to my Dodge Ram extended cab and slid in behind the steering wheel. Even for a white vehicle, it was hotter than Satan's balls after a vigorous round of whipping and flogging sinners. I put the key in the ignition, turned it on, and immediately rolled down the windows.

Because Winter Harbor—my new place of residence for the next year—was a tiny-ass coastal town in Oregon nothing was more than a ten-minute drive and that included the hardware store.

I was there before my leather steering wheel had a chance to cool off or for my left nut to stop sticking to my thigh.

There were loads of angle parking spots, so I picked one beneath a big ginkgo tree in full bloom that would hopefully shade my truck so it wasn't the depths of hell hot inside when I left.

For the summer in a tourist hotspot, the sidewalks were surprisingly empty and all the storefront doors were closed.

Maybe everyone had their A/C cranked because of the heat.

I paid this unusualness no mind since I hadn't lived in the town long enough to really know its character and I headed for *Pete's Hardware and Garden.* I heaved on the door but it didn't budge.

What the fuck?

I tried again.

It still didn't move.

Cupping my face, I peered through the glass door into a dark and empty hardware store.

This didn't make any

fucking ... oh shit.

Goddamn quirky-ass little town.

Everything was closed on Tuesdays.

Why Tuesdays? I don't fucking know. But this wasn't the first time we'd needed something on a Tuesday, driven into town only to have to turn around and do without until the following day.

I'd never lived anywhere in my entire life where a place was open every other day of the week, but closed on a Tuesday.

I pulled my phone out and double-checked the date. Sure enough, it was mother-fucking Tuesday and every single store in the entire strip mall was closed today. Nearly everything in town would be closed—because that's how Winter Harbor rolled.

The only places that would open were the bank, the hospital and *Ned's Necessities* a puny corner store hovel on the other side of town where *Ned* the geriatric owner defied the town laws and stayed open on Tuesdays, jacking up his prices and selling weird canned meats on his dusty shelves.

No way was I driving all the way over to Ned's Necessities for ice cream, beer, paint rollers or screws. Not that I figured he carried the latter two.

"Fuck!" I growled, spinning on my heel to head back to my truck.

But I wasn't even two steps from the hardware store when strolling toward me with her pale, slender arm linked through the arm of a tall, decent-looking man was the woman who ghosted me over six months ago.

The woman who broke my heart.

No.

Destroyed it.

Shattered it. And then for good measure crushed those tiny fragments into dust beneath the heel of her

boot.

Amaya.

"C-Carson," she stammered, stopping directly in front of me. Well, not *directly* in front of me, seeing as she had a pretty significant baby bump under a long gray dress taking up a large portion of the space between us.

My eyes dropped to the human in her belly.

"What are you doing in Winter Harbor?" she asked, her voice just as soft and breathy as it'd always been. Normally, I didn't like women with that kind of voice, it struck me as ditzy, but when Amaya spoke it did nothing but make me hard.

My eyes were still glued to her stomach, but the gentle throat clear of the man who was obviously her baby-daddy and the man she'd jumped into bed with probably seconds after ghosting me—quite possibly before—had me lifting my head.

"What am *I* doing in Winter Harbor? What are *you* doing in Winter Harbor?" I countered. My heart was thumping so loudly I felt like I was yelling in order to hear over it.

The delicate line of her throat bobbed and her green gaze bounced from the man beside her then back to me. "I ... *we're* here helping my aunt. She fell and broke her hip, and since I'm between jobs and Stanton works freelance, we offered to come to help her until she was back on her feet. What about you?"

My eyes were back on her stomach.

Well, and her tits. She'd always had great tits, and now they were even bigger. Her long, dark red hair fell in chunky waves over her shoulders, the ends landing right where her nipples would be. Fuck, I'd loved sucking on those nipples.

She loved it when I sucked on them, too.

The man she'd called Stanton cleared his throat again.

Dammit.

Lifting my eyes once more to Amaya, even though it was seriously painful to look at her, and my heart was beginning to seize in my chest, I pushed through the pain and opened my mouth. "I live here."

Her brows bunched. "Since when?"

"Since a while ago."

"You're not in Portland anymore?"

I shook my head. "Not if I live here."

When she stopped returning my calls and messages, she lost the privilege of knowing more about me. And now that she'd so very clearly moved on, like hell was I going to waste any more of my time pining over her, let alone standing there talking to her.

"What happened to your arm?" She pointed to my cast.

Hooking my thumb over my shoulder at my truck, I turned. "Gotta go." I was unable to continue looking at her. She was fucking gorgeous, and pregnancy had only enhanced that beauty. I couldn't continue to torture myself like this. I'd never felt about a woman the way I had about Amaya, hell the way I still did about Amaya.

Even after she ghosted me. And had probably cheated too. Given the size of her belly—unless there were twins in there. But either way, I needed to get fucking gone and go take my pain and anger out on something productive. Like trying to open that motherfucking hobbit door on the side of the house. Maybe a few rounds with a sledgehammer might convince the fucker to finally open.

I showed her my back.

"I-it was nice seeing you."

I could not say the same.

"Where are you living?"

I turned back to face her, her expression earnest and curious. She blinked those long, thick lashes and one hand fell to the top of her swollen belly. My own belly formed a tight knot and an agony so fucking fierce I thought I might collapse on the street throbbed in my chest. "Why do you care?"

Pain filled her eyes and her bottom lip wobbled.

Her baby-daddy took her hand and made to pull her away. "Come on, Amaya, let's go."

"I know you hate me," she said, her words coming out like the croak of a chain-smoking frog.

"Can't hate what you don't care about," I said, the pain in my chest intensifying.

Well, that was a big ol' fucking lie.

Not only did I care about this woman, but I'm also pretty sure I was fucking in love with her. Which was why her ghosting me and now showing up on the arm of another man and carrying his baby gutted me like a rusty bayonet. Sepsis or tetanus would be a welcomed alternative to this feeling of complete and total heartache.

A tear slid down her cheek, but she nodded, wiped her wrist beneath her nose, and turned to go, taking Stanton's arm again.

I barely made it to my truck before my legs gave out and a ringing formed in my ears.

Amaya was in Winter Harbor and she was pregnant.

What other sick fucking surprises did the universe have in store for me?

TO FIND OUT IF THE BABY IS CARSON'S GO HERE TO GET YOUR COPY OF THE ASSHOLE HEIR—> https://mybook.to/the-asshole-heir
FOR A DELETED BONUS SCENE OF
THE BASTARD HEIR GO HERE—>-
https://dl.bookfunnel.com/i7l3swmqeg

THE BASTARD HEIR

If you've enjoyed this book, please consider leaving a review. It really does make a difference. Thank you again. Xoxo Whitley & Ember

ACKNOWLEDGMENTS

There are just so many people that we have to thank for helping bring this book to life.

First, we'd like to thank all the eyes that took a gander at our words and helped us craft a better story. Author Jeanne St. James, Author Kat McIntyre, Author Brooke Burton, Landra, Kelli, and Elisabeth. Thank you!

To our editor, Jacqui Nelson, you rock! Thank you so much.

To our cover artists, Roberta Cottam and Megan Squiers, thank you.

To our proofreaders and ARC team. Thank you! Our promo companies and bloggers, thank you.

To our readers who have been patient with us as we navigate motherhood, sick kids, a pandemic, husbands, careers and all the other crap life throws at us when all we want to do is write. Thank you for sticking by us and remaining steadfast and loyal fans. We hope you love the Winters brothers as much as we do and we can't wait to give you a wonderful small-town world you can get lost in and also lose your heart in.

To our children who are the beasts and beats of our hearts. Your mothers love you, but leave us the hell alone so we can write ... please. Also, we love you.

To our husbands who are so supportive and help us figure out certain "positions" when we're not sure if it's actually possible for two people to bend and connect that way, and for just being our rocks when life just gets a bit tough. Thank you and we love you.

ABOUT THE AUTHORS

Whitley
A West Coast baby born and raised, Whitley is married to her high school sweetheart and together they have two beautiful daughters and a fluffy dog. She spends her days making food that gets thrown on the floor, vacuuming Cheerios out from under the couch and making sure that the dog food doesn't end up in the air conditioner. But when the kids are in school and it's not quite wine o'clock, Whitley sits down, avoids the pile of laundry on the couch, and writes.

A lover of all things decadent; wine, cheese, chocolate and spicy erotic romance, Whitley brings the humorous side of sex, the ridiculous side of relationships, and the suspense of everyday life into her stories. With single dads, firefighters, Navy SEALs, mommy wars, body issues, threesomes, bondage and role-playing, Whitley's books have all the funny and fabulously filthy words you could hope for.

Ember
Ember Leigh has been writing erotic romance novels since she was far too young. A native of northern Ohio, she currently resides near Lake Erie with her Argentinean

husband, where they run an Argentinian-American food truck and wrangle two wild boys.

Don't forget to grab The Bastard Heir bonus scene HERE-->
https://dl.bookfunnel.com/i7l3swmqeg

FIND EMBER HERE

Website: http://www.emberleighromance.com/
Instagram:
https://www.instagram.com/emberleighauthor/
Facebook:
https://www.facebook.com/emberleighauthor

Exclusive Facebook
Reader Group, Ember's Blossoms:
https://www.facebook.com/groups/19207350413372
07/
Goodreads:
https://www.goodreads.com/author/show/8045833.E
mber_Leigh
Bookbub: https://www.bookbub.com/profile/ember-
leigh
Subscribe to my newsletter here: http://bit.ly/EL-
newsletter

FIND WHITLEY HERE

Website: WhitleyCox.com
Email: readers4wcox@gmail.com
Twitter: @WhitleyCoxBooks
Instagram: @CoxWhitley
TikTok: @AuthorWhitleyCox
Facebook : https://www.facebook.com/CoxWhitley/
Blog: https://whitleycox.com/fabulously-filthy-blog-page/

Exclusive Facebook Reader Group:
https://www.facebook.com/groups/234716323653592/
Booksprout: https://booksprout.co/author/994/whitley-cox
Bookbub: https://www.bookbub.com/authors/whitley-cox
Goodreads:
https://www.goodreads.com/author/show/16344419.Whitley_Cox
Subscribe to my newsletter here:
http://eepurl.com/ckh5yT

OTHER BOOKS BY EMBER LEIGH

**THE BAYSHORE
SERIES**
Make Me Lose

http://mybook.to/make-me-lose
Make Me Fall

http://mybook.to/make-me-fall
Make Me Yours

http://mybook.to/make-me-yours
Make Me Choose

http://mybook.to/make-me-choose
Make Me Hot

http://mybook.to/make-me-hot
Make Me Smile

http://mybook.to/make-me-smile

The
Breaking Series
Breaking the Rules

https://books2read.com/breaking-the-rules-emberleigh
Changing the Game

https://books2read.com/changingthegame-breaking
Breaking the Sinner

https://books2read.com/breakingthesinner
Breaking the Habit

https://books2read.com/breakingthehabit
Breaking the Fall

https://books2read.com/breakingthefall

OTHER BOOKS BY WHITLEY COX

Love, Passion and Power: Part 1

https://
mybook.to/LPPPart1
The Dark and Damaged Hearts Series Book 1
Kendra and Justin

Love, Passion and Power: Part 2

https://
mybook.to/LPPPart2
The Dark and Damaged Hearts Series Book 2
Kendra and Justin

Sex, Heat and Hunger: Part 1

https://
mybook.to/SHHPart1
The Dark and Damaged Hearts Book 3

Emma and James

Sex, Heat and Hunger: Part 2

https://
mybook.to/SHHPart2
The Dark and Damaged Hearts Book 4
Emma and James

Hot and Filthy: The Honeymoon

https://
mybook.to/HotandFilthy
The Dark and Damaged Hearts Book 4.5
Emma and James

True, Deep and Forever: Part 1

https://
mybook.to/TDFPart1
The Dark and Damaged Hearts Book 5
Amy and Garrett

True, Deep and Forever: Part 2

https://
mybook.to/TDFPart2
The Dark and Damaged Hearts Book 6
Amy and Garrett

Hard, Fast and Madly: Part 1

http://
mybook.to/HFMPart1
The Dark and Damaged Hearts Series Book 7

Freya and Jacob

Hard, Fast and Madly: Part 2

https://
mybook.to/HFMPart2
The Dark and Damaged Hearts Series Book 8
Freya and Jacob

Quick & Dirty

https://
mybook.to/quickandirty
Book 1, A Quick Billionaires Novel
Parker and Tate

Quick & Easy

https://mybook.to/quickeasy
Book 2, A Quick Billionaires Novella
Heather and Gavin

Quick & Reckless

https://
mybook.to/quickandreckless
Book 3, A Quick Billionaires Novel
Silver and Warren

Quick & Dangerous

https://
mybook.to/quickanddangerous
Book 4, A Quick Billionaires Novel
Skyler and Roberto

Quick & Snowy
The Quick Billionaires, Book 5

*https://
mybook.to/quickandsnowy*
Brier and Barnes

Hot Dad

*https://
mybook.to/hotdad*
Harper and Sam

Lust Abroad

*https://
mybook.to/lustabroad*
Piper and Derrick

Snowed In & Set Up

*https://
mybook.to/snowedinandsetup*
Amber, Will, Juniper, Hunter, Rowen, Austin

Hired by the Single Dad

*https://
mybook.to/hiredbythesingledad*
The Single Dads of Seattle, Book 1
Tori and Mark

Dancing with the Single Dad

https://
mybook.to/dancingsingledad
The Single Dads of Seattle, Book 2
Violet and Adam

Saved by the Single Dad

https://
mybook.to/savedsingledad
The Single Dads of Seattle, Book 3
Paige and
Mitch

Living with the Single Dad

https://
mybook.to/livingsingledad
The Single Dads of Seattle, Book 4
Isobel and Aaron

Christmas with the Single Dad

https://
mybook.to/christmassingledad
The Single Dads of Seattle, Book 5
Aurora and Zak

New Years with the Single Dad

https://
mybook.to/newyearssingledad
The Single Dads of Seattle, Book 6
Zara and Emmett

Valentine's with the Single Dad

https://
mybook.to/VWTSD
The Single Dads of Seattle, Book 7
Lowenna and Mason

Neighbors with the Single Dad

https://
mybook.to/NWTSD
The Single Dads of Seattle, Book 8
Eva and Scott

Flirting with the Single Dad

https://
mybook.to/Flirtingsingledad
The Single Dads of Seattle, Book 9
Tessa and Atlas

Falling for the Single Dad

https://
mybook.to/fallingsingledad
The Single Dads of Seattle, Book 10
Liam and Richelle

Hot for Teacher

https://
mybook.to/hotforteacher
The Single Moms of Seattle, Book 1
Celeste and Max

Hot for a Cop

mybook.to/hotforacop
The Single Moms of Seattle, Book 2
Lauren and Isaac

Hot for the Handyman

https://mybook.to/hotforthehandyman
The Single Moms of Seattle, Book 3
Bianca and Jack

Doctor Smug

https://
mybook.to/doctorsmug
Daisy and Riley

Hard Hart

https://
mybook.to/hard_hart
The Harty Boys, Book 1
Krista and Brock

Lost Hart
The Harty Boys, Book 2

https://
mybook.to/lost_hart
Stacey and Chase

Torn Hart
The Harty Boys, Book 3

https://
mybook.to/torn_hart

Lydia and Rex

Dark Hart
The Harty Boys, Book 4

https://
mybook.to/dark_hart
Pasha and Heath

Full Hart
The Harty Boys, Book 5

https://
mybook.to/full_hart
A Harty Boys Family Christmas
Joy and Grant

Love to Hate You

http://mybook.to/love2hateyou
Alex and Eli

Coming Soon

Rock the Shores
A Cinnamon Bay Romance

https://
mybook.to/CBR-rocktheshores
Juliet and Evan
May 10, 2022

Mr. Gray Sweatpants
A Single Moms of Seattle spin-off book

https://
mybook.to/mrgraysweatpants
Casey and Leo
September 10, 2022

Raw, Fierce and Awakened: Part 1
The Dark and Damaged Hearts Series,
Book 9
Jessica and Lewis

Raw, Fierce and Awakened: Part 2
The Dark and Damaged Hearts Series,
Book 10
Jessica and Lewis

Printed in Great Britain
by Amazon